Sherwood Monastery Press
An imprint of Sageline Publishing
502 Oella Avenue
Oella, Maryland 21043
sherwoodmonastery@sageline.com

First U.S. Printing: April 2014
Second Edition U.S. Printing April 2025

ISBN 978-1-931936-03-3

9 781931 936033

Book design and composition by William Meisheid

Cover design and composition by William Meisheid
Cover and Chapter Illustrations by Carolyn Lyons
Small illustrations, maps, and timeline by William Meisheid
The Chronicles of Moses the Lawgiver:
Book One: Beginnings (Second Edition)
Book Two: A Warrior's Heart (Battle of Kadesh)
Book Three: Remembrance (Moses, His Sons, His Story, and the
    Burning Bush)
Planned:
Book Four: Exodus (Leaving Egypt and crossing the Red Sea)
Book Five: Law and Rebellion (Ten Commandments and a Rebellious
    People)
Book Six: Passing (Death of Moses and Joshua crossing the Jordon)

Dedication

This is an updated second edition of this story. I edited this book in preparation for the release of Book Two: A Warrior's Heart in 2025.

I would like to express my sincere gratitude to the numerous individuals who have contributed significantly to this book. Besides my wife, who stuck with me through all the trials it took to bring this to fruition, there are several people without whom this never would have been finished.

Keith, you believed in me and the story from the beginning, and your constant refrain of "Moses, Moses, Moses" kept me going. Thank you for sticking with me to the very end.

Sally, several key characters and events owe their existence to you. Thank you for broadening my vision.

Jim and Mary, you are real and prolific readers who liked the story from the beginning and constantly encouraged me to finish it.

Pam, you were my first editor and helped me overcome the early stumbling blocks every new author faces. Thank you.

Steven, your challenge at your writer's workshop spurred me to stick through the endless rounds of edits, revisions, and more edits. We agree that writing is rewriting; an author's task is to refine the text until the story speaks clearly with as few stutters and stumbles as possible. Thank you for your example and encouragement.

Pam number two (interesting that both my editors were named Pam), this book would not have been possible without you. You hung in there through rewrite after rewrite, always encouraging, blunt, and to the point. You, too, liked the story and helped me flesh out what was lacking. I believe a successful book is always a collaboration between the writer and the editor because, without someone to help us refine our vision, we scribes tend to wander far afield. You helped me focus, cut where necessary, add what was needed, and constantly improve. Thank you. Thank you.

Lastly, this book is for all readers who will find new insight into an epic tale through this adventure. May you discover the extraordinary story behind the narrative you thought you knew. Enjoy.

Prologue

To the Egyptians, the Hebrews were a people apart—stubborn, defiant, and growing too numerous to ignore. For over 300 years, measured by the yearly inundations of the Sacred River, these interlopers had lived primarily as separate people within the borders of Egypt. The Hebrews had come to this land because of Joseph, one of their patriarchs—known to the Egyptians as Imhotep. He saved the Egyptians from seven years of famine by correctly interpreting Pharaoh's dream and using the earlier seven years of rich, plentiful harvests to prepare them for the later lean years. Though Joseph's descendants had settled throughout Egypt, they had rejected the gods of the land where they dwelt and worshipped their singular deity, an invisible and nameless one.

As their numbers grew, they mainly spread through the region bounding the lower Nile, especially within its broad and fertile delta. Their increasing numbers eventually became a burden to the Egyptians. Then, as political and religious difficulties descended on the land, a new Pharaoh arose who did not remember what Joseph had done. He decreed to the midwives that when a Hebrew child was born, if it was a son, then he must be killed, but if it was a daughter, then she could live. However, the midwives feared the God of the Hebrews more than Pharaoh's wrath. With whispered prayers and trembling hands, they defied his command, letting the sons of the Hebrews live. But still, their numbers grew.

After this merciful deliverance, another Pharaoh ascended the throne of Egypt, and he decreed to all his people, not just to the midwives, that every newborn son of the Hebrews should be cast into the river, but no daughter should be harmed. Therefore, the Egyptians honored their great crocodile god, Sobek, and his priests offered the infant sons of the Hebrews as sacrifices to the river beasts. The agents of Pharaoh also punished anyone hiding a male baby, and there was wailing and misery across all of the dwellings of the Hebrews.

Then, a male child was born to a Hebrew couple on the outskirts of Memphis. His cries could mean death, yet his silence could not last forever. He would upset everything. Hidden by his parents, he began a journey that would forever change his family's destiny, Egypt, and that of his Hebrew brethren

Departure

A fluttering of wings swept past the high eastern window. The unexpected sound, filtering through the heavy covering, sent a chill down Jochebed's spine. She froze, her hand suspended in midair, sticky waterproofing dangling from her fingers.

She held her breath, straining to hear beyond the thick silence.

Nothing.

"It was only a bird," she said aloud.

No one was outside. We had not been discovered.

She took a deep breath and forced herself to return to the task.

I can't make a mistake, or he will drown. Pay attention to what you're doing.

With renewed determination, she went back to sealing the basket.

The curtain to the bedroom where the two older children were asleep parted, and her husband, Amram, slipped through the doorway. The smell of pitch filled the air.

"Is it finished?"

"It will be done when it is done," Jochebed snapped. She bit her tongue, regretting the sharpness, and forced the sealant deeper into the weave, her hands trembling with urgency.

After an awkward silence, she stopped and looked at Amram. "I know you're concerned, but it is hard to work with only a lamp for light. It takes time to fill in all the spaces in the weave, and I cannot leave a gap." The persistent fear that stalked all her efforts accused her:

The water will leak through a place you missed.

"I'm sorry. I made you wait too long before starting the waterproofing," Amram said apologetically. "I was just worried that the sealant would dry out and crack when the basket hit something. Now it is getting late, and you must get to the river before you lose the darkness."

Jochebed relented. "I'm almost done. While I finish, go out and check the village to make sure no one will see us leave."

Amram headed toward the door. As he put his hand on the latch, he turned to her and said, "It will be enough."

Jochebed unhooked the lamp from its drop cord and covered it without replying. No light spilled out into the darkness as her husband slipped out. As the door shut behind him, she uncovered and rehung the lamp, allowing the meager light to refill the room.

It had taken Amram a long time to agree to her plan. It took him even longer to get enough sealing material to waterproof her double-woven basket. She'd pushed him hard. She had heard about too many sons vanishing into Sobek's jaws because of that accursed edict.

It took a while, but she had finally convinced him that their son's only hope was the possibility of adoption by a childless Egyptian couple who would take him as their own. Every day, barren mothers scanned the Nile, hoping for a gift from their gods. Unwanted babies throughout Egypt were given another chance at life and family by being placed in papyrus boats and cast adrift on the mercy of the river. While this wasn't a boat, it was a desirable basket that someone would want to make an effort to retrieve.

Amram had accepted the alternative, believing that his dreams meant the Lord God would protect their son and find him a home where he would be safe from the death that stalked him.

Jochebed worked the last of the pungent mixture into the remaining empty spaces. She prayed it would be enough, but more than that, she prayed someone who wanted him would find him.

Unhooking the lamp, she examined the inside of the basket. She hoped the smell would not create a problem for her son. Satisfied that the entire inner surface was adequately sealed, there was one thing left to do. To keep the blanket and their son from disturbing the waterproofing, she took a piece of heavy cloth, cut it to size, and pressed the fabric around the inside of the basket, setting it into the sticky coating. That should protect the sealant.

Pleased with the results, she rehung the lamp, stepped back, put her hands on her hips, and said, "Good."

Standing in the doorway, Amram said, "You're satisfied?"

Startled, she reached for the lamp, but Amram held up his hand, signaling her to stop.

"No one will see," he said. "I went from one end of the village to the other. Everything is quiet. Is the basket finished?"

"I've done everything I can. It will hold."

Amram secured the door and came to the table. Placing his hands on his wife's shoulders, he leaned forward and touched his forehead to hers. With a quiet gentleness, he said, "Then it is good enough." He kissed her cheek and added, "Before we wake Miriam, let me test the lid."

Picking up the cover, he slowly pressed it onto the basket. It was a snug fit. The lid's looser weave would let in air but still keep out any snakes. Jochebed had made two places to tie it to the basket to keep it from jostling loose.

"Perfect! You can leave it on until you reach the river."

She paused, her eyes catching his in the dim light, "I'll go and wake Miriam. We have to leave."

"Try not to disturb Aaron." As she turned away, he said, almost too quietly for her to hear, "I will hold my son one last time."

Reaching into the large old basket they had used as a hiding place, Amram lifted the sleeping child into his arms. His hands, strong enough to carve the ribs of a ship, now trembled as he cradled the fragile warmth of his son against his chest. Would the God of his fathers truly watch over him? Or was this nothing more than desperation wrapped in faith?

His heart ached as he looked at his son's sleeping face, and all his fatherly expectations, the strange dreams about his son's destiny, welled up and threatened to overwhelm him. Fighting back the rising tide, he struggled to rein in his emotions. His heart reached for a prayer, diverting the pain to his only hope.

"I am your father. I will always be your father." He raised his trembling fingers and pressed them against his lips. Then, with his kiss still lingering on his fingertips, he anointed the child's forehead, blessed him, and quietly prayed, "Oh God of Abraham, Isaac, and Jacob, I trust the promise of the dreams you have given me. Save my son as you saved your servant Joseph. Protect his life. Give him a home where he, like Joseph, will find favor in your sight and in the eyes of the Egyptians who find him. Use him like you used Joseph, and save us from this oppression."

Amram felt Jochebed's hand on his shoulder.

"It is time."

He turned and saw Miriam, still half-asleep, standing beside his wife. He reached out and caressed her head. Though she was only ten, she was strong for her age. Her dogged determination would keep her going through the long walk to the river.

He pushed open the sling hanging from her shoulder and placed his sleeping son into the blanket that lined the carrying cloth.

"He's gotten heavier," Miriam moaned.

"Don't be afraid. You can do this. Now, listen to your mother."

"I will, father." She stood as tall as she could and said, "I am not afraid."

"One last thing, don't start talking to yourself. Sometimes, you don't even know you are doing it. You have to be careful."

Miriam looked down at the floor. "I will be careful."

Amram gave her one last caress, turned to Jochebed, and said, "Remember, treat the basket gently. No harm can come to the water seal before you get to the river."

"Don't worry, I'll be careful," she said.

"I know it is late, but try not to rush."

"Husband, you have told me many times that hurrying causes mistakes."

"Well, don't forget it." Amram knew he had begun to babble. Taking a deep breath, he called up all of his resolve, reached out, and pulled his wife close. He wrapped his arms around her and squeezed her hard for a long time, trying to press into her every bit of his strength.

"We must go."

He reluctantly released her. If only he could go instead, but the demands of his work prevented it. Reluctantly, he picked up the basket and placed it carefully into her hands.

"Go with God," he said. "May his wisdom guide your steps."

Amram unhooked the lamp, placed it on the table, and covered it, darkening the room. He moved past his wife, found the door, and carefully opened it, cracking it enough to look outside. After satisfying himself that no one was there, he opened it the rest of the way.

"Be careful," he whispered as he guided them into the night.

As she stepped into the night, Jochebed clutched the basket tighter. The wind carried the distant cry of a jackal, and for a fleeting moment, she imagined another mother somewhere, mourning a child already lost. She swallowed hard and walked faster. She could not afford grief—not yet.

They had chosen to leave during a new moon, and the starry sky was further dimmed with clouds. Despite the darkness, a lone star pierced through, watching them go. As their footsteps faded into silence, Amram sighed and closed the door, the hand gripping his heart squeezing tighter.

Demanding Voyage

The Royal Dispatch Pouch pressed against Sunsamen's hip, heavier than any before. This mission required the swiftest boat available, and unlike most vessels that traveled the Nile, they did not put to shore during the night, although they were forced to move at a significantly reduced speed.

The craft was long and sleek, built from full-length planks of Syrian pine. With each pull of the four pairs of oars, it cut a shallow draft as it skimmed across the surface.

During the day, they moved quickly down the river. For several hours on good water, before the day's heat taxed their endurance, the craft reached sustained speeds twice as fast as any other river vessel.

A moonless night. A sky choked with clouds. The darkness was absolute—blacker than Sunsamen had ever seen. The stars, smothered in the heavens, offered no aid. The river was a shadowy void beneath them, the hidden hazards lurking just beyond their fragile pool of lamplight. What remained of the shadowless light failed to show the slight surface disturbances that signaled a hidden hazard. Despite the danger, he had no choice; his duty required him to press on, though he chafed at their limited speed.

The steady drone of the rower counting the strokes echoed across the water and rebounded back from the near shore to Sunsamen. Joined by the rhythmic swish of the oars and the intermittent sound of the hull slipping through the water, it gave the night an eerie feel.

Sunsamen, seated in the prow, had the rowers match the boat's meager speed to his limited vision. He was aided by a triple-wicked lamp extending from a long pole stretched forward from the boat's prow.

A large cloud passed overhead, deepening the brutal darkness, and Sunsamen called out, "Slow your speed by one count."

The stroke counter adjusted his rhythm, and the steady swoosh of the oars perceptibly slowed. Twice, they had run aground on one of the constantly shifting sandbars, losing precious time as they struggled to free themselves.

Their greatest danger lurked beneath the surface. A submerged hippopotamus, startled in the dark, could shatter their vessel in an instant, its massive bulk flipping them into the river's waiting jaws.

Exhaustion blurred his eyes, bringing back memories of Buhan's frantic departure. But failure gnawed at him more than fatigue. It was approaching the ninth day since he had left the fortress at Buhan, situated just below the Second Cataract. He had stopped at the garrisons at Elephantine, Thebes, and the port that serviced the quarries at Hatnub to rotate his rowers and restock provisions before pressing on. Now, they were on the last leg of his journey, and the fourth and last crew was nearing the limit of their endurance.

His duty was speed, but he feared they wouldn't arrive until late tomorrow night. He did not want to rouse the noble Seti, may he be merciful, from his sleep, especially since he was the bearer of troubled tidings.

He had not been told what was in the sealed scroll tucked away in the leather satchel. Messengers only bore the dispatches; what they learned about their contents came from the rumors circulating among the soldiers and retainers who had ears within the private counsels.

This time, much of the dispatch was not a secret. Everyone was talking about the gold caravan from Nubia that was attacked four days from the Salima Oasis, about a four-day chariot journey southwest of the fortress. An exhausted chariot driver had arrived requesting aid. The garrison commander responded with a single chariot group rather than the whole corps, thinking twenty-five chariots were more than enough to deal with the problem.

It was not. Rumors of a disaster circulated throughout the fortress, along with conflicting reports. Many said Pharaoh, may he avenge the honor of Egypt, would be roused to anger. Speculation among some of the soldiers was that Amunthuya, the husband of the Pharaoh's sister and commander of the relief force, had been seriously wounded.

Sunsamen had learned to ignore the shifting winds of rumor. As a messenger, it was his duty to be swift, and these idle imaginings distracted him from the water ahead, thereby increasing the risk to his mission. Listening to the steady strokes of his rowers, he focused his attention on the outer edges of the advancing pool of light, searching for any change in the water's flow.

Overland Passage

They had practiced the journey by day, using reed-gathering as their excuse. No one had paid them any mind. But now, under the cover of darkness, every step felt different—slower, heavier, more dangerous. Thankfully, their night journey would be cooler than the earlier trek through the day's oppressive heat.

"It's so dark," Miriam said.

"Don't worry," Jochebed said. "You have good eyes, and we have practiced the journey."

The road toward Memphis was little more than a cart path swept free of rocks and debris by the passage of endless travelers.

As they began their journey, Jochebed pictured the milestones in her mind. She had used small piles of rocks to mark where they should leave the road before they got too close to the two villages the road would pass along the way. Despite the intermittent starlight, the small mounds should still be visible. During their earlier attempts, it had taken them a little over two hours to reach the river by the direct route. She knew it would take much longer in the dim light with the planned detours around the villages, but the only thing that mattered was that they reached the river before first light. No one must see them putting the basket in the river.

"Mother, I can hardly see," Miriam whispered, her voice tight with worry.

"You can do it. Just take your time. Your eyes will adjust."

Jochebed understood her apprehension. Her daughter's growing concern about unwelcome surprises was to be expected; the night was home to the silent predators: dangerous creatures that roamed across the rocks and sands. While they had taken precautions—they had wrapped their lower legs with thick cloths for protection against the less perilous hazards, and Miriam carried a long, thin stick to sweep the ground before her. There were many clouds, frequently obscuring much of the starlight, making it difficult to see potential dangers, especially unexpected dips in their rugged route around the village.

"I have to slow down."

"All right. We don't need to hurry," Jochebed said, though going slower could become problematic if they had to hold this pace. Right now, she needed to keep her daughter focused. If her fears took over, the shadows would fill with imaginary dangers. The real ones were bad enough.

Barely loud enough for her daughter to hear, Jochebed said, "Remember your father's prayers before we left. We must trust that God will guide our steps and clear our path. Let him deal with what lies in the darkness." She said it as much for herself as for Miriam.

Their route would take them past another Hebrew village and a medium-sized Egyptian community. These settlements had grown up east of the fertile ground along the river opposite Memphis, around places where successful wells had been dug. Water was everything in this arid place. To the south of their route was the sizable royal estate owned by the sister of Pharaoh. It stretched into the distance as far as the eye could see. Numerous small farms lined the river to the right of the road, opposite the port of Perunifer. Another large estate belonging to another less-connected Royal family took over the land north of the city.

Jochebed had chosen to stay on the road as it passed along the edge of the small Egyptian farms. She and Amram had agreed it was the safest route. He took it every day to work at the shipyards north of Perunifer. However, no one should be on the road this late at night, and since the farms bordering the road were smaller and had fewer resources, they lacked the same level of security as the Great Estate further to the south. The same families had worked these small plots of land for generations. They were all that remained around Memphis from when small, commoner-run farms dotted the banks of the great river.

Every farm, no matter its size, depended on the floodwaters of the yearly inundation and its fertile silt deposits. The surge of life-giving water from the great river submerged all the lowlands near the river, creating fertile fields for planting. This demanded special preparations. The living and livestock areas, the walking and cart paths that allowed passage through the farms, and any roads, such as the one on which they now walked, were elevated high enough above the walled fields that contained the yearly flood. They stayed dry and usable. The inundation was still a moon away. A long shadow hung over the kingdom as everyone awaited this year's promise. There was growing unease throughout Egypt because the last two gifts of the Nile had flooded considerably short of expectations, causing meager harvests. If they experienced another cycle of shortages, it would be difficult for everyone, especially her family and the rest of the Hebrews.

Even so, their planned route ran against the northern edge of the Great Estate. Considering its size and royal importance, it should have regular night patrols, which meant they would be close enough to require careful vigilance.

"How are you doing, Miriam?"

"I can see better now. We can go a little faster. I'll let you know when I get tired."

"Remember," Jochebed said, "we planned several rest stops. Do not push yourself too hard."

"I won't."

Jochebed balanced the basket on her head in the traditional manner of working women. This gave her a clear view of the ground ahead, which was important since her primary concern was tripping. Any fall might damage the waterproofing.

The carry sling freed up Miriam's hands, allowing her to sweep the area ahead with her stick for any potential dangers. However, carrying her brother was tiring and difficult. A fall could injure or startle him. Also, a baby's cry carried a long way, alerting anyone within hearing to their presence.

Jochebed wished this journey were their only concern. Ever since the overthrow of the Pharaoh, whom no Egyptian would name over a generation ago, the priests of Egypt, especially those of Amun-Ra, blamed the Hebrews for his heresy. Like her people, he had claimed that there was only one god, the Egyptian deity Aton, the life of the sun and lord of all creation. He had almost destroyed the country before he died. Some said he was poisoned; others credited the gods with reasserting themselves. After restoring the historic divinities of Egypt, the pharaohs, with the support of the various priesthoods, began controlling the movement of Jochebed's people. They broke up the larger Hebrew communities and relocated the people to various building projects throughout the country. They wanted to keep the Hebrew settlements small and separated to limit their ability to organize against the edict that took their newborn sons, as well as their steadily growing oppression. This became critical once the soldiers began searching Hebrew homes for newborn males, who were then taken to the priests of Sobek.

Jochebed's husband, Amram, had argued that the advisors who guided Pharaoh's decisions did not understand the complex tribal rivalries of the Hebrews. Their sordid history made uniting for any reason doubtful. Each tribe, which traced its origins to one of the twelve sons of Jacob, was suspicious of the motives of the other eleven. They were more likely to be at odds with each other than unite and turn against the Egyptians.

Jochebed was a Levite, a descendant of Levi who, along with his brother Simeon, avenged the rape of their sister Dinah. Despite the covenant their father Jacob had made to settle the issue, they killed the offender and his entire Hivite clan. Jacob disinherited the two brothers, and in his dying blessing, he denied any inheritance to Levi, Simeon, and their entire lineage. They would have no place in the lands God had promised to the descendants of Abraham. Ever since, the other tribes have looked down on these two tribes almost as much as the Egyptians have looked down upon the Hebrews. No one expected anything good to come out of the descendants of Levi or Simeon. Jochebed, her husband, indeed her entire village, knew that scorn.

The Hebrew village should not be far. Getting past it would be easy; it was another Levite settlement, and Jochebed knew it well. No one would be up, and no guard would be on patrol. The much larger Egyptian community would be another matter. It was filled with tradesmen and had regular night patrols, making her anxious.

"We should be close to the first place where we will leave the road," Jochebed said. "You should see the pile of stones off to the left."

"I think I see them up ahead."

Miriam adjusted the carry cloth as best she could without stopping. Her brother seemed undisturbed by the jostling. As she moved off the road around the small pile of stones, she said, "I have to slow down, and I may have to stop suddenly."

"Do the best you can. I will drop back a little."

Miriam cautiously started forward, expanding her sweep to either side over the rough ground.

They were about halfway around the village when Miriam stopped and whispered, "My arm is getting tired."

"Go back to only sweeping the area in front of you."

They made it around the Hebrew village without incident, one hurdle out of the way. Back on the road, they picked up their pace. It was an easy walk. The night was quiet except for the occasional cries of a few distant jackals. How close were they? Those desert dogs are dangerous.

As the Hebrew village disappeared behind, the Egyptian lights appeared dimly ahead.

This meant they were nearing the halfway point of their journey. They were making good time.

"I see the next marker," Miriam whispered.

As they approached the pile of stones, Jochebed's gut twisted tighter with each step. She was unsure where this uneasiness came from, but she couldn't shake the feeling. Trusting that the Lord might be trying to tell her something, she decided to swing farther away from the outer wall of the village than they had initially planned. She wanted to avoid even a chance that a night patrol might see them.

"I want you to swing out wider to the south," Jochebed said.

"What's wrong?" Miriam asked.

Jochebed could hear the tinge of fear in her daughter's voice. Her own apprehension had grown, not dissipated, and now she had begun to alarm Miriam. "Nothing. I'm just being careful."

"We have reached the marker. Miriam said. "I'm leaving the road now and will swing out wider."

Jochebed could hear the distress running along the edges of her words. "Don't worry, Miriam. We have time."

Without answering, her daughter turned left and moved off the road onto the rougher ground.

The new moon was an ideal time for thieves and criminals to engage in their illicit activities. That meant the local police would patrol their towns and villages with extra vigilance tonight. In Egypt, the civil police force had long been separated from the standing army. The two duties were considered significantly different in both training and function. The Egyptian police took pride in their unique responsibility and status.

Even so, it was common knowledge that you could bribe these outlying officers. Unfortunately, Jochebed had nothing to offer despite Amram's promising working conditions at the shipyard. They had exhausted their meager funds on the waterproofing materials for the basket. So, unless they happened upon a band of criminals, the village policemen would be their greatest threat. Two Hebrew women walking past an Egyptian settlement in the middle of the night would arouse suspicion, especially off the road, and would need investigation. It was something they had to avoid at all costs.

They swung in the broader arc Jochebed wanted and were almost halfway around the village, off to their right, when suddenly, Jochebed saw Miriam's hand fly up as a warning. Her anxiety clutched at her throat, and she could feel her heart pounding at an alarming rate. As her daughter slowly crouched, she cradled her brother in the space between her knees and chest, afraid he might cry out from the jostling. Jochebed, trying to keep her emotions under control, moved close behind her and, as quickly as possible, gently set the basket on the ground.

They remained as still as their anxiety allowed. As Jochebed's ears adjusted to the sounds of the night, she could hear two men off towards the village. Their voices were low and hard to hear, but it sounded like they were coming straight toward them.

Jochebed anxiously pleaded a silent prayer: "Help us, Lord of Heaven." They were exposed, but they had one hope: God would not fail them.

"Are you sure you heard something?" one of the men said.

"Yes, and it wasn't a hyena either."

Sniffing the air, his companion asked, "Does the night feel strange to you?"

"Now that you mention it, something is in the air."

"Maybe we should go back."

"Not until I find out what made that scraping noise," the second man said, striding forward a short stone's throw from Miriam and her mother. "What if thieves are looking for a way into our village?"

Jochebed was sure they could hear her heart hammering in her chest when a fluttering of wings suddenly broke through the tension. From a short distance to her left, she could barely distinguish the form of two large birds as they took off and flew over her head toward the two searchers.

As the birds flew overhead, the first one asked, "Is that what you heard?"

"I don't know," the other replied and then cursed loudly.

His companion laughed. "Did you just get hit by their droppings?"

"I don't want to talk about it," he said, turning and spitting, cursing every bird that ever existed; he angrily stormed back toward the village.

"Tell me," His companion called after him, with a slight laugh, "which is worse: having to make rounds outside the wall or being spooked by a couple of birds?"

Jochebed heard an exceptionally robust string of curses fill the air as the two men disappeared into the dimness toward the village's southern gate.

Miriam finally exhaled, but neither she nor her mother moved. After the sounds of the two men had died away, Jochebed's heart finally began to slow down. A sense of calm replaced her distress, and the knot in her stomach began to unwind. Her upset had been a warning, after all. Taking a deep breath, she reached forward and placed her hand on Miriam's shoulder. Jochebed could feel her daughter still trembling as she offered a quiet prayer of thanks.

"That was dangerously close. We would have run right into them if we had not taken the wider route," Jochebed whispered.

Miriam reached back and caressed her mother's hand. Then, to give voice to her earlier private prayer, her mother said, "God be praised for his protection."

"Amen," Miriam answered.

They slowly stood up. Miriam took a deep breath, which helped stop most of her shaking. She carefully resettled her brother in the carry sling. Amazingly, he had not moved or made a sound the whole time, for which Jochebed thanked her God again. Stretching her aching legs and stiff back, she recovered from the long, motionless squat. Feeling better, Jochebed reached for the basket and swung it onto her head. Cautioning Miriam with her hand, she waited quietly, trying to discern any movement or noise, but heard nothing.

"It is safe to leave. But go even farther away from the village. I want to make sure we don't run into anyone else."

Miriam set out and adjusted her course without answering. Jochebed knew the precaution was probably unneeded, but she didn't want to take any chances.

They eventually found the road, and once on it, they quickly put the Egyptian settlement behind them.

The brush with the two policemen left Jochebed shaken. While the immediate upset from the encounter had disappeared, it was replaced by another apprehension. Her original plan to cross the smaller farms using the road to Memphis now felt wrong. As they approached the first farm, her distress grew so much that she decided to alter their course. It might take a little longer, but she couldn't afford to disregard this continued foreboding since the earlier sense of danger had proven true.

"I want to take a different path to the river," Jochebed said.

"Where?" Miriam asked, confused by the change.

"Up ahead, at the edge of the first farm, there will be mounds on either side of the road. They run along the edge of the fields to keep the water contained. I want to turn south and follow the short wall around the southern edge of the Great Estate. It will guide us around the fields to a more deserted river area."

"Do we have enough time? That is a much longer way to go."

"We can do it. It will be close, but we should change our route. I had doubts after those two policemen almost found us. This should be a safer river path since it goes south of the estate's living quarters and is far away from the buildings along the riverbank where the road meets the ferry. We don't want to keep depending on God's deliverance by not being careful."

"I see the mounds up ahead."

They went a short distance, and then Mirian cautiously turned off the road. Jochebed followed close behind. They angled toward the mound, marking the edge of the field. It was a well-constructed wall, almost a cubit high. The ground beside it was rough compared to the road they had just left. There were loose stones everywhere. Cleared from the field over many generations, they had been tossed over the mound and littered the ground, making walking difficult.

It did not take long for them to begin to exhaust themselves walking through the loose stones. They were so numerous that it had been impossible to avoid any but the largest. While they had good leather on their feet, sheepskin with the fleece turned inward for cushioning, they were sore and tired. Also, carrying the basket was awkward, and Jochebed's neck, arms, and shoulders began to join her legs and feet in rebellion. Miriam's shoulders and back showed the strain of carrying her brother and enduring the constant sweeping motion with the stick as she searched ahead.

"Mother," Miriam said. "I think the mound is large enough to walk on. It's almost like a small path. We could walk on that and get away from all these rocks."

"Are you sure you won't fall?"

"It is not that high, and yes, I think I can do it."

"Alright," Jochebed answered. "Let's try that."

Getting onto the mound's smoother ground helped. They made good progress, but their bodies and feet eventually began to rebel.

Jochebed called out, "We've gone far enough. It is time to rest."

Miriam let out a sigh of relief. "A cart path cuts across the mound just ahead, and a ramp leads down."

They probably use that to access and inspect the wall, with the ramp for turning around. Sweep a place nearby so we can sit down for a while."

Miriam thrashed the ground near the ramp, finding nothing. Jochebed settled atop it, facing east, knees raised. "Lean back," she said. Miriam sighed, easing against her mother's legs, and lifted her brother from the sling. "He slept through it all," she marveled, handing him over. "A blessing," Jochebed replied, cradling him.

Miriam gave her mother the blanket, stretched, and leaned back, folding the sling under her head.

Jochebed took the blanket, then reached into her robe and removed a small waterskin. "Here, have a drink. You haven't said anything, but your throat must be parched. I thought the air would be less dry at night."

"I didn't want to say anything," Miriam replied, "but this was harder than practicing."

Miriam took a long drink and handed the waterskin back.

"Yes, it has been, but we're almost there. Get some rest."

As Miriam looked up at the sky, only a few small clouds remained. Her village was somewhere in the distance. She had never been out this late on the night of a new moon. The stars shone brightly against the surrounding darkness. The wonder she felt was an unexpected gift amidst the long and challenging night. She marveled at the night sky's vastness and the countless little lights spread across the heavens, some brighter than others, especially one bright one above her village. As the immensity of it all rushed in, a strange feeling almost overwhelmed her. It was both wonderful and scary, making her feel small and insignificant, yet at the same time, curious and awestruck. Miriam gazed skyward. The stars shimmered—some blinking, some swaying as if caught in a distant, unseen current. They felt impossibly far away, yet closer than ever.

"I wonder what they are," she whispered, feeling, for the first time, how small she truly was.

What did you say?" her mother said.

"The stars, I wonder what they are."

"Our elders say that God put them there to be lights for signs and seasons. They also show us that even when the moon is at its lowest, as it is tonight, God has not abandoned us to darkness."

"Signs? I would like to see a sign. When I meet God, I will ask Him what the stars are."

"I think if God were here now," her mother said, "he would tell you to hold your curiosity for later. Right now, you need to rest because the most important part of our journey is still ahead."

Royal Disturbances

Tuya, startled by a sound that lingered in the space between sleep and wakefulness, bolted upright. A faint recollection of disturbing dreams remained like a mist in her memory, but it was already drifting away, like the last wisp of clouds that moved beyond the horizon. Though Tuya seldom remembered her dreams, these vapors had left behind a reminder—a cold dread that touched an apprehension deep within her womb.

The high windows were dark, and the new moon did not help. The only light came from a small lamp trimmed low at the far corner of her sleeping chamber. She could see almost nothing in the murky dimness, and the stillness, broken only by the sound of her breathing, added to her sense of foreboding.

Then she heard the sound again. It was coming through the curtain that separated her husband's quarters from hers. As she heard Pharaoh's voice rise and fall, her trepidation turned from her distress to his.

Were dreams also disturbing his sleep?

She waited to see if he would quiet down. Instead, his voice grew louder, and he shouted, "Watch out!"

Tuya rushed from her bed into her husband's sleeping chamber. In the dimness, she could barely make out his arms reaching toward the ceiling, grasping at the air as if he were trying to grab something.

She felt her way to the edge of his bed, where she sat down and then gently took his outstretched hands in hers. She leaned forward and kissed his fingers, whispering, "Everything is all right. It's only a dream."

Seti awoke suddenly, sitting up and knocking Tuya off balance. He caught her, pulled her close, and put his arms around her. "I'm sorry," he said softly. "You surprised me. Did I hurt you?"

"No. I'm all right, but I was concerned."

"Why?"

"You shouted in your sleep."

"I did? What did I say?"

"At first, I wasn't sure; you were murmuring, but then you yelled, 'Watch out!' When I rushed into the room, you were trying to grab something in front of you."

Seti reached up and gently stroked his wife's face. "I had a strange dream, that's all."

"Tell me about it."

He hesitated and then said, "We can talk about it in the morning."

"You know I won't go back to sleep if you don't tell me. I'll lie awake, wondering, making up things."

"In the morning," he said softly.

"Seti..."

"All right."

Tuya waited, but he seemed reluctant to say anything, so she said, "I'll just sit here, and then neither of us will get any sleep."

Seti relented. "When the dream began, it was early morning in the northern marshes. Ramses, who appeared fully grown, and another young man were hunting."

"Who was with him?"

"I will tell you in a moment. The important part is that Ramses was older, and he was using his spear to face down a leopard when he was ambushed from behind. I yelled, but he didn't hear my warning, and I couldn't reach him."

"Someone tried to harm our son!"

"Not a man," Seti quickly reassured her. "A viper struck from behind, coiled and ready to sink its fangs into Ramses. I shouted, but my voice was swallowed by silence. I could do nothing."

"And then?" Tuya whispered, unable to stop herself.

"A boy stepped forward. He was unarmed, yet he moved with certainty. He seized the viper, his hands steady, and cast it into the reeds. He saved our son."

When he said nothing else, Tuya grew impatient and asked, "Was it the young man you mentioned earlier?"

"Yes."

"Who was he?"

Seti did not answer. She almost pleaded when she asked again, "Who was the young man who saved him?"

Silence. However, as her distress increased, Seti said, "He was a young Hebrew."

Her upset quickly turned to astonishment, and she said, "A Hebrew? Is he the same as those whose infant sons are offered as sacrifices to Sobek every day?"

"Yes, the same."

"How can that be?"

"I don't know. Ramses was older; he looked fully grown. That is why I believe it was more than a dream."

"Is this an omen about the future—that he's not in any immediate danger?"

"I don't think he is in any immediate danger. But the dream was strange, and I'm not sure what it means."

"The priests will help."

"Maybe. We'll see about that in the morning, but enough about my dream. I'm sorry I woke you."

Tuya remembered the lingering ache and felt a shiver go through her body.

"You're trembling. Were your dreams as dramatic as mine?"

As Seti pulled her closer, Tuya buried her face in the crook of his neck. Her husband was a strong, well-trained warrior and yet surprisingly gentle. Whenever he held her, she felt safe and protected.

Her words were almost a whimper. "When I woke up, I couldn't remember anything, but I had a deep sense of dread, and there is an ache that remains in my womb."

Seti leaned over and gently placed his hand on her lingering pain. "Are you...?"

"No. But now you tell me you saw Ramses' life threatened, and I think that might be the source of my pain. Maybe your dream or my dreams? Maybe they are related."

"I don't know. It's possible." He reached out and pulled her close; his embrace gradually comforted her trembling, but she needed reassurance. Ever since the death of their firstborn, Shaanar, two inundations ago in a chariot accident, she had become extremely protective of Ramses, their only remaining child.

Seti kissed her forehead and said what she needed to hear, "I'll keep Ramses with me today. He can miss Temple School. It would be good for him to be with me at court and learn how the priests interpret the dreams of Pharaoh."

"And he'll be safe with you?"

Seti responded to the quiet pleading behind her words. "Yes. He'll be safe with me."

Tuya held onto his comforting words and gradually settled into his warmth. Her breathing began to slow and eventually became smooth and rhythmic as she drifted off to sleep, temporarily freed from her maternal distress.

Seti leaned back into the cushions, careful not to wake his wife, as he gently moved her alongside him.

His mind began sifting through what had happened: the ache in his wife's womb and the disturbing nature of his dream. Seti wondered whether the two together might mean more than either one alone.

Saved by a Hebrew, what a strange twist of fate. Were the gods trying to tell me something? Was Ma'at asserting herself, demanding that the balance of justice be restored, that I stop the sacrifices?

As Pharaoh, I can demand the edict be rescinded, and everyone would comply, at least publicly. Rebellion would stir behind that façade, jeopardizing the hard-won religious and political peace his family had brought to the throne of Egypt. The country was finally healing from the depredations inflicted by the Pharaoh Who is Not Named. His father, may he rest with the gods, had sacrificed much to gain the support of the influential priesthoods. He could not take a chance without a more precise direction. His family's dynasty was only in its fifth year; now was not the time for him to confront this issue on his authority alone.

If the gods willed this, they would need to speak louder, much louder. One dream would not silence the priests, least of all Nephura, the First Priest of Amon-Ra in Memphis. He despises the Hebrews beyond reason. Even if I command the edict's repeal, he and most of the other priesthoods will resist unless the gods force their hand. No, if Ma'at demands justice, she must make it known—to all of Egypt, not just me.

Disturbing Dreams

Princess Asati tossed fitfully on her bed as a cold sweat broke out, making her gown cling unpleasantly to her skin. Most nights, her sleep was peaceful and dreamless, like a gentle lover caressing her in the darkness, but tonight, powerful visions upset her usual tranquil stillness. She'd awaken with a start, her breath shallow, her heart hammering against her ribs. The dream refused to fade. Even in the darkness, the image burned behind her eyes—etched like a vision from the gods.

She was on the edge of a vast sea. Rising from the distant horizon, the sun fanned luminous rays out from the center of its fierce brightness. A breeze rippled across the water's surface, carrying undercurrents of anticipation and premonition. The hair along the nape of Asati's neck bristled as the wind brushed past her, sending a chill down her back. As she looked out from the shore, the water's surface began to boil and foam.

She wanted to flee, but her feet had sunk into the wet sand, which held her ankles fast. Imprisoned, she could not turn away but had to face the chaos and wait. Slowly, out of the middle of the upheaval rose a baby, a male child with strong, noble features.

Spellbound, she watched as the child drifted toward her, weightless upon the water. His skin, rich as the desert earth, glowed softly beneath the fractured light. Dark curls framed his round face, his eyes wide, piercing, filled with recognition. His tiny arms stretched toward her as he softly called to her, saying, "Momma." The word flew across the water, boring into the deepest yearnings of her heart. But he was circumcised, and floating in the water below him was a coarse blanket of the type used by the Hebrews. He was not Egyptian. Recoiling, she wanted to turn away, to deny what she saw. And yet—something in the child's eyes caught her, held her. A strange stirring, barely more than a whisper, brushed against her heart before she shoved it away.

As she held back from his pleading, large clouds began to darken the sky, and powerful bolts of lightning filled the air, arching between the thunderheads and the churning sea below. An overwhelming sight, one Asati had never seen, only heard about. But here it was, happening right in front of her. Despite the gathering squall, the child waited persistently and unafraid at the edge of the water, his small arms still outstretched, repeating the haunting assertion, "Momma. Momma. Momma. Momma."

As the dream faded, Asati's heart pounded in her chest, its beating spurred on by the word reflecting back and forth across the cavern in the center of her being. Even with her hands clasped over her ears, she could not shut out the sound. It found its way into every part of her, its taunting refrain echoing in her inner emptiness.

Over the five inundations since her marriage, despite the continuous offerings, the innumerable potions tried by the priests, and her plea-filled prayers, Asati's womb had remained barren. She had begun to think her name was a curse. In naming her Asati, her father had dedicated her to Satis, the Goddess of the First Cataract, the Protectress of the Nile, and the symbol of fertility and love. Instead of blessing her with abundant children, the goddess had allowed her field to remain fallow.

At court, whispers floated behind veiled lips, suggesting an ill omen had overshadowed her. Asati's husband, once drawn by her beauty and grace into an endless stream of passion, now sought less the pleasure of her bed than the diversions of his concubines.

The vision was seared into her mind, stirring a hunger she could no longer silence. The ache in her womb was a ravenous beast, a jackal, voracious and relentless. She curled into herself as if she could shield her empty center from the truth.

Terrified by this sense of inward dissolution, she offered a crying prayer to the gods, asking that this vision, despite its ominous implications, be a sign her prayers would be answered, her emptiness filled. The possibility that the baby might be a Hebrew was pushed aside. Her remaining hope grasped the idea of a child, please, a child, a son for the prince, an end to the whispers.

After what seemed like hours, Asati unfolded and slowly began moving her legs, stretching the stiffness and lethargy from her body. She had made a decision. She would bathe early, and it would be a special, sacred bath. Then, she would ask the priests about this night vision.

Although not even a hint of light was visible through the high window, a vague sense of urgency prompted her to call out for her chief maidservant. She closed her mind to the fear that stirred in its depths that this tenuous hope might only be a mist in the night. She left her bed as the door opened, and Nari entered.

"You called, my princess?"

"Yes, Nari. I know it's still dark, but I want to bathe in the Nile at first light."

Debating whether to confide in her servant concerning the night's events, even though the woman had watched over her since birth, Asati paused and said, "I had an omen during the night. Now that the inundation is about to begin, I want to present offerings to Hapi and receive the anointing of the sacred waters. After that, I will consult with the priests to investigate the meaning of the omen. Begin preparing what is needed."

"We shall be ready before Ra's barge breaks the horizon."

Turning from the retreating servant, Asati went to the alcove, which held the altar and statue of Satis. A sacred lamp was kept burning as an ongoing tribute to her patron, illuminating a small female figure wearing a horned white crown, the reservoir of the seed of life and protectress of the yearly inundation.

Looking at the statue, Asati voiced her concern.

"Oh, Mistress of Heaven, did you send these visions?"

There was no answer. The goddess's blank eyes and fixed mouth showed Asati no response, no concern. An old doubt that had grown stronger since the last inundation edged its way into her thoughts: had the gods abandoned her? Were they dead, as some who still followed the heresy of the forgotten Pharaoh whispered? Maybe they were only a memory, kept alive by the priests' ministrations?

With cold determination, she quenched those thoughts. She poured a libation to her mistress into the waiting bowl and lit a small lump of incense using the lamp's flame. Then, kneeling on the hard tile, Asati whispered her final plea and lifted her gaze to the altar. The tiny flame of the sacred lamp flickered. For a breath, she dared to hope. But the light held steady. The stone face of the goddess remained as empty as ever. There was no sign. No answer. Only silence.

Celestial Signs

The searing bright light in the night sky of his dream faded from memory as Saisa felt a hand on his shoulder, gently shaking him.

"Saisa. Wake up."

Opening his eyes, he saw one of the elder priests crouched in front of him, his hand still on his shoulder.

"Are you awake?"

"Yes," he replied, the sleep still tugging at him.

"Get up. Dress to go outside. The Chief Priest has a special mission for you. He is waiting in the Audience Room." Without waiting for a response, he turned and left.

Upina, his purification partner, stirred in the bed next to him. Still half asleep, his voice sounded like a groan. "Is it time to get up?"

"Not yet. I'm going on a mission."

"Need help getting ready?"

His tender skin rebelled at the thought. During their daily cleansing ritual, Upina's razor frequently nicked Saisa's out-of-reach places. He was worse with tweezers, often grabbing the skin along with the hairs. It had gotten so bad that some of the older priests had begun to call him "the wounded one" and had jokingly suggested that he might be better off in the army; at least there, his injuries might serve to advance him.

"No, don't worry about it. I don't need my toilet." The last thing he wanted was his purification partner "helping" him.

With a grunt, Upina rolled over and went back to sleep.

Saisa took a common linen wrap from the set of pegs that held his clothes and hastily adjusted it around his waist. Slipping his feet into his work sandals, he quietly made his way to the purification area. Splashing water on his face, he rubbed his wet hands around his head and neck.

It wasn't much of a purification, but it would have to do. He could finish when he returned. He found the Audience Room in the dim light, and Sostris, the Chief Priest of Satis, was waiting outside the entrance.

"You called for me, my lord?" he said, bowing.

"I have an important task for you, and you need to go quickly. It's a long way, and there isn't much time."

"I will do my best, my Lord."

"I know you will, Saisa. That is why I chose you. Many older priests dreamt strange things last night, but your sharp eyes may yet see what they cannot. The gods favor the vigilant. We need better water for this morning's procedures. I want it to be fresh and pure, taken directly from the Sacred River, untouched by its journey through the city. The water in our temple supply is not pure enough for these special circumstances."

The sacred pools within the city's temple enclosures relied on small canals connected to the central waterway that ran through the capital. The water levels were extremely low in the lead-up to the coming inundation, and the temple pool had become murky due to overuse.

Sostris pointed to the two jars and carry pole waiting for him. "Hurry."

Saisa bowed and picked up the bag of cover materials and carry straps. After tying the bag to his waist, he slung the jars on the pole using the carry straps and left.

The Chief Priest led him to the service entrance in the side wall of the temple enclosure. He lifted the locking bar and opened the door.

Turning to one side so he could maneuver the jars through the opening, Saisa went out into the night.

"May Satis give you strength and speed, my son," Sostris called after him as the door closed, sealing him outside.

The predawn air was cool, and Saisa was soon glad for the exertion. Carrying the two water jugs required enough physical effort to warm his muscles as he walked toward the Great Southern Gate. He needed to go as far south as possible, where the Nile first encountered the city, to get the clean water Sostris wanted.

Saisa was studying to become the village's resident magician. That meant starting at the bottom of the temple's hierarchy as a wa'eb, a minor assistant to the priests of Satis. This left him with mostly menial and tedious duties, like gathering water for the morning procedures. It was not often he got a chance to be out of the city so early, and despite the effort, he looked forward to the physical labor, which helped take his mind off his loneliness.

The priesthood of Satis was small. Only five others were studying the course of magic at the same level as him. While the goddess was a favorite of the family of the new Pharaoh, her following was minuscule compared to the established deities of Egypt. However, it had recently begun to grow.

He was thankful the Temple of Satis was near the Great Southern Gate. It was a new structure, much farther from the palace than the other temples, which filled every available space at the city's northern end.

As Saisa neared the great doorway, one of the guards called out.

"Stop! Identify yourself."

"I am Saisa, a wa'eb from the Temple of Satis."

"What are you carrying so early this morning?"

"Jars to get pure water from the Sacred River for the temple's morning rituals."

"Come forward."

As he approached them, the head guard checked his jars and then looked him over, poking and prodding him from head to foot.

"You will have to go through the small door over there. It is too early to open the main gate."

"Thank you," Saisa replied, relieved to have gotten past their inspection.

One of the guards led him to the side passageway, pulled the restraining bolts, and opened the small but heavy door. It was a tight fit as Saisa moved sideways through the opening.

As the guard shut the door behind him, Saisa saw he still had to go further south for the clear, untainted water Sostris wanted. Despite the new moon's lack of light, the starlight reflecting off the towering white expanse of the Great Wall provided him with enough illumination to see the road ahead.

He walked south along the wall using a well-worn track. The southern end of the wall was close to the Nile as it angled past the city and then turned to flow parallel to Perunifer, the burgeoning port that filled the space between the river and the city walls. Up ahead, beyond the southern edge of the city and its port, stood the great locks with their massive gates. These vital structures prevented even the most extensive inundation from flooding the central canal running through Memphis. To protect the locks, the authorities had prevented anyone from building within an arrow shot of these essential barriers. That meant most of the land he had to cross was completely open.

As he passed the last buildings marking the southern edge of the port to his left, Saisa left the path and angled across the open ground toward the river. Long ago, the pharaohs had raised the land between the white wall and the river to prevent the yearly inundation from flooding the port. He needed to find a place to climb down to the river.

He came to the last public shaduf station, which was used to lift water from the river. Using the long-counterbalanced pole to get what he wanted would have been more straightforward, but he had specific instructions. Too bad, since it would also have been safer. The stations sat high on the raised edge of the riverbank, well above the usual path of the crocodiles, who usually kept to the shallow and marshy areas close to the steep banks. Anything could be hidden in those reeds.

He peered over the edge of the bank and found a suitable spot to enter the river. A sharply angled path worn into the bank's side looked well used. Many people must have used it to go down to the water.

The distance down the bank to the river, now at the lowest point of the yearly cycle, was over twice his height. The little trail passed around the Shaduf station's heavy stone base, which provided a solid foundation for the endless water lifting from the river and protected its supports during the yearly flooding.

The stars provided just enough light to guide his feet. To his chagrin, he knew seeing any crocodiles in the area would be difficult. While he  respected their deadliness, the water beasts did not usually intimidate him, but this darkness made it hard to know if any were in the area. He had grown up on a Nile farm and was strong and quick. Besides, he carried his newly sharpened bronze knife in a sheath always attached to his thigh. It was a gift from his village when he left home to pursue his studies in Memphis. In addition, his carry pole made a stout and effective weapon that could ward off almost any of the beasts. Most important, though, was the Wedjat Eye amulet Sostris had given him when he became a wa'eb and apprentice magician. The Wedjat Eye was the most powerful amulet in Egyptian magic, and it dangled from his neck. The temple's seer priest had blessed it with the most potent magic available. And there was one last item in his assembled defenses. As part of his studies, he had memorized the prayer of protection to the great crocodile god, Sobek, which he began to recite earnestly.

Despite all of his preparations, Saisa knew he needed to keep a sharp and vigilant eye in the direction of the river's edge. While the crocodile-headed god might hear his petition and the amulet perform its assigned magic, it did not pay to act foolishly. Over the years, many inexperienced apprentices had become an unintended casualty because they had stepped on a log or stone that unexpectedly became a death trap. Thinking about crocodiles and being at the river reminded him of the small Temple the priests of Sobek had built on the other side of Memphis. It was there they offered the Hebrew male babies as sacrifices to their god. He was glad he had never seen that.

Putting that chilling image out of his mind, he slowly made his way down the path to the river's edge, carefully balancing the jars as he tried to keep them from striking the receding wall of the riverbank. When he reached the bottom, he went through an area cleared by the many who had gone before him to the water's edge. He set down the jars, removed the carry pole, and drove it into the damp sand. Then he took one of the jars and worked the pointed bottom securely into the sand next to the pole. He took the bag of cover materials and the carry straps and placed them on the top of the anchored jar.

After scanning the river from one end to the other for any signs of a river beast and seeing nothing, he took the remaining jar and waded out into the cool water. He moved as far as he could toward the center of the river until he could feel the bottom starting to give way. He was a short stone's throw from the bank.

Looking up at the night sky, he enjoyed gazing at the vast expanse of stars, which held so many pinpoints of light that he could not begin to count them. He turned and faced south so the river flowed directly toward him. Feeling the current gently push against his chest, the ghostly outline of the Nile appeared almost as a straight line, starting from a single point far in the distance. The vastness and majesty of the moment nearly overwhelmed him. It was a humbling sight. Ever since he came to the temple, he had begun to appreciate things that had previously gone unnoticed.

Putting the experience away for later reflection, he returned to his urgent task. Grasping one of the handles with one hand and the pointed bottom with the other, he lowered the mouth into the slow-moving water. As it began to fill, the increasing weight pulled down on his arms, but he was strong and held it steady until it was full of the precious water. Then, using the river to reduce the effects of the increased weight, he kept the jar almost submerged, with only the top of the rim above the surface, as he waded back to the bank. Keeping the jar almost submerged made it feel lighter and easier to maneuver. He did not know why it worked, but it did.

Climbing out of the water, Saisa lifted the water jar and easily anchored the tapered end into the soft sand on the other side of the carry pole using its significantly increased weight. He removed the pouch from the top of the other jar and took out a piece of clean cloth, a circle of leather, and the tie string used to secure the two pieces over the mouth of the jar. These would protect the pure water from any dirt or debris. After securely fastening the cloth and leather cap, he put the pouch on the sealed jar and the carry straps through the jar's handles. He then picked up the other jar. Looking again for evidence of crocodiles and seeing none, he headed back into the water.

He was only half the distance to where he would fill the jar; the water was only up to his mid-thighs when he noticed something strange in  front of him, high in the eastern sky. Among the many stars was a long streak of slow-moving light, as if one of the heavenly bodies had left its place and was now traveling across the heavens. Following the line of its path, it looked as if it might come close to where he was. Saisa had heard stories about stars falling from heaven but had only seen the brief flashes, which sometimes dotted the night sky.

Everyone knew falling stars portended significant events, though he never thought he would live to see such a thing. He remembered his dream and the bright light he had seen in the night sky just before the priest had awoken him. His body began to tremble excitedly as he followed the light's descent. To steady himself, he widened his stance, shoved the pointed end of the jar into the riverbed, and tightened his grip.

A ball of blue-green fire began to glow more intensely at the head of the streak of light. The nearer it came, the more he was sure it was heading toward Memphis and him. Saisa had no idea of what to do. Should he run or kneel in the water and pray? How do you avoid a star? Frozen by indecision, he saw the streaking ball of light suddenly begin to flicker, then fade, and finally disappear.

Amazed, he searched the sky for any movement, any sign of the falling star. Where could it have gone? Then, a rushing sound began to build to the east, coming from the same place where the star had disappeared. Still, despite the steadily growing noise, he couldn't see anything.

The closest thing Saisa had ever heard to this sound was when his older brother, who worked on a Nile cargo ship, took him on a trip south to the First Cataract. As they approached the base of the great rapids, he heard the crushing sound of the river as it crashed down in torrents, cascading through the rocks.

Whatever was making the noise sounded as if it were heading straight at him. He hurriedly searched the night sky, but there was nothing to see. Suddenly, the noise increased to a deafening roar, followed by a tremendous whoosh as the air buffeted him. He saw something strike the river to the south near the great locks. It hit between mid-river and the bank, causing the river to shriek as the star dove through its surface, sending a high-arching torrent of water, steam, and earth into the air. Much of it hurled across the western bank toward the Great Lock and the southern edge of the city wall. Most of the river and a large portion of the riverbed were now arching through the air, and a lot of it was coming toward him.

Every muscle in Saisa's body froze in a rigid clench as the earth shuddered beneath his feet, almost knocking him down. As he regained his balance, aided by the jar anchored in the riverbed, he broke free from his rigor. He began to run toward the bank, but the remaining river, shallower now that much of the water had rushed toward the point where the star had struck, still resisted every thrust of his legs. With his body rebelling from the extreme exertion, Saisa's mind raced through a quickly narrowing set of options. Then, unexpectedly, everything seemed to slow down. Though his legs burned as he thrashed through the knee-deep water, it was as if time was being stretched out like dough when it was drawn out on a baker's table.

He was not going to make it to the bank. The bulky jar was slowing him down, and in that instant of clarity, he knew what he had to do. He heaved the pointed end of the jar toward the riverbank. Then, unhindered, he turned to the river itself for protection. Taking a deep breath, he dove under the water as an ear-splitting sound burst from the air over his head. He had barely made it beneath the surface when a massive fall of water and debris smashed into the river above him. His back felt like a thousand fists were pounding him, and he was forcefully driven into the riverbed. He was a good swimmer and had often practiced holding his breath. Despite that, he felt like his lungs were going to burst as the pounding continually hammered him to the bottom. He was just about to pass out when the beating stopped, and he was able to thrust his face above the surface. Battered, bruised, and gasping for air, he stood up. He was wet and trembling, while the water around him was thick with mud and debris.

"Ugh!" Saisa coughed, spitting muddy water out of his mouth. His heart pounded in his chest, and he could barely steady himself. But he was alive. As he slowly turned and started to push through the debris-filled water, his legs were almost too weak to support him. With each step, his strength grew, and it didn't take long before he started to feel much better, though he still sensed a slight tremor in his hands. When he reached the bank, he was surprised to see the full jar still embedded alongside the pole he had driven into the sand. The empty jar he had heaved was stuck in the slope, and although covered with mud and debris, it looked undamaged. He found the bag embedded in the mud uphill from the first jar, with the carry straps still looped through its handles. As he turned to look up the river, his knees felt wobbly, and he had to sit down.

After taking a short rest and praying his way through several litanies of thanksgiving, a sense of calm descended over him. The gods had not struck him down. They had chosen him. He had seen the fire descend, had felt its power, had survived its fury. His hands trembled, not with fear, but with the weight of a new certainty. The river had been marked. And so had he.

It was then he heard voices off in the distance, and light began spilling over the riverbank in several places in the port downstream. He could hear the people who had come out to investigate what had happened.

He wondered about the Great Lock. It regulated water flow into the city, especially during the inundation, which was due to begin within one moon. It was the only means of preventing the impending flood of water from overwhelming the central canal and inundating the waterway that led into the city. There would be serious problems if the star had damaged the mechanism.

As the events began to sift in his mind, he wondered whether he might be the only person in Memphis or the surrounding area to have seen the whole event. What a story he would have to tell the temple priests, his village, his family, and eventually his children and grandchildren. It would give him real status at home and enlarge the prestige of his office as Village Magician. But most of all, it would raise his stature among everyone back at the temple.

It was time to complete his task and finish filling the second jar. Despite this extraordinary event, he still needed to complete his charge. Mud and debris covered the filled jar, but at least he had protected its opening. From what he could make out in the dim light, the river appeared to be filled with mud and debris as he looked toward the place where the star had struck. How was he going to fill the second jar with clean water?

Then Saisa had an inspiration. He would still fill the empty vessel with the sacred water from the river, but despite the mud, it would be water blessed by the star, the messenger of the gods. It would be extraordinary; it would be twice blessed. He hoped his master, Sostris, would appreciate his initiative, as the priests could filter the muddy water through several layers of cloth and use what they collected to fashion a specially blessed vessel. Afterward, they would pour the water into a large holding container. Over time, the water would begin to clear as any remaining mud settled to the bottom, allowing them to draw clean water off from the top. Besides, they had one jar that was sealed and still clear for the morning's special offerings.

After testing his legs and deciding he had recovered enough to complete his task, he cleaned the mud and debris off the filled jar using the dirty water. When the jar was reasonably clean, he carried the empty one back into the flow of the river. Instead, what had begun as a chore had become a unique blessing, and the determination in his actions spoke to his new sense of destiny. The gods had chosen him to witness and live through a great wonder. That had to mean something auspicious for his future. Saisa strode out into the water, mud still streaking his grin. One jar sealed, the other star-blessed—a destiny etched in water and fire awaited him.

Divine Voices

Miriam and Jochebed

Miriam saw one of the stars move. It started like those sudden flashes of light that sometimes shot across the canopy of heaven but always lasted less than a breath. Instead, this streak of light was more than a sudden flash. It slowly grew into a fiery ball with a tail trailing behind. It appeared to be coming in their direction.

"Momma, look!" Miriam exclaimed, and then, getting control of herself, she pointed. "A falling star!"

Jochebed looked up to where her daughter pointed.

Miriam watched the bright blue-green flaming light move through the sky, trailing a distinctly glowing tail. This was different from the streaking flashes that usually disappeared in a blink. It was a lot larger, and it continued to glow in the eastern sky, increasing in brightness as they watched.

"Maybe this is one of the signs our elders talked about. God is telling us that something important is about to happen," Jochebed said.

"What's he saying?" Miriam replied, sitting straight up, the anxiety evident in her voice.

"I don't know," her mother answered. "We'll have to wait and see, but it looks like the star is falling in this direction."

As they watched, the streaking fireball unexpectedly dimmed; its light sputtered and then disappeared.

"Did you see where it went?" Miriam asked.

"No. I don't understand what happened."

"Strange," Miriam said as she continued to explore the night sky. Then, out of the expanse in front of her, she heard a distant rushing sound. It grew in intensity and was coming right at them. Jochebed leaned forward and grabbed her daughter, the blanket falling over her son, sheltered in the space between them.

Fearing she was going to die, Miriam leaned hard against her mother's legs and put her hands over her ears as the sound screamed over their heads and, with a resounding crash, hit near the city to the west of them. Buffeted by a hot wind, with the ground still shuddering beneath them, a thunderous sound struck them from the sky above. It was stronger, deeper, and almost earsplitting like a deafening clap of thunder had struck right next to them. She felt her heart trying to pound its way out of her chest. In the distance toward Memphis, through the ringing in her ears, she heard a brief sound like heavy rain falling.

Then, it was eerily quiet, as if the whole of creation had been shocked into silence. Beyond the dust slowly settling on them, only a soft cry from her brother interrupted the stillness, and then it faded as he settled back into sleep. When nothing else happened, Miriam felt her mother gently stroking her back, trying to calm her. She removed her hands from her ears.

"It has passed, Miriam. It has passed."

With her brother safely settled in the cradle created by her mother's lap, Jochebed reached up and stroked Miriam's head reassuringly and said, "It's all right."

Miriam was astonished they were still alive. She did not know what to say or think. After a series of deep breaths, the pounding in her chest slowly quieted, but the shudders still rippled through her. Taking care not to disturb her brother, who was resting quietly in her mother's lap, she slowly got up. Reaching down, she carefully removed the blanket from over her brother, keeping any of the accumulated debris from falling on him.

Everything was covered with dust and dirt stirred up by the wind from the passing star. Miriam took the blanket and carry cloth and shook both items clean. She brushed away the remaining dirt from her gown, put the carry cloth over her shoulder, and approached her mother. Kneeling beside her, Miriam arranged the blanket around her brother and, with her mother's help, lifted him back into the carry cloth. After ensuring he was safely settled, she asked, "Can we still go to the river?"

Jochebed thought for a moment. "It looks like it struck close to Memphis. That had to wake everyone from our village to the city…except for your brother." Jochebed marveled how he had come through the event undisturbed. "It will not take long before everyone is out investigating what happened. We can't go back. It is a good thing we chose to go around the Royal Estate."

Adding weight to her words, torches began appearing in the distance. As she stood there watching the number of lights grow in the distance, Jochebed thought about how their new route had become their only option. God works in mysterious ways. The royal estate's villa and surrounding buildings were near its northern border with the small farms they had planned to cross. It was close enough to the edge of the estate that their vast fields to the south would be far enough away from the current activity to be safe. With the disruptions caused by the falling star, it was unlikely anyone would pay attention to the southern fields, at least not until later in the morning. If they hurried, they could still make it through the estate's fields to the south and get to the Nile before they lost the darkness. They needed to move.

Jochebed said, "We are continuing south." She placed an encouraging hand on her daughter's shoulder. "We must hurry. I hope we have enough time."

Temple of Satis

The Book of Dreams was opened across Sostris's lap as he, three of his elder priests, and the temple's Seer Priest sat conferring in his private Audience Room. Each temple in Memphis had a designated room where the Chief Priest received special visitors, typically high-ranking officials or wealthy patrons seeking a favor from the deity. Sostris had even received Seti; may he live forever, the new Pharaoh in this room. Ramses the First, his father, had commissioned the building of this temple to Satis. Seti, may the goddess bless him, had recently finished the work.

With the aid of Sostris and the Seer Priest, the three elder priests tried to understand the disturbing dreams that had awakened them during the night. However, the overwhelming sense of foreboding in the air was disrupting their efforts.

Many throughout Memphis believed Sostris was an instrument tuned to the gods' intent, especially concerning dreams. He often used his reputation to benefit the goddess and advance their priesthood. It helped their temple in the constant jockeying for prominence between the priests of the lesser gods. While Amun-Ra and Ptah held the preeminent places in the pantheon worshipped by the people of Memphis and Pharaoh's court, the perceived importance of the other gods changed constantly with current events and the whims of those in power.

During their discussion, they were startled by a growing rushing sound, followed by a strong vibration that passed through the floor of the room. Before anyone could react, a resounding clap of thunder shook the temple, as intense as if lightning had struck in the courtyard.

Before Sostris could move, one of the priests jumped up and ran outside. He called back, "I can't see anything that could have caused it. The night sky is clear except for a few clouds. It couldn't have been a storm."

It was yet another strange event that disturbed the night. Even in the dim light of the lamp, Sostris could see the anxiousness on their faces.

"I believe something significant just occurred," Sostris said. He remembered the young wa'eb, Saisa, and offered a quick prayer for his safety. He then turned his attention to the possibility the gods might be speaking. "Whatever that was, I think the gods are trying to get our attention."

"Could this be connected to our dreams?" one of the priests asked.

"It is too soon to know. We need more information, but first, someone must go to the southern gate and ensure Saisa is all right. Then, we should send some lesser-known priests and our remaining students to the other temples to find out if they have experienced any omens. If these things are connected, and if what is happening to us is happening elsewhere, then the more we know, the better we will deal with it."

The other priests agreed, and together, they began drawing up a list of temples and the people they would send. They decided to have Satyu, Sostris' senior priest, oversee the investigation since he would not have to be the pure priest for several more days.

"All of the temples in Memphis will be jockeying for position," Sostris said, "to cast the events, whatever they prove to be, positively for *their* god and *their* priesthood."

"We should also increase the morning offerings and add entreaties for wisdom," Satyu said.

"I agree," Sostris replied, "but getting information is our first concern. We need to learn as much as possible about what happened. We need to know if the gods are speaking and, if so, what they are saying."

Royal Household

A rushing sound invaded the high southern windows, disrupting Seti's sleep. Then, a crash and a shudder passing through his bed roused him completely. Almost immediately, out of the same high windows, he heard a deep, powerful sound, which reminded him of very close thunder, but deeper so that he could feel it in his chest.

Tuya stirred in the crook of his arm and mumbled something, but surprisingly, she did not awaken. Her breathing settled in the silence that followed, and she drifted back into sound sleep.

Seti knew something momentous had happened. Were the gods sending the sign he had asked for? As pharaoh, it was his duty to investigate. A seasoned commander, Seti was not the type of leader who relied on second-hand accounts when he could see something for himself.

Gently supporting Tuya's head, he carefully got up and left the bed. He could hear his servant stirring in the room next door. Wanting to let his wife sleep as long as possible, he went to the door and whispered into the adjoining room, "Danar, I am getting up, but the queen is still asleep in my bed. I do not want her disturbed, but I need to investigate what happened. So, be very quiet and prepare my things."

"Yes, my Pharaoh," Danar whispered and began making preparations.

Temple of Amun-Ra

Startled from a dreamless sleep by the bed shuddering beneath him, Nephura, the Chief Priest of Amun-Ra in Memphis and Second Priest of Amun-Ra in all Egypt, was instantly alert, a learned ability he constantly reinforced with each new awakening. Then he heard the sound, like a muffled thunderclap, but he could not tell its direction. His quarters were situated deep within the walls of the Temple of Amun-Ra, with fresh air supplied by an ingenious system of small tunnels, providing him with a tranquil and private space to rest and think. It also meant only the loudest sounds could penetrate his sanctuary.

Alarms began going off in his mind. At first, he thought it might be an earthquake, but they usually lasted much longer. The closest thing to that kind of shudder he had ever experienced was when they had set the great stone statue of Amun-Ra in the temple courtyard, but that paled when compared to what had bolted him awake. The accompanying sound had to be extremely loud for him to hear it in his chamber.

Something crucial had happened, and he had to find out what it was. As the Second Priest of the god and the First Priest of the temple in Memphis, he was the representative of Amun-Ra to the court of Seti. Something this significant would soon become the concern of the Pharaoh.

Getting out of bed, he grabbed his robe from the hook on the wall and called to his servant, "Amunsa, get up!"

"I was already up, master," he said, entering the chamber. "Did you feel the ground move?"

"Yes, I did, and I need to find the cause. Go and find Mioa. Tell him to use whatever resources are necessary to discover what has happened and then report back to me."

As his servant bowed and left, Nephura wondered if this new concern would complicate his efforts at court. Initially, the new dynasty had made concessions to the priesthood of Amun-Ra, but there were signs that Seti was beginning to assert himself. Any crisis would allow this new Pharaoh to expand his influence beyond the current dutiful reverence given to the Great House. Whatever this event was, its implications needed careful scrutiny.

The Royal Estate

A strange rushing sound coming through the high eastern windows interrupted Asati's prayers. It reminded her of the sound the Nile made as it passed through the rapids of the First Cataract, a sound she had not heard since childhood. The noise grew increasingly louder until it sounded as if it had passed right over the northern wall of the villa, followed immediately by a thunderous crash. The floor beneath her knees shuddered, then stopped. A few heartbeats later, a monstrous clap overwhelmed the room like lightning had struck outside.

She was still on her knees, with her hands over her ears, when an anxious Nari came rushing into the room.

"Are you all right, my princess?"

Asati nodded but did not speak.

"I was crossing the courtyard to wake Sephra when a great rushing sound came from the eastern sky and passed almost above us to the north. It sounded like it struck something a short distance away. From the sound of water raining down, which followed the strange thunderclap, I think it must have struck the river between here and Memphis. There are cries of confusion throughout the villa. I came immediately to see what you wanted to do, my princess."

Asati was still kneeling and, though she had recovered from her initial alarm, did not immediately reply. Then, looking up at Nari, she said, "Do you have any idea what it was?"

"It sounded like something was falling from the sky, but I couldn't see anything. Should I call the head of the night watch to ask if they've seen anything?"

As she finished speaking, Semri, the captain of the guard, called from outside the doorway, "Forgive me, my princess, but I have urgent news."

Asati got to her feet and replied, "Enter." The word came out more like an entreaty than a command.

Semri entered her chamber and stood just inside the door. He had a lamp in his hand and seemed not to notice her distress. He bowed slightly and didn't seem affected by what had just happened. Asati marveled at how some men, especially those who sought the warrior's path, appeared to take the most significant events in stride while she trembled to her core.

"Tell me what you know," she said, exerting her most practiced calm to cover her inner turmoil.

"According to the night watch, my princess, a falling star has passed by to the north of us and struck the Nile at the southern edge of the city, near the great lock. It not only woke the whole household and probably everyone in the Memphis area, but now everyone is upset, wondering what this great portent could mean. Lights are starting to appear on both sides of the river. People are gathering to try to see what the gods have done. I came to find out what your orders were, my princess."

Asati took a deep breath and tried to quiet her distress. She looked questioningly at Nari, who had regained some measure of composure. The chief maidservant took a step forward, and Asati saw she had an opinion. After coming up with nothing herself, she said, "What do you think, Nari?"

"It is possible your dreams are related to this star, my princess. It appears there is no damage to the estate, only a little upset. It looks like it struck an isolated area of the river, so there is no immediate danger to worry about. Shouldn't we at least continue with your original plan?"

Once Nari had made the suggestion, Asati sensed something shift deep inside her. It was as if everything that had been out of order abruptly found its place. Instead of the former confusion, a strange sense of purpose began to build within her. It was empowering.

"I agree. After everyone calms down and we can prepare, we will go to the Nile for my sacred bath and make the offerings to Hapi and the coming inundation. The place where we are going is well upriver from where Semri said the falling star struck the water, so it should be unaffected by what has happened. However, now more than ever, I must go to the Temple of Satis and inquire of the priests. I want to start as soon as possible. Nari, go and calm the servants and get everyone moving."

After Nari had left, Asati looked at Semri, who remained standing at the doorway and said, "As you heard, I am going to the Nile for a sacred bath, and then I will go to the Temple of Satis to inquire of the gods. Choose a reliable messenger. Tell him to go to the Ferry Master. I want him to be ready when I arrive so I can have immediate passage across the river. Being the sister of Pharaoh should count for something, despite the chaos that will grip the port this morning. Afterward, he should go to the Temple of Satis and tell Sostris to prepare for my arrival. I will come to inquire of the goddess and for a dream reading."

"I will see to it immediately."

As he started to bow, Asati stopped him and said, "Semri, I want you to choose your best men to accompany me to the temple. The city will be in an uproar, and we wouldn't want an incident to occur."

"I will lead them myself."

Semri bowed and left, taking his lamp with him. Asati was alone again, the fluttering light of the votive offering her only company.

"The dreams, the star, what does it all mean?" she said aloud, almost prayerfully. Then, looking at the statue of Satis, she said, "When my heart begins to question, you send a miraculous sign to strengthen my faith."

The smoke from the incense she had lit earlier still spiraled upward. Asati went over to the alcove and poured a fresh libation. Kneeling, she began offering new and heartfelt petitions to the goddess.

The Nile Messenger

Everyone lurched forward as the boat struck sand, but after the sudden stop, the craft broke free and continued moving, though at a slower pace. The port-side oars struck the bottom below the surface for a few strokes before rowing in clear water. As Sunsamen regained his position, he noticed the lamp was dimming and needed refilling.

He called for the men to stow their oars and get something to eat. After applying grease to the loops of their oar ties, they refreshed themselves from the provisions while he replenished the light.

After relighting the triple-wicked lamp with the aid of the oarsmen, he slid the lamp pole along the boat, extending the light beyond the front of the craft until it reached its maximum length. He reset the pin, which prevented the lamp from twisting, and retied the lashings that anchored the pole to the craft.

"Would you look at that," one of the oarsmen unexpectedly bellowed, pointing high in the eastern sky.

Following his direction, Sunsamen saw a bright falling star heading earthward somewhere to the north of them. By now, all of the rowers were staring at this unique sight.

The fiery ball, trailing a long luminous tail, moved steadily downward. It appeared that it would strike close to the river, somewhere ahead of them. Then, to his surprise, it disappeared. As he searched the sky for the star, he heard a faint rushing sound. It reminded Sunsamen of the sound of the waters rushing past the First Cataract, which he had forded on his third day out. Despite the disappearance of the wayward star, the sound continued to build in the distance. It ended abruptly, but was followed several heartbeats later by a resounding boom that sounded like distant thunder.

Sunsamen was surprised to find his hand wrapped around his stone sailor's amulet, which hung from his neck. Looking back down the length of the boat, he saw that his four rowers were also holding theirs. The gods had shouted out a message, and whatever it was, it looked like they had spoken somewhere near Memphis.

He said to get the men's attention, "I know you are all tired, and I do not want to speculate on what happened ahead of us; I will leave that to the gods and the priests. However, dawn will soon arrive, and I am sure we need to reach Memphis before nightfall."

For a while, his rowers grumbled among themselves; they were all tired and hungry, and now the falling star added one more concern, but they all looked at him and nodded in agreement. Stowing their unfinished food, they took up their oars and began rowing downstream, quickly settling into a safe rhythm. The faster they got to Memphis, the sooner they would discover what had happened.

Helping Hands

Having gone as far as possible into the river, where the water seemed less muddy, Saisa filled the second jar, keeping its mouth near the top of the river where the water was cleaner. Torches were everywhere as he returned to the shore, though most were along the opposite bank. People were trying to see what had happened, and it would not be long before gawkers filled the entire area. Witnessing a star fall to earth was a once-in-a-lifetime experience.

Stepping out of the water, his foot slipped, and his weight yanked him to one side. He barely caught himself, his knee slamming into the wet, shifting earth. The jar teetered dangerously, and for a horrifying moment, he thought it would spill its sacred contents into the mud. His heart pounded as he fought to regain his footing, sucking in a deep breath through gritted teeth. He finally anchored the tapered bottom of the newly filled jar in the soft, miry sand opposite its partner. He took the carry straps and bag from the shaduf base and shook off the muck. Opening the bag, he took out the cover cloth and leather cap, and then, using the tie string, he secured the top of the jar. After tying the bag back on his waist, he examined the path back up the bank and saw it was a mess. He took a few steps to test the route, and despite the gentle slope, he slipped and slid back down. There was no way he would be able to get the filled jars up the slope by himself, at least not in time for the morning procedures.

Over the crest of the embankment, he saw a flickering light parallel to his location accompanied by animated voices. Hoping to find someone to assist him up the bank, Saisa cupped his hands around his mouth and yelled, "Help! I am stuck down here!"

The voices stopped, so he called out again, "Help! I'm down by the river. I can't get up the bank."

A torch appeared at the bank's edge, held by a policeman, who quickly spotted him.

"What are you doing down there?"

"I am a student magician at the Temple of Satis. I was gathering sacred water for the morning procedures when the star struck the river."

"You are lucky to be alive."

"I know. I was able to fill my jars, but I cannot get them back up the bank. It is too slippery. Can you help? I have to get this blessed water back to the temple in time for the morning rituals."

The man called to his companions, "It's an apprentice priest who can't get his water jars up the bank because of the mud."

One of the officers frowned. "The gods may have spared you, but we're not supposed to meddle in priestly matters." Another grunted, crossing his arms. "And yet, if we leave him here and the goddess is displeased, maybe we're the ones who will suffer."

The first officer ordered, "Go and get a rope so we can haul him up." Turning back to Saisa, he said, "Did you see what happened?"

Saisa told him the whole story while they waited for the rope. He could not resist embellishing the account just a little. He made his experience — and, of course, his being chosen by the gods to witness the event — dramatically more compelling. He was careful not to overdo it. After all, he needed their help getting up the bank. If he exaggerated too much, they might become disgusted and leave him there. He had finished his description when a rope fell out of the darkness and landed across his shoulders.

"Tie that through the handle of the first jar," the officer said.

They quickly pulled up the two jars, followed by Saisa and his carry stick and straps. By the time he reached the embankment, torches covered the other bank of the river.

"Watch yourself. The way back to the gate is very slippery, so I suggest you carry your sandals and use your toes to grip the ground," the officer said. "You will also have to pass through the crowds before you reach the gate. If you take your time and move slowly, you should be able to proceed without incident. I'm sure you would hate to spill those jars after all that has happened."

"You're right," he replied. "One of them is filled with water blessed by the star. That one at least has to return to the temple."

"Your temple is fortunate to have such a gift, and you, despite your low station, have been blessed by the gods to have seen the whole thing," the officer said, and the others murmured their agreement.

"The gods are gracious," Saisa said. Taking the officer's advice, he removed his sandals. After banging them against his knee to shake off the residue, he tied them together and looped them over his shoulder. Picking up his carry pole, he stooped down so the officers could attach the carry straps through the jar handles and over the notched ends. He straightened up, and as the burden pressed down on his shoulders, he tested his balance. The weight of the jars helped him sink deeper into the mud, allowing him to get a better grip. He seemed to find decent traction as long as he curled his toes.

"May the gods give you a safe journey," the first police officer said.

"And may the gods bless you for your help and keep you safe," he called back. Saisa started north toward the small door next to the Great Southern Gate, sludge-streaked jars his prize. Ahead, crowds loomed, and the morning rituals called as destiny weighed heavily on his shoulders.

Turmoil at the Lock

"The night watch said a falling star struck south of the city," Seti said to his son as his chariot came to a stop in front of him. "Are you ready to investigate?"

"Yes, father. This will be exciting."

Seti let Ramses climb into the chariot first and stepped in behind him.

"Forward," he commanded, and his driver fell into line behind the two chariots, following a herald who ran ahead. Two additional chariots fell in behind them. The four chariots were filled with his personal guard.

As they neared the city's southwestern edge, torchlight revealed a growing crowd pressed against the gates. The guards, reinforced by the Memphis police, had refused to let anyone out of the Great Southern Gate, which was still locked for the night. This caused a severe blockage on the thoroughfare leading to the gate.

His herald ran ahead of the lead chariot, shouting above the din, "Make way for Pharaoh; he who is blessed of the gods approaches!" Despite the upset over the closed gate, made stronger by the visceral expectation driven by a falling star, the crowd began to part, making way for their Pharaoh. He was their direct link to the divine and was coming personally to see what the gods had done.

Seti was pleased he had brought Ramses with him. His son stood in the front of the chariot next to the driver, his hands clenched around the top rail, filled with excitement. It was good he had let Tuya sleep. Always overprotective, she would have objected to him going to the impact site. However, this was a holy event and probably would never happen again in his son's lifetime. Moreover, Ramses was approaching his eleventh inundation. That made him old enough to begin experiencing the demands of sovereignty on a ruler's life. Besides, as a father, Seti wanted to share the joy of this unique event with his son.

He put his arm around Ramses' shoulder, leaned close, and said quietly into his ear, "Stand strong like the prince of Egypt you are, my son. The people will remember how you look this morning."

"I will, father!" Ramses replied, holding his head high and broadening his shoulders even further.

His son, strong and tall for his age, was also finely featured. Ramses' skill with the bow and lance was already turning the heads of his instructors. The court physician said if he continued growing at the same rate, he might be a hand taller than Seti, who was taller than the Pharaohs before him. Ramses already approached Seti's shoulder, and despite what some thought, it pleased him. A true father always wanted his son to surpass his stature and accomplishments. Having a strong and worthy heir was an essential part of his plan to revive Egypt's greatness and reclaim what the forgotten Akhenaten and his heretical ideas had squandered.

Seti turned his head and spat the vulgar name from his mind, uttering under his breath, "I spit you out. Repelled is the enemy that is in my mind. Cast out is the evil that was in my thoughts!"

Ramses was too excited to notice his father's reaction. Composing himself, Seti watched as the police pushed the people back and blocked the road for a short distance leading away from the swing point of the gates. They needed to prevent the crowd from rushing the gate after he passed through it.

As the front chariots led him through the crowd and then the partially opened gates, fear and excitement erupted from the roiling mass of people. Seti could not remember a public crowd expressing such a rich mixture of emotions. He typically experienced this intensity among his troops in the moments leading up to a battle. The air was filled with the scent of men when they faced eternity. For a soldier, it was strongest in those fateful heartbeats before they reaped either death or glory. The gods had spoken—but what had they said? These people stood at the edge of fate, like soldiers before battle, uncertain whether it would bring them ruin or glory.

That was what Seti had come to find out.

"Hold tight, Ramses," Seti said, increasing his grip on his son and the top rail as his chariot driver passed through the gate and turned right. Their pace increased as they intersected the path that ran along the great white wall. It would take them to the Great Lock.

There were torches everywhere. Seti saw a great mass of people lining the opposite bank of the Nile. While a few people from Perunifer had managed to get through the lines south of the gate, another police line barred their path.

His herald, running ahead, repeated the warning that their Pharaoh was approaching. The eager crowd reluctantly parted. Seti saw some of them so wide-eyed with excitement that they were almost beyond control. Barred from approaching further, they had jammed against the police line, trying to see something, anything. In the river, a few adventurous souls from the other side had ventured into the water, oblivious to the dangers posed by the river beasts. They were attempting to swim across to reach the impact site.

As his chariot moved through the parted crowd, Ramses spoke first as they broke into the open: "Look at the mud, father. It is everywhere. See, even the papyrus rushes have been thrown against the wall."

Seti looked around. It seemed as if a mythic giant had heaved a great mountain of sludge and debris against the city's eastern edge.

He ordered his chariot driver to pass the two lead chariots and then looked down at his son. Ramses' eyes darted from one sight to the next, trying to take everything in.

"I heard your excited response. Now, tell me, my son, what do you see?"

"The star must have hit close to the riverbank, Father. I have thrown rocks at puddles that splashed mud and water, just like what I see; only this is bigger, much bigger."

"Do you see anything else?"

"It is hard to make out with only the light of torches, but it looks like the debris sprayed out like a fan. So..." Ramses paused, his hands coming together in front of his face, showing he was in deep thought. After a moment's pause, he said, "If you follow the flow back to its source, you should be able to tell the exact place where the star struck the river." He hesitated, then added, "If the riverbed shifted toward the city wall, it could weaken the lock even if the surface looks undamaged?"

"Very good, my son," Seti said, squeezing the boy's shoulder in a sign of proud encouragement.

"The power of effective observation, the ability to take in what you see quickly and accurately, is essential in a leader. It can pull victory from the brink of death and defeat in battle. Here, it will help us separate the facts from the wild speculations we have already begun to hear. When the gods visit men, my son, people often forget how to think."

An appreciative smile spread across Ramses' face. Giving his son's shoulder another squeeze, he felt deep pride stirring in his heart. Seti knew experiences like these were a treasure and extremely rare. While Paser, his vizier, oversaw the customary lessons his son and heir needed to learn, nothing substituted for the real thing at his father's side.

The horses snorted in protest as their hooves fought for purchase in the sucking mud. This was as far as they could go. The debris was much deeper here, both along the ground and what still adhered to the wall on their right. While they were almost to the southern corner of the city, the edge of the dikes and the all-important Great Lock were still some distance ahead.

A small group and a torchbearer approached the chariots through the slimy mess. Their balance was precarious. It was tough going, and they almost fell several times. One of them was Merba, the night police supervisor. Seti prided himself on his memory, remembering the names and positions of everyone he met, which he used to his advantage. In the years before his family ascended to the throne, it had enhanced his authority and helped him advance in the army. Now, he used it to cement the power of his new reign as Pharaoh.

Merba stopped in front of the horses, a little to Seti's right, and bowed.

"Give me your report," Seti said, noticing the man was ankle deep in the muck.

"Do you want to wait for the Chief Scribe, my Pharaoh?"

"No, Merba. You can give me an initial report." There was an immediate response from the police captain when he heard his name from Pharaoh's lips, as well as when he was asked to give a status report himself.

"I am at your service, my Pharaoh," Merba replied, bowing with pointed precision. "As you can see, what the star threw up has made the ground very slippery," he said. He was using a staff to keep himself from falling. "Until the sun rises and does its work, the way to the dikes and the Great Lock will remain treacherous."

Seti caught the warning hidden beneath Merba's careful words. The man had a practiced tongue—he would go far if his actions matched his speech. It would not do for Pharaoh or his son, Ramses, to slip in the mud and fall, or worse, the gods forbid, be injured. Getting any closer was both unwise and unseemly.

"We will remain here. Continue."

"As far as we can tell, no one was killed or injured. The damage is still being assessed. The Chief Engineer and Chief Operator arrived to inspect the Great Lock, but it was difficult to see well with only lamps and torches. While much of the river bottom covers the mechanism, there appears to be no obvious damage. However, the star struck close enough to the bank of the river to cause a large section of the ground to rupture and shift noticeably to the west, directly in line with the lock. The earth's movement may have weakened the lock's foundations. The operators are testing the mechanism now, but even if it functions, it may still require repairs."

"Other than the section of ground that moved and the mud and debris thrown about, have you found any pieces of the star itself?" Seti asked.

"No, my Pharaoh, we have not found anything yet. It appears it buried itself deep into the riverbed before the west bank, but the water is still so fouled that no one has been able to investigate. The mud continues to churn up from the area that was struck, and we do not know how long it will take for the water to clear itself. We have no experience with such an event."

Seti's attention shifted as he considered the broader concern.

Was this the sign I asked for? If so, the gods have answered swiftly, yet their meaning remains unclear. A soldier wants direct orders— why must the gods be so cryptic?"

He had come personally to investigate the site because he wanted to see firsthand what had happened. It also elevated his position in the eyes of the priests and the people. It said their Pharaoh was in control. He was acting as Egypt's mediator with the gods. Fortunately, there was no severe damage to the lock, but that only dealt with one concern. The city and countryside would be in uproar, and the priesthoods would compete to claim the gods' message as their own, each vying to elevate their temple.

The gods had spoken, but had they given the answer we needed? They had shaken the heavens yet left only silence in their wake. Many things were happening. This was just the loudest. The days ahead would be rife with speculation and self-proclaimed interpreters.

I have to act quickly and deliberate with the priests.

Omens have been twisted before—each priesthood shaping the gods' will to serve their own ends. Rumors and wild stories will leave on the first boat leaving port. The gods are sending us a message, with a powerful demand to listen.

We must reach an agreement on what they want, so we can replace this confusion with a response that demonstrates we have listened and will act on their demands. There is a lot to do.

From the direction of the Great Lock, a light was approaching them.

"That should be the Chief Scribe, my Pharaoh."

"I will wait."

As the light drew closer, they recognized it was Sekmet. He came up beside Merba and bowed to Pharaoh.

"You have good men working for you, Chief Scribe. Your Night Captain, at my request, has given me an initial report."

"My Pharaoh, you are too kind. After further inspection of the lock, they found no serious damage. The mechanisms still function. Some minor repairs are required, which can be completed within a few days. The gods have been merciful."

"Excellent. Your men seem to have everything under control. They have handled the crowds well. I will return to the palace. Send me messengers every hour with updates."

"It will be done as you command, my Pharaoh."

"Chief Scribe, come to court as soon as you are finished here. We must plan to deal with any potential turmoil that may arise. It will take a while for the people to calm down. You're welcome to join me at the morning meal."

"It will be my great honor," Sekmet replied, with evident excitement as both he and Merba bowed.

"Back to the palace," he commanded his driver. The call echoed to the other four chariots, and they began the delicate maneuver of turning around.

"Father?" Ramses asked, looking up at Seti. "What will you do now?"

"I will be Pharaoh, my son. I will gather Egypt around me and help her interpret these messages the gods have sent."

"Messages, father? What else has happened?" Ramses asked.

Seti put his hand on his son's shoulder as their chariot began to move. He gave it a firm squeeze—approval, but also a reminder of the weight Ramses would one day bear. He was pleasantly surprised by how much his son had deduced from one word.

"Dreams and portents, my son. Dreams and portents." He tightened his grip on the rail. "And soon, we will learn what they mean."

Waiting

Sostris paced his garden, worry tightening his chest. Saisa had not returned. To the east, the first hint of light pried apart the night's darkness. He had been praying that Satis would keep the young wa'eb from injury ever since he had heard about the star striking the Nile at the city's southern edge. He had sent his purification partner, Upina, to look for him.

Frustration gnawed at him. Seven priests and three student wa'ebs had been sent to investigate, but only one had returned—with nothing but more questions. Sostris had also sent someone to inquire, as discreetly as possible, of the policeman who was a friend of the goddess. Knowledge is power, and every temple would strive to acquire it.

The less the other temples think we know or are trying to find out, the less of a threat we will appear to be. It's easier to maneuver if we seem to be wearing a cloak of ignorance.

As he looked up at the first dim signs of morning beginning to expand across the horizon, a prickling sensation ran along his skin. The involuntary shiver subsided, but he could not shake the sense that something extraordinary was happening. Even the air seemed to carry portents of things to come.

Despite the upheaval, morning rituals could not be ignored. The sacred routines bound them to the gods—the steady rhythm of life, death, and eternity. The world might shift, but the gods' rites remained unchanged. Even amid such wondrous occurrences, the day must begin as it always does. However, since they were a small temple, they were short of priests this morning because of those sent out to gather information. That meant those remaining and their servants had to assist.

Sostris was about to send his servant to get an emergency jar of water from the sacred pool when there was a coded knock at the doorway in the wall. His servant rushed over, unlocked the door, and pulled it open. Saisa and Upina trudged through. He thanked the goddess that the young wa'eb was safe, and Satis be praised, he was carrying two fully loaded jars.

As Saisa approached, Sostris could see he was disheveled and exhausted. His garment was dirty, and his legs were covered in dried mud. But what mattered most, he appeared unharmed.

"Praise be to Satis that you have returned safely, my son."

Sostris motioned to Upina and his servant to relieve Saisa's burden and immediately deliver the blessed water to the pure priest.

Saisa pointed to one of the jars and said, "Be very careful. This water is special, twice-blessed. It was gathered from the water after the star struck, but it is muddy and needs to be filtered."

"Sit down. Sit down. Tell me what happened."

He listened intently as Saisa told his story. What a story it was. His well-practiced ear could hear the little embellishments, but still, it was a remarkable tale of an extraordinary event. The gods had blessed this young aspiring magician—not just to witness a star strike the sacred waters and live, but to weave this tale so vividly it felt as though you were there yourself. He was an exceptional talent; his village would be incredibly blessed to have him as its magician.

"My lord, did I do right in bringing the specially blessed water?"

"Yes, you did well, my son. You have given a great gift to our temple."

"May I ask a question?"

"Of course. What is it?"

"As we neared the temple, two falcons descended—one on either side of the gate. Upina believes Amun-Ra sent them to honor our goddess. Could it be true? What does it mean?"

This new revelation caught Sostris off guard, but he managed to control his surprise. This could be very important and needed immediate investigation. Looking at Saisa, he said calmly, "It is possible. We will need to investigate the matter. Now, go and cleanse yourself and report to the pure priest. The morning rituals are understaffed, and we must prepare to awaken the goddess."

As Saisa hurried back to his quarters, Sostris saw his servant returning and called him over.

"Quickly, find someone to go outside to see if the falcons are still on our temple gate. If they are, keep a watchful eye on them and report back on anything of significance they observe."

As his servant rushed away, Sostris began contemplating the strange cacophony of events unfolding this morning. The gods were stirring. Their will was moving throughout the land. He had to understand what they demanded before it was too late.

Adrift

Bone-tired from the night's events, Jochebed carried her child's only hope on her head—a lidded basket of bulrushes woven from the very reeds that now concealed them. Throughout their arduous journey, she had protected the basket's waterproofing—even in their final sprint to the river. She had succeeded. They got to the river before dawn.

Several birds flew overhead as they went down the embankment to the river's edge. This time, Jochebed could see they were ibises. All around her, the sounds of the retreating night gave way to the muted stirrings of predawn.

Trying not to disturb the tall reeds more than necessary, Jochebed crept through the rushes toward a small opening along the river's edge. Miriam followed cautiously behind. To the north, she could see torches moving along the river. They did not worry her. The change of direction had put their path far enough south that anyone exploring the miraculous event was too far away to see them.

She stopped and signaled for Miriam to wait. The concern now was crocodiles. She scanned the riverbanks. Nothing stirred. The strain of their twisting journey, aggravated by the falling star and the changes it forced upon them, had stretched her nerves to thin strands that, if plucked, would be dangerously out of tune. Reaching deep into her diminishing reserves, Jochebed steadied herself.

"God of Heaven, don't let your servant falter now," she quietly prayed.

Partially concealed by the thinning rushes, they moved to an open stretch just ahead. Placing the basket on the narrow bank, Jochebed carefully removed its lid. Her daughter lifted their delicate cargo from the carry sling around her neck and handed her brother to her mother, undisturbed. Amazingly, he had slept the whole journey, even with the commotion caused by the falling star.

Against her people's tradition, they had not named him, fearing the increased bond that the usually joyous time would bring. What she had to do was already hard enough.

As she knelt in the wet sand, Jochebed gently held her son to her breast for the last time. He instinctively responded and, without fully waking, began nursing. He was so warm, so close to her heart, it almost overwhelmed her.

All during their careful preparations, she had put off thinking about the difficulty of parting, telling herself it was not a significant concern. She had always prided herself on her firm resolve, but now the anguish fueled by the abyss they were about to cross bit deeply into her determination. She knew she couldn't falter now. Despite the heart-rending sadness that began to well up inside of her, she had to push those feelings aside and continue to nurse him. The child would get no more nourishment until someone found him.

Three inundations ago, the current Pharaoh's father had begun seriously enforcing the decree of the elderly Haremhab. Egyptian soldiers now actively sought out all newborn Hebrew males. Following the decree, now overseen by the priests of Amun-Ra and carried out by the priests of Sobek, they would cut the infants' throats and then toss them into the Nile as offerings for the glory of Egypt and food for the waiting crocodiles. Many of her people believed the cause of this horror was the priesthood of Amun-Ra's hatred of the Hebrews. They blamed them for the apostasy of the long-dead Pharaoh, the one whose name Egypt had tried to blot out of her memory. Others believed the real cause was their rapidly increasing numbers, which troubled the royal house and led some around the throne to say they were becoming a threat.

At first, Jochebed and her husband had fiercely argued over their son's fate. In a dream, Amram had seen greatness foretold for the child. He believed their young son would be the deliverer for whom everyone was praying. He had argued that the Most High God would protect the child and that they should keep him. They were able to hide her pregnancy and the birth from everyone, and their son did not cry out at his circumcision. Despite the danger that God-ordained ritual had subjected them to and how it forever identified him as Hebrew, her husband had wanted him numbered among the children of Abraham.

Jochebed had countered it was only a matter of time before they would be caught. Paid informers were everywhere, even in their village. No, an anonymous voyage on the Nile was the child's only realistic hope.

It was common knowledge that Egyptian women used the river to free themselves of unwanted births. The penalties for murder, including newborns, were very harsh, so it was safer to offer the unwanted child to the gods and let the Nile, viewed as sacred by the Egyptians, become the easy solution. Eventually, the cycle was complete; barren couples would scan the waters of the river and its canals for a reed basket, ferrying their only hope for a child, a much-desired gift from their gods. Better for an unknown Egyptian mother to raise him than to be an offering the priests gave to the river beasts.

Besides, she had argued, what greatness could a child of the Hebrews, who are now treated almost as slaves, aspire to? Yet, she held onto her slender hope. The God of their Fathers could use this means to fulfill her husband's vision. Just as their ancestor Joseph's bondage in Egypt had prepared the way for him to fulfill his destiny, this fragile voyage could provide him with a similar opportunity. Finally, her husband had relented and grudgingly agreed to the plan. They would put the fate of their son in the hands of God and the Egyptians he chose to raise him.

What had seemed like a good plan as they had started was now fraught with uncertainty because of the falling star. There was no way to know what lay ahead in the section of the river that had been struck. Despite this uncertainty, they had no choice. There was no going back; that was sure death.

At least on the river, he has a chance at life. Oh God of our fathers, I pray this journey is according to your will for our son.

Jochebed's gaze drifted to the suggestion of light on the eastern horizon. Time was short. Dawn was almost upon them. Steeling herself against the growing anguish and increasing uncertainty, she reluctantly removed the child from her breast. She placed him gently in the basket where Miriam had carefully arranged the blanket.

He moved for a moment but remained asleep, peacefully unaware of the journey that lay ahead. Taking a deep breath, she replaced the lid and tied it securely, feeling as if she had bound her heart in the process. She signaled her daughter, and together, they carefully lowered the basket into the shallow water at the river's edge.

The inundation had not yet begun, and in the last few moons, the Nile's level had dropped lower than anyone could remember. As a result, the river's flow was unhurried and unlikely to upset this fragile voyager as the currents carried him downstream. There was no way to know what the star had done as it had struck closer to the city, but Jochebed knew she could wait no longer. So, with another faltering prayer, she released her son into the hands of the God of Abraham, Isaac, and Jacob.

A hollow ache pulled at her chest as the current nudged the basket from her fingers. The river quickly took the little bulrush ark from her shaking hands, and then he was gone.

Almost out of sight, the basket drifted downstream before becoming wedged in a clump of reeds. Jochebed watched for a few tense breaths, a desperate anxiety fighting against her withering resolve. She prayed and willed for it to continue, but it refused to break free. She considered moving north along the bank and trying to free it herself, but she was unable to. The growing light urged her to leave before someone connected her to the basket—and sealed her son's fate.

She stood frozen in a state of anguish and indecision. She exhaled. Finality closed around her heart like a cold fist. Her son's fate was out of her hands. Nothing had changed because she had seen the first snag in his journey. He was now in God's hands.

Turning away in resignation, she took the carrying cloth from her daughter and said, "We can do nothing more, Miriam. It is almost dawn. Hide yourself nearby and see what becomes of your brother."

"Momma, how long should I wait?"

"All day, if necessary."

Reaching into her robe, she pulled out a cloth from which she took a piece of bread.

"Here, eat this. If you cannot get home by the evening meal, then stay here. I will return with something for you to eat. If there is still a problem and no one has found him, we can then decide what to do."

Looking Miriam directly in the eye, Jochebed said, "Be careful and stay hidden."

"I will, Momma. I will."

Bending down, Jochebed took a small flint knife from an interior pocket, cutting some of the nearby reeds and piling them onto the carrying cloth. When there was enough to satisfy any casual inquiry, she hoisted the bundle onto her back, supporting it with a loop across her forehead. Looking around to ensure no one could see her, she gave her daughter a weary caress, then disappeared through the curtain of rushes.

Aftermath

"Wake up, my lord."

Sekmet, the Chief Scribe of Investigations and Secrets and head of the Memphis police force heard his servant trying to rouse him. His voice was full of restrained panic.

"What's the matter?" Sekmet asked groggily. Last night, he and his wife had entertained a group of friends. Everyone had stayed late and consumed too much wine. His head began throbbing as he sat up.

"Excellency, there was a great shaking of the ground and a large noise from the east. I was unsure whether to wake you, but now the night supervisor is here and asking for your advice."

"Tell him to wait," Sekmet said as he struggled to his feet and grabbed his robe from the peg on the wall. He had not heard or felt a thing, but then he had barely heard his servant waking him.

"What's going on?" his wife groaned, lifting her head from the bed.

"Go back to sleep, my dove. I will get you up if anything interesting is happening."

His wife lay back down and pulled the linen sheet over her head.

Sekmet exited their sleeping quarters and went down the hall to the room where Merba, the night supervisor, was waiting. Sekmet was short and wiry. He had risen through the ranks on the strength of his wits and investigative skills, but his stature always made him feel insufficient, especially when dealing with a possible crisis.

Going into the room, he said in his most official-sounding voice, "Give me your report," though the pounding in his head rebelled at every word.

"Yes, sir," Merba replied. "We have had reports of a falling star hitting the Nile on the western bank, near the Great Lock. It has aroused all of Memphis and the surrounding area, and crowds are already gathering outside the city walls on both sides of the river. I have sent for the morning shift to arrive early while the reserve contingent is already at the site, trying to maintain order and hold back the onlookers. The various priesthoods will want to inspect the area. I would not be surprised if Pharaoh, may he live forever, decided to show up."

"Was there any damage? Was anyone killed?"

"As far as we know, no one was killed or even injured. Preliminary reports from the guards at the Great Southern Gate only mention mud and water being thrown up from the river, striking the lock, canals, the southern part of the eastern wall, and all along the western bank. We have not yet investigated the condition of the Great Lock to determine if it has been damaged. Still, with the inundation soon to begin, we will need to have the Chief Engineer inspect everything as soon as possible. People are already suggesting that this is a significant portent from the gods, so we are trying to keep the area clear. However, we will still hear complaints from the priests, no matter how well we protect the site."

"You have done well, Merba," Sekmet said, noting his subordinate's slight but visible reaction to his praise.

"I will dress and join you at the river as quickly as possible. We need a leadership presence at the site, so hurry on ahead...Wait! First, send someone to fetch the Chief Engineer and then dispatch runners to retrieve half of the men from the southern district. We cannot allow the crowds to get out of control. Everyone will want a souvenir. If Pharaoh arrives. No, knowing Seti, it will be when. We do not want him to use his guard to maintain order. That would not do. Hurry!"

As Merba rushed away, Sekmet, trailed by his servant, hurried back to his sleeping chamber to prepare himself for the possible presence of Pharaoh. Sekmet sighed, rubbing his temples. This was more than a crowd-control issue. The temples would claim this was a divine sign. The merchants would want the roads cleared. The noble houses would demand protection. And Pharaoh...He decided not to reawaken his wife. She would insist on coming and want to be in the middle of everything. The situation was too uncertain for him to waste precious time and resources worrying about her. Sekmet and his servant slipped quietly out of the sleeping chamber with their arms full of clothes and other necessary items.

A Pharaoh's Concern

As the familiar portico of the palace came into view, Seti recognized Osri, the scribe to Paser, his vizier, waiting for him. He instructed his driver to stop with Ramses' side of the chariot facing the scribe. He wanted to include his son in the discussion.

The scribe bowed as the chariot came to a stop. Despite the early hour, Seti could see that he was properly dressed and had accomplished his full toilet. Situations like this demonstrated a man's respect and dedication to his office. Seti made note of the scribe's effort.

"You may speak, Osri."

The scribe straightened and replied with a slight nod, "Most noble Pharaoh, my lord Paser seeks your guidance on how to proceed after this morning's events."

During the return ride from the impact site, Seti had been mulling over several courses of action. He was unsure of everything he wanted to do, but it was important to have wise counsel before making a decision. The battlefield had taught him that those choices made in haste often led to disaster. Good advice was like fresh reinforcements. But this—this was something different. A sign from the gods demanded that I listen. But, was it a message—or a warning? Already, wild speculation was taking root in the streets. He had to act before fear and rumor took hold.

While the falling star may have been an answer from the gods to his earlier request, it was an unprecedented event that, without proper interpretation, raised more questions than it answered. Wild speculations were already circulating—he had heard them whispered along his journey to and from the locks. The people would demand answers. He had to act before the storm beneath their feet became a flood.

He placed his hand on Ramses' shoulder and said to Osri, "Have your master come to the palace for the morning meal. Tell him his Pharaoh seeks the benefit of his learned counsel."

Osri bowed and replied, "As you will, my Pharaoh, so shall it be."

He then turned and hurried away.

As they exited the chariot, Seti told Ramses, "Always treat your advisors and chief officials with respect, my son. Never be too proud or too hasty to seek their advice. Like a good general, a wise ruler knows the importance of good counselors. Never forget that we each have our role to play, and the gods honor every man who embraces his duty. We should do no less; as Pharaoh, we should always lead by example."

Nodding at his father's words, Ramses accompanied Seti onto the great steps that led into the portico of the palace.

"Father?" Ramses asked.

"Yes, my son," Seti replied and turned to face the young prince.

"What if a man dishonors his office? Must we still honor him?"

Seti was pleased at the depth of the question. His son was inquiring into the problems that all leaders faced, which meant he was beginning to grasp the insights necessary to rule and become a Pharaoh after him.

"Then you respect the office. When a man lets down his office, he alone has failed. If you disrespect the office because of the man, then when a good man later takes the position, he will inherit a seat of diminished authority. This is not good for Pharaoh or Egypt."

"You are a good Pharaoh, father. I will pray to the gods to grant you a long life. I want to learn everything you have to teach me."

Seti smiled, reached down, and put his arm around Ramses' shoulder as the new sun's first rays began to touch the dawn, driving the grey away with piercing bursts of gold.

"A day unlike any other," Seti said as they ascended the remaining steps, passed between his guards, and disappeared into the palace.

Defiled

Despite the momentous events that were unfolding, the priesthood of Amun-Ra followed the timeless tradition governing all Egypt's temples; they awakened their god the instant the new sun touched the eastern horizon. As the first rays of Ra's rebirth struck across the sky, a lookout at the top of the temple signaled to the attending priest that their god had been reborn. The lookout removed the covering from the hole in the roof, allowing the specially positioned and polished bronze mirror to reflect the rays of the first light down into the inner sanctuary of the god. The appointed pure priest, who had broken the seals of the previous night into the Naos, the holy place within the sacred space, would open its doors to receive the reborn light of Ra reflected into the sanctuary. At the entrance of the first light, the pure priest would unveil the face of the god to celebrate the rebirth of the sun, incarnated in the face of the god's statue. When this happened, the god was considered awake and ready for washing, anointing with oils, perfuming, and, after the proper makeup was applied, dressing in the appointed clothes for the day. Each day had its own requirements.

As Nephura, the Chief Priest of the Temple of Amun-Ra in Memphis, returned from his morning purification, a commotion erupted inside the temple. Irritated that such a disturbance could desecrate the god's awakening, he hurried through the nearest doorway into the side of the columned hall at the front of the sanctuary.

As he scanned the usually finely ordered space now in an uproar, he heard, over the cries of the shrieking priests, flapping wings coming straight at him. He instinctively ducked as a vulture flew past his head and out through the doorway he had just entered. Feeling something wet strike his forehead, Nephura wiped it with his hand.

The fleeing bird had fouled him with its droppings!

His mind recoiled at the impossible sight. Not only was he now ceremonially impure, which meant he could go no farther and could not enter into Amun-Ra's sacred presence, but he could not fathom where the vulture had come from.

He screamed at the attending priests that he had been defiled by the fleeing vulture and commanded that someone come and explain what had happened. At the sound of Nephura's voice, the raucous confusion instantly gave way to hushed whispers. After a long pause, during which the Chief Priest's irritation began to boil over, a single set of footsteps padded through the columns from the entrance to the Naos. The pure priest, wringing his hands and with the same foul droppings spotting his head and robe, hesitatingly approached his master.

"This is unprecedented, my Lord. We are beside ourselves. We have no idea what to do. No one has ever seen such a thing. There is no..."

"Quiet!" Nephura shouted. If he had let him, the babbling idiot would have continued like that well past his limited patience.

"Tell me what happened, and be quick about it!"

The pure priest took a deep breath and waited for his shaking to subside before finally saying, "We were beginning the Open the Mouth ritual. I approached the doors of the Naos, and the seals were still intact. I broke them, just like we do every morning, and opened the doors to the inner sanctuary. But as the first rays of sunlight signaled the rebirth of Ra, and I lifted the veil from the god's face, this vulture burst out of nowhere from within the ceiling of the Naos. It just appeared! Its wings could barely be contained in the sacred space, and it scarcely missed my head as it flew out of the opening. It thrashed through the sacred air, scattering filth across the god and offerings alike. Then, as suddenly as it appeared, it turned, flying this way, and vanished. Right after that, we heard you calling, noble one."

The priest spoke hurriedly, nearly without taking a breath. He acted as if his mouth would lock up if he failed to get it all out at once. However, if he did not stop wringing his hands, he would wipe the skin right off of them.

"Stop!" Nephura commanded, pointing at his hands.

The priest's hands immediately separated and shot down alongside his legs.

"The vulture was behind the sealed doors of the inner sanctuary, inside the Naos itself?"

"Yes, my Lord. It flew directly out of the Naos. If I hadn't been holding onto the god while removing the cover from his face, the bird might have knocked him over."

"But how did it get in there? It's a small space, barely big enough for a bird that size to fit!" Nephura stopped. He heard the shrill edge creeping into his voice, dancing on the edge of control. With great effort, he managed to calm his upset.

"It just appeared, noble one. The Naos is dark this time of morning. There is only one small lamp in the outer sanctuary, supplying all of the light until the announcement of the rising sun is complete. Even so, the bird seemed to emerge out of nowhere. First, a star hits the sacred river, and now this vulture. What is happening, my Lord? What should we do?"

Never, in the annals of the Amun-Ra priesthood, including the hidden books that recorded things only the Chief Priests saw, had he read about anything as strange as this. This foul bird could be taken as an evil omen, and if word got out, it would appear that the god was rebuking his own priests and reproaching even him! He had to find time to figure out the meaning of these events, but he was already sure he would not like it. However, nothing about this strange portent could leave the temple.

Nephura reached deep into his practiced demeanor and, speaking with his most authoritative voice, said, "Have fresh water drawn from the sacred pool. Clean and purify the sanctuary. Clean the god and put him back in the Naos. Re-purify yourselves and then, with fresh offerings, begin the duties of the morning ritual as if nothing had happened."

The pure priest started to say something and then thought better of it. "As you command" was all that came out.

"Now, listen to this, and I want you to ensure that everyone, and I mean everyone, understands clearly what I am about to say. Not a single priest, apprentice, or servant, and I mean no one, is to talk of this ever again. Not one word, or they will be cursed by my own hand."

The pure priest's features grew pale as he cowered at the thought of Nephura's curse.

Nephura knew they whispered about his powerful, dark magic in fear. Throughout Memphis, hidden counsels knew that the Chief Priest of the Temple of Amun-Ra was someone to be feared.

As the pure priest shrank away, Nephura said under his breath, "That should silence them—at least until I find an answer that erases this stain."

Watching

Miriam waited before moving, giving her mother a chance to get a good distance away. The semi-darkness quickly gave way to morning twilight, and she wanted to be sure that no one would connect her to her mother retreating in the distance if she were seen. However, with all the upset surrounding the star, she doubted that it would be a problem.

After checking whether the rushes still held her brother's basket, she considered reaching for it and freeing it, but decided against it. It could free itself. If it didn't, she might make an effort, though she didn't look forward to getting wet again and possibly exposing herself to the river beasts. Instead, she went through the reeds and up the shallow embankment. Seeing no one, she followed the cart path that ran along the river and marked the field's boundary. Her goal was a palm tree near the edge of the downstream bank. Reaching the palm, she could still see her brother's basket through the thinning rushes. He was a long stone's throw downstream. She was close enough, but not too close. Someone seeing them both might not make the connection. Clearing off a spot at the base of the palm, she settled down beneath the tree to keep watch.

As Miriam fitted her back against the rough curve of the trunk, she turned her attention back toward the fields where her mother had disappeared. As she looked toward the eastern horizon, the luminous rim of the sun touched the edge of the land, its first rays shooting across the grey landscape, turning everything they touched to gold. She wondered why the sun moved so quickly and appeared so large as it gradually dawned into view.

"I can see it move as it climbs up from the horizon, and I can watch its color change from a deep golden orange to a brilliant yellow," Miriam said aloud.

Embarrassment washed across her face as she realized she was doing it again, talking to herself.

"It doesn't matter," she said to the tree behind her, "no one listens to me anyway."

Remembering her father's admonition, Miriam set her resolve and reined in her curiosity. Thoughts like this would soon start her daydreaming, and then she would fall asleep in two blinks of an eye. Folding her arms across her chest, she pressed her back hard against the tree's rough bark, determined to stay awake, even if it meant being uncomfortable. She had to see what happened to her little brother.

Mother will never forgive me if I fall asleep.

Laughter rang out in the distance. Miriam looked farther downstream, past where her brother had come to rest. She saw a procession winding its way from a cart path along a well-worn trail to the water's edge. As she shaded her eyes with her hand, she saw there was a cleared and leveled area next to the river, making it easier to access the water's edge. Four men, armed with spears and swords, guarded a group of female servants carrying bundles. They preceded a litter carried by four large Nubians, their black skin standing out in the early morning sun.

The servants immediately began preparing the cleared area along the bank. The entire party seemed elated about something. Their laughter and joyful banter easily carried to where she was sitting. Maybe they were excited about the falling star. The women erected a bathing enclosure out into the river, and then a young woman clad in a delicate linen gown stepped out from the curtained chair and made her way down to the water. While the woman was beautiful, what caught Miriam's attention was the gown. As sheer as the webs spun by spiders, a lustrous white cloth draped her body.

She wondered who this woman could be. The most likely possibility that she was the estate's mistress, the sister of Pharaoh, sent a cold chill down Miriam's spine.

With the group so close to her brother's basket, it was only a matter of time before someone saw it. She cautiously moved closer, near enough to hear their conversation. If necessary, she would go to the water and pull his basket into the reeds to hide him. She slowly approached the edge of the river. She would have to try to reach her brother's basket through the rushes along the riverbank, praying to God, they would not see her.

Carefully making her way through the thinning stalks, her innate sense of adventure overcame her initial fear of discovery. Miriam began to imagine herself as a lioness stalking its prey, edging ever closer and closer to her objective. Because the water level was exceptionally low, the sandy edge of the bank where the plants grew thickest was wider than usual along this section of the river. Partially hidden by the growth of rushes, she was only a short stone's throw from her brother. The boisterous party was near enough for her to make out what they were saying, their words skipping across the placid river.

From the servant's chatter, she discovered it was Asati, Pharaoh's sister, who had come to bathe. Miriam's heart leaped to her throat—her worst fear realized. There was no doubt in her mind that if the princess found him, she would have her brother killed. It was her father's edict, rigidly enforced by her brother, the Pharaoh, that condemned him to death.

Moving with almost reckless haste, she was no longer concerned with the possibility of crocodiles or snakes. She still tried to imagine herself as a hunter, unafraid as she confronted danger. She almost lost her balance and barely prevented herself from tumbling head over heels through the rushes and into the water. She stopped. Her heart was pounding, and she was breathing heavily. She had to quit this headlong rush. She had to reach her brother undiscovered.

Looking at the area around the basket, she realized that to reach her brother, she would have to expose herself, at least for a short distance.

I have no choice.

As she cautiously made her way to the edge of the rushes, she decided to wait until the group's attention was away from the river before trying to reach the basket. She was no longer able to pretend she was a hunter. Instead, as her brother's fate teetered on discovery, she felt the bone-numbing fear of the hunted wash over her.

The Babe Discovered

A vibrant expectancy lifted the morning; unlike the sullen days they had spent tending to their mistress. The night's mysterious events had turned this early bath into an eager, even exciting outing.

"The water is cool. Do you still want a full bath?" Nari called back as she tested the shallows with her feet.

"Yes. It's necessary. I want the sacred waters to cleanse me completely. This anointing is an offering to the gods. Nari, these omens must be true—my dreams, then the star..."

"You must trust the gods have a purpose, my princess."

Sighing, Asati turned and stepped with Nari into the open-ended linen enclosure, which projected well out into the water and angled into the river's flow. Raising her arms, she let Nari remove her gown. The early morning air was crisp on her naked skin, and the first touch of the brisk water sent a chill coursing through her body, almost draining the fragile hope she had clung to all morning. Gritting her teeth, she steadied herself and continued into the river until the water was above her knees.

Nari followed her mistress into the river, carrying a stubby, wide-mouth pitcher, which she filled with the sacred water. She raised the container above the princess' head. As Asati recited her petition to the river god, Nari sent the crisp water cascading over the princess's shivering body.

"Oh, the fertile waters of Hapi, a source of nourishment and life, overflow my womb with the same fruitfulness you are now preparing for the land. Bless the coming inundation. Bless my night dreams as a gift sent by Satis and grant a man-child to blossom in the garden of my prince."

Nari gave the pitcher to the servant who had come up beside her and took from her two small stelae: one gold and the other silver. The estate's metalworker, their mesniti, had hastily prepared and engraved them with Hapi's image and prayers. She gave these to her mistress.

Asati first raised the two stelae to the sky and intoned a dedication to the god of the inundation. Then she tossed them, one at a time, as an offering into the deepest part of the river's flow upstream. As she watched the second one splash into the water, she noticed something nearby, barely visible from the edge of the enclosure. There was a basket wedged in a tangle of rushes.

At first, the sight merely intrigued her, but a strange pull, half hope, half dread, drew her to it. The unexpected feelings grew as she pondered what it might be. She knew she had to see what it contained. Turning to her chief maidservant and pointing upstream, she said, "Nari, while you anoint me with the oil, send someone up the river to bring that basket to me."

"Yes, my princess," Nari replied. Calling to one of the servants outside the enclosure, she said, "Sephra, take someone with you and retrieve that basket from the rushes. Float it down to the princess. You better take one of the guards and watch out for crocodiles."

While the servant obeyed, Nari retrieved towels and scented oils to complete the anointing of her mistress.

Asati left the water onto the bank where Nari was waiting. Raising her arms, she let her servant dry her and then anoint her with fragrant oils, rubbing them in with stimulating strokes that warmed her chilled skin. As she lifted her head and adjusted her arms to let Nari put on her sheer linen gown, she saw two falcons flying from the direction of Memphis. They circled overhead three times and then headed back toward the city.

"Did you see that, Nari?" Asati asked as the birds disappeared.

"I did, my princess. It seems you are being favored by Amun-Ra this morning."

"Do you think so? Falcons, especially at the rising sun—they must mean something important. Maybe my prayers have been heard."

Asati could barely contain her excitement as she finished dressing. The servants dismantled the enclosure, and Sephra, the other servant, and the guard returned, carrying the basket along the water's edge. They waited for the others to finish packing away the enclosure, then picked up the woven container between them, carried it across the sand, and carefully placed it at the princess's feet.

"What do you think it is, Nari?" Asati asked.

"It could be a gift from Hapi in response to your prayers and offerings."

"Do you think so?"

"We will know better when we remove the lid."

All the servants began to crowd around the basket, but Nari shooed them away, leaving her alone, except for the guard, with the princess.

The lid was tied shut. Asati knelt in the sand and, with Nari's help, unfastened the knots. Trembling with anticipation, she placed her hands on the cover. However, as her fingers wrapped around the rough weave of the reeds, she froze, her apprehension overcoming her initial curiosity.

Seeing her hesitation, Nari said, "There is nothing to fear. This is a gift sent by the gods, my princess. Open it and see what they have granted you."

Buoyed by Nari's confident words, Asati tightened the fingers of her right hand around the cover and tried to lift it from the basket. It wouldn't budge. After several failed attempts, a petulant irritation replaced her apprehension.

"Help me, Nari."

Nari quickly knelt beside her in the sand. She had to keep the princess's mood from turning dark. She used an ivory comb to pry at the lid until it began to give way.

"Let me," Asati said. She reached down and grasped the loosened lid with both her hands, her spirit lightening.

She felt like a child unwrapping a sacred offering. As she started to lift the cover, a husky cry burst out of the woven container. Everyone turned to look as the startled princess fell backward onto the sandy bank, the lid still clutched in her hands.

Asati stood up, holding the cover in front of her like a shield. She approached the edge of the basket, cautiously lowered her protection, and peeked inside. Lying naked on a rough, woven blanket, she saw a beautiful male child. He was crying. Tears flowed from his scrinched eyes while his little arms and legs thrashed wildly about him. Suddenly, he opened his eyes, and amid his flailing, he looked directly at the princess. Asati stared at him, her heart beating widely, her mouth half open in surprise. He immediately became still, looking up at her with his arms still outstretched.

Conflicting emotions surged within Asati. Her dream: this was the same child from her dream, a Hebrew child; the blanket under him was the same one she had seen floating in the water. A war of emotions surged inside of her. The deep longing for a son clashed with her father's edict, her brother's continued enforcement of it, her duty to Egypt, and her husband's expectations. At the same time, her heart was overwhelmed by a sudden and unexpected maternal instinct as she responded to the infant's pull before her. Utterly confused, she turned imploringly to Nari.

"This is a Hebrew man-child."

"And apparently, a gift from the gods, my princess," the wise, elderly woman said. "Let the priests decide what it all means."

Despite hearing the demands of the edict urging her to turn away, she turned back to the basket, her sudden maternal emotions and curiosity overcoming her concern. Asati wondered why the baby had become suddenly quiet once he had seen her. He seemed unafraid. Then, as if it were the natural thing to do, his eyes and hands reached out to her. Unbidden, she felt her heart quickly warming, and despite the contradictions, before she knew what she was doing, she reached down and removed him from the basket. Cradling him, her arms responded as if he belonged there. As she looked down at him, he reached up and touched her chin, sending a rush of warmth that spread across her face, down her neck and coursed through her body.

Asati's impetuous heart took over. "He is given to me. I will not offend a gift from the gods. I will keep him." She looked down at the child and blurted out, "Since he was born to me out of the sacred waters of the Nile, I will give him a name Hapi would approve of: Moses, son of the river."

Then, a sudden movement in the rushes upstream drew her attention. A young girl partially emerged from the growth along the river's edge. Their eyes met across the distance. The girl froze, a reed snapping under her trembling hand, her Hebrew features plain in the dawn light.

Asati wondered, "Is this another omen?" She called out to her. "Wait there, child." Turning to Nari, she said, "Bring that girl to me."

Nari told two of the guards to fetch the child, and they escorted the frightened girl to the princess.

"Calm down; I won't hurt you. What were you doing in the rushes?"

Though young and scared, Miriam was quick-witted and tried to divert the question by flattering the princess. She went to her knees and bowed her forehead to the sand. With a shaky voice, in the common Egyptian she had picked up from the traders and sellers in the marketplace, she said, "I came to the river because of the star, but then you came to the water. I have never seen a real princess before."

Just then, Moses cried again, diverting Asati's attention. She tried to comfort him without success, and the familiar irritation that had become more common with her expressed itself: "What is wrong with him?"

"He's probably hungry," Nari replied.

"How am I supposed to feed him? I've no milk!"

"Give him to me."

Before the princess could give her brother to the maidservant, an idea had leaped into Miriam's mind from the princess's words. Not giving her fear a chance to dissuade her, she coughed pointedly, her forehead still kissing the sand in deference to the princess.

Asati glanced at the Hebrew girl face down in the sand. Her frustration with the crying baby was evident in her voice, "What is it, child?"

Without looking up, Miriam seized the opportunity. "Shall I go and fetch a Hebrew woman to nurse the child for you, Your Highness?"

Asati wondered if this was a new omen, a solution provided by the gods. She knew that there were mothers in the Hebrew villages who had lost their children but not their milk. She was tired from the difficult night, and this was one more decision she did not want to think about. Before Nari could dissuade her, Asati accepted the easiest course; she took advantage of the offer.

"Alright, child. Take my servant, Moses, and find a nurse for him. I will give fair payment to both you and the woman you choose. Two of my guards will accompany you while the arrangements are made."

His crying stopped, which reinforced Asati's sense that she had correctly interpreted the omen. With the cause of her irritation calmed, she looked at her new son; the word felt strange and frightening yet somehow right. As the child looked at her, he seemed to find his place, a long-awaited home deep within her. Reluctantly, she placed Moses in Nari's arms.

"Take good care of him and see that whatever he needs is done. I will return home, dress, and consult with the priests. When everything is settled, bring the wet nurse and Moses to me." The word came so naturally off her tongue that it startled her when she realized it. Moses.

"Yes, my princess," Nari replied.

Asati waved over two of the guards and, motioning Nari and Miriam to go on ahead, said to the two men, "Escort them to wherever this young girl leads you."

They looked to Semri, who nodded and then turned to the princess, bowed, and left.

Asati watched as they departed. As they crested the bank, the overwhelming nature of the morning's events began to take over, and her heart started to pound. The dreams, the star, this child, and now her hasty response, she almost called after them, but couldn't do it. "Oh," she exhaled, her heart twisting. "What will my brother say? My husband? Will they believe this child is a gift from the gods? What am I doing?" She almost called Nari back, but as she hesitated, torn over the complications, the group disappeared from view. Resignation replaced doubt and indecision. Turning to Sephra, she said, "Take another servant, go into Perunifer, and get what we need for the nursery. Buy the best cradle, bedclothes, and wrappings in the whole port. Everything must be new. Get the necessary oils, ointments, and perfumes. You know what we need. We've discussed this many times before. Also, I want the best bed you can find for the baby's wet nurse."

"Yes, my princess."

As her servant left, Asati called after her and said, "Sephra. Do this as quietly as possible. We want to keep this within the household until I have consulted with the priests and my brother."

Sephra nodded and hurried up the slope with another servant in tow.

"Take me home," she said, stepping into the litter. Semri and the remaining guard positioned themselves at the front and back of the procession as the company began to move forward, all realizing that something momentous had happened.

As the litter swayed homeward, the memory of Moses' quiet eyes lingered in her soul, a fragile promise riding the storm she'd unleashed.

Growing Concerns

The rising sun brightened the Temple of Satis as the pure priest dressed the goddess in fresh linen. Sostris sat alone in the garden, relieved that the rituals were held despite the day's strangeness.

Though the day had begun unlike any he had ever known, at least the temple had settled into its daily rhythm. Performing the familiar duties had a calming influence that helped offset the growing disturbances. That was the strength of Egypt. Its deep-seated traditions nourished its historic greatness: the regular rhythms of its many temples and the people's time-honored customs. These measured cadences maintained the balance and covenant between the gods and men and gave daily life a measure of stability.

Egypt took a long time to recover from the depredations of the Pharaoh Who is Not Named. This morning proved how far they had come. Despite the disruptive events, the ongoing turmoil, and public excitement, daily life continued its familiar cycle. He knew that as long as this partnership and its orderly expressions continued, so would Egypt, drawing from this deep well of strength.

Sensing movement out of the corner of his eye, he looked up to see his servant hurrying toward him. Accompanying him was another man he recognized, a guard who served Princess Asati. This unexpected arrival piqued his curiosity.

Standing up, Sostris accepted the guard's bow and asked, "How may I be of service to your mistress?"

"Great priest, the princess had a dream during the night and desires to inquire of the goddess about its meaning. Even now, she is preparing to come."

Sostris maintained his calm demeanor, but this new development meant the disruptions had spread far beyond the falling star and his priests' dreams into Pharaoh's family. "We will receive her petition and assist in any way we can," he said, betraying neither surprise nor concern.

As Asati's guard bowed and left, Sostris' servant got his attention.

"Noble one, I apologize for the delay, but I have just learned that the falcons left the gate some time ago and flew to the southeast."

"I wonder where they went. No matter, we will continue to express our gratitude for their visit. Now, go and tell the pure priest to prepare special offerings and intercessions for the princess' visit."

As his servant hurried away, Sostris sat down. He wondered about the dream that caused the princess' unexpected visit.

At first, Pharaoh's sister had been a great blessing to the Temple of Satis. Her father, Pramesse, who would become Ramses I, named Asati in honor of the goddess. This benefited the priesthood when he grew in importance in the court of Haremhab. It also helped that the princess was a favorite of the childless Pharaoh. When he produced no heir, Haremhab made Asati's father his successor. This led to a shift in power throughout Egypt. A rise in status for those favored by the new royal family, including the goddess and her small but growing priesthood. This new temple in Memphis was only the beginning of their rapidly expanding prospects.

"But nothing is guaranteed, and not everything happens the way you believe it should," he thought.

What had begun as a blessing now threatened to become a curse. Princess Asati's continued barrenness was becoming a worry, a possible blot on the goddess's name and growing power. It threatened to undo the years of careful positioning Sostris had charted through the tortuous politics inherent in the power struggles between the resurrected influence of the temples and Pharaoh's court.

"What else can we do?" he mused. "We have employed every known temple lore and Egyptian medicine to the problem. We even tried exotic potions from the East and had Nubian priests brought up from the South to invoke their magic fertility rites. Nothing has worked. Even his most faithful priests had begun to lose heart. With everything else happening today, maybe the princess is coming to inquire about a good omen. Maybe, by the grace of Satis, this time she has good news."

"Noble one," his servant called, hurrying across the garden, "The falcons have returned."

"I wonder where they went," he murmured, but there was no answer.

Making Plans

Still unsettled by the morning's chaos, Nephura retreated to the temple garden for solitude and a private meal. He knew instinctively that more was happening than just the falling star and the strange events in his temple. Hearing a cough, he looked up to see Mioa, his special confidant and the manager of the temple's day-to-day activities.

"Well? Do you have anything?"

"Soon, my lord. Soon. So far, what we have is little more than rumors. There's a lot of talk about strange events happening at several of the other temples."

"Do you know any specifics?"

"Not yet."

"Rumors are smoke on the wind," Nephura said. "I need facts. Have you heard anything from the two priests who checked where the star struck the river?"

"One has returned. He reported that no one searching the area had found anything. The Chief Engineer believes the star is buried deep in the riverbed, close to the western bank. But the lock is not damaged."

Stifling frustration at the scant news, he bit his lip. This would be a long day.

"Go get something to eat, and then make sure the pure priest has successfully dealt with the morning disturbance; he can explain. Come back when you have something to report."

"Yes, my Lord."

After Mioa left, a prickle of foreboding crept up Nephura's neck. It had never failed him before. He loathed being blind to unfolding events, and now the insistent voice in his mind warned—there was no time to waste. He called to his servant, who was waiting a respectful distance away.

"Have Mioa get back here immediately!"

Whether it was a long day or not, it was time to expand their efforts and put their vast network of informants to good use. Before the day was over, they needed to know everything important that was happening in Memphis, whether from the other temples, the port, the police, or the palace.

Mioa came quickly across the garden, still chewing his last bite of food. Stopping a few feet away, he bowed slightly and, after hastily swallowing, said, "You called for me, Noble One?"

"Take whomever you need and seek out as many of our sources as possible on short notice. Be discreet but insistent. Focus on Pharaoh, his family, and the police. Once you have taken care of them, check the temples and the port, except for Satis and Ptah. The royal family favors them, so check them immediately. Use whatever means necessary. I want to know about anything unusual, no matter how small or insignificant. I will decide what is important. Now, hurry, be off!"

Mioa bowed and rushed away.

Nephura knew it would be a while before anyone returned with any useful information. After leaving orders with his servant that he should only be disturbed by someone returning with something significant, he went to his private quarters.

He needed to prepare for several possible contingencies. His position in Memphis and the secrecy with which he carried out his business meant that Mioa was one of the few people with whom he could confide. He did not mind being isolated; he hated being in the dark about what was happening. He was unsure how to proceed or where a possible attack might come from. That he no longer doubted—an attack was coming—but from whom? He felt paralyzed by his lack of knowledge, and that disturbed him most of all.

Despite all the uncertainty, there was one thing that Nephura was sure of. At some point during the day, Pharaoh would call together all the Chief Priests in Memphis. He would ask for their counsel about the falling star. It was an unprecedented event, and Seti would want public counsel, if for no other reason than to calm everyone and assure them that the gods were not angry at Egypt or her people. As Pharaoh, he would seek an interpretation of the events that all the priests could agree upon so that when he spoke about the matter, it would be with confidence about the will of the gods.

"Enough waiting. I must be ready," his mind locked onto a path ahead. "I can use these events to my advantage," he growled, pulling the cord that summoned his servant.

Gathering Information

Mioa sent two of the least known, though reliable, priests to check with their sources at the palace. He sent two to Satis and Ptah, dispatched most of the others to the remaining temples, and assigned Ameny, his favored young priest, to monitor the royal estate from the Great Southern Gate ferry. He wanted to know if they had sent any messengers and, if possible, to whom.

He would go himself to the office of the Chief Scribe of Investigations and Secrets. Though they knew him well, his inquiry would not stand out. All of the temples in Memphis would have high-standing representatives seeking information from Sekmet. It helped that some high-ups in the police looked kindly on the priesthood of Amun-Ra. Although these men worked for Sekmet and, ultimately, for Pharaoh, they still sought the favor of Nephura. They had occasionally looked the other way, quietly not pursuing certain investigations with the utmost vigor.

When Ameny arrived at the dock, the ferry had just left, though the resting crew was sharing dates awaiting their next turn. These ferries were spread along the river and provided much of the city's and port's fresh food.

As he approached the dock, Ameny prepared to strike up a conversation with the crew that was resting. But before he could speak, one of them beat him to it.

"What temple do you serve?" the ferryman asked.

"I serve at the temple of the great god Amun-Ra," Ameny said.

"Has your god spoken about the meaning of the falling star?"

"It is not for me to say. The Pharaoh will speak for all the gods when the time comes. What do your passengers have to say about it?"

The bold speaker hesitated, then turned back and talked in hush tones among his brothers before again facing Ameny.

"Some believe it is an evil omen. Others feel it signals a great event. Many of those who cross the river head to the temples to make offerings and hear what the priests have to say. Others hope to find a souvenir, a special blessing from the star. This morning, the stalls in Perunifer's market are filled with odd pieces of rock that their sellers say came from the heavens."

"I thought the star buried itself deep into the riverbed."

"It did, but that doesn't stop the hawkers from claiming that their little stones are pieces of heaven itself."

"Have many passengers made the trip to the port since this morning?"

"The barge has been filled on almost every trip. If you look across the river, you can see the crowd still waiting to cross. They are mostly people from the farms and outlying villages. However, one of the first passengers this morning was a guard from the Great Estate sent by Princess Asati. He was in a hurry and argued with the Ferry Master to let him go ahead of others who were already waiting for the first crossing."

Ameny recognized the lure when he heard it and wasted no time letting the ferryman pull in his catch.

"If I knew where he was going and why, it would save me a trip across the river. In that case, I am sure my lord would want to suitably reward those who assisted me."

The ferryman extended his hand expectantly. Surprised by his boldness, Ameny pulled a piece of copper from a hidden pocket—enough for the crew to buy a round of beer—and tossed it over.

The man snatched his prize and said, "The guard wanted to reach the Temple of Satis and alert the priests that the princess was coming. She had several disturbing dreams and wanted an interpretation from the goddess. He said the princess would be coming shortly, and the Ferry Master should be ready for her arrival. That got him to the front of the line."

"Is that all?"

"It was all *he* said."

Ameny looked at him, intrigued by the way the man emphasized *he*. For a ferryman, he appeared smart, ambitious, and surprisingly subtle. He knew how to draw out the possibilities for effect. He probably heard a lot of interesting gossip while ferrying people across the river. Ameny wondered what his implied information might be. This man might be useful. Taking a chance, he reached into his pocket and raised the stakes. Taking out a small piece of silver, he tossed it over. That would get his crew as much beer as they wanted for the rest of the week.

The ferryman caught the metal strip, showing no surprise at the increased encouragement.

"There were two servants of the princess riding on our last load. They tried to keep quiet, but being young and very excited, they couldn't help but talk."

"What did they say?" Ameny fought to contain his excitement. He did not want to give away how vital this information might be.

The man paused, obviously for effect, and said, "While Pharaoh's sister was taking an early morning bath along the river's edge, she found a Hebrew baby boy floating in a basket." He paused again, allowing the significance of his words to take hold. "She believes the child is a gift from the gods. Her servants were on their way to the market to buy items for the nursery."

Though the ferryman spoke in a matter-of-fact tone, the revelation stunned Ameny. His pulse quickened, but he kept his face stone-still. Trying to keep his voice from betraying his concern, he asked, "Did they say anything else?"

"No. They spoke very quietly. I only heard them because they were excited and standing beside my rowing station. They did not notice that I was listening. Most people using the ferry forget we are even here."

Ameny fished out another piece of copper and flicked it to the ferryman.

"Keep your ears open. If you hear anything else of interest, come to the temple and ask for Mioa. Tell him Ameny sent you. You will be amply rewarded. By what name are you called?"

The ferryman tucked the piece of copper away. He bowed slightly to Ameny and replied, "I am called Wasur." He then casually turned back to his companions and the bowl of dates as if nothing had happened.

The young priest rose and slowly left the area, trying not to betray his anguish. As soon as he was out of sight of the boatmen, he hurried off, pulse racing—this news would infuriate the Chief Priest.

The Weight of Dynasty

Seated on low chairs in the great hall, officially called the Hall of Reception, Seti and Ramses waited as the servants began bringing in the morning meal. This was the room where Pharaoh held official gatherings and public banquets. When there were only a few people, the space was large enough to allow quiet conversations far from prying ears, reducing the risk of eavesdropping. A number of those who labored in the service of Pharaoh had spent their entire lives in the palace. Due to the changes at court and in the palace over the last five inundations, some individuals had mixed loyalties when the new dynasty took residence.

Seti knew that bribes found their way to those who knew the worth of secrets, especially those with sharp ears and careful tongues. Juicy tidbits of information were commonly available to those who worked in the court and palace, and many would pay to access that knowledge.

He knew the priesthood of Amun-Ra had their dedicated ears sprinkled among the palace servants. Along with his attendant Danar, whom Seti trusted with his life, he believed they had identified most of them. Seti, the wise strategist, chose to leave the disloyal in place, unaware that their treachery had already been accounted for. An enemy in sight was someone he could manipulate to his advantage.

Hearing footsteps, Seti turned to see Tuya coming to join them.

He knew his wife loved the small honeyed cakes, but she would stay only long enough to ensure he would keep his promise: Ramses would remain with him all day. While she was not happy that the young prince had joined his trip to the impact site, they had returned safely. She had little choice but to accept his decision—easier now that the outcome was known. Even though he had recently appointed their son to the official positions of Chief Commander of the Egyptian Armies and Supervisor of all Construction, it did not make it easier for her to deal with her fears. Ramses was growing up, and that meant he would face more dangers. She would have to learn to deal with what was expected of the one in line to become Pharaoh. It did not matter that he was barely eleven inundations old and now her only son.

Seti could see that Tuya was struggling with her emotions. Not being able to remember her forgotten dreams, yet feeling their upset, was upsetting; yet when she spoke, she gave no hint of her increased anguish. "I want to hear more about the morning's events and enjoy some sweetbread," she said.

"I know you are curious," Seti said as she picked up one of her favorite delicacies. He purposely avoided mentioning her distress. "We are waiting on a report from the Chief Scribe of Investigations and Secrets. So far, little is known beyond the assurance that there is no significant damage to the Great Lock."

"Thank the gods." Then she nodded toward Ramses and said, "How is my son this morning? Are you enjoying the time with your father?"

"Yes, I am, mother. It has been very exciting."

Tuya could see his eagerness in how he sat, his eyes, and his voice, which pitched slightly higher than usual. She tried to be happy for him despite her anxiety, which this morning's adventure had only increased. She smiled bravely and said, "Make sure you pay attention to everything, Ramses. Today is special, and you will learn important things about being Pharaoh."

"I will, mother. Father has been teaching me a lot already," he said, his eyes sparkling with every word.

"I knew he would." She looked at her husband and said, "I won't stay long. I am going to visit the Seer Priest at the Temple of Ptah." She did not mention any further her dreams or the deep ache that had grown all morning. It would disturb her son, and her husband had his own worries.

The Temple of Ptah was the largest and oldest in Memphis, and its god was the city's historic protector. The Seer Priest had helped her in the past, and his reputation for recalling lost dreams was well-known throughout Egypt.

Tuya was glad to leave the palace. She did not enjoy the subtle maneuverings of priests and court officials. That was what the day held for her husband and son. The mere thought of the endless bickering, how the priests would twist every little thing to gain an advantage, would increase her discomfort. Seti had a formidable task ahead, with the whole city buzzing with rumors and wild tales. In the short time she was with him, two messengers reported events at several temples.

"I must go. I will leave you to the things that men must do."

Seti smiled at her subtle jibe and said, "What my Queen must do is come to see me when she returns, no matter what I am doing."

"I will, my husband," she said, hoping she would have something to tell him, something that would quiet her upset. She forced a smile, gave him an affectionate nod, and then turned and left.

Paser, Pharaoh's vizier, accompanied by his scribe, Osri, came in as the queen was leaving. Seti motioned for his counselor to take a seat and ordered more food, calling for some of the sweet date bread cakes that were Paser's favorite. His vizier took the seat to his left while Osri discreetly sat on a cushion in front of the impromptu court. Paser depended on his scribe to be his second ear, to remember everything as a reliable counsel.

Seti's chief counselor sat quietly and began to eat. He concentrated on the food and waited for his Pharaoh to start the discussion.

Seti studied him. Though his counselor was five inundations older than his Pharaoh, he seemed much younger. A thin but sinewy man with superb fighting skills, he had an incredibly sharp mind. His vizier came from a long line of warriors. His family had a distinguished history of service in the armies of Egypt. Paser was one of his father's captains when Haremhab appointed him Chief Commander of the Armies of Egypt and designated him as his chosen successor. Paser's loyalty to the Pharaohs of Egypt, as well as his personal loyalty, was as sure as the sun rising each morning. Seti recognized that his vizier was the one man the wiles of the priests would find no purchase. That is why he had given him the two most important tasks in his kingdom: the position of Vizier and Chief Adviser to Pharaoh and the Keeper of the Royal Crowns, which made him responsible for Ramses' education. This duty included instructing the prince in the affairs of state, warfare, finance, and the responsibilities of Pharaoh's relationship as the link between the gods of Egypt and her people.

"We cannot let the day's events dictate their own course," Seti said, "or others will use them to advance their agendas. We need to understand what the gods are saying and know what they are demanding. How else can we make an official proclamation?"

"I agree, my Pharaoh. The star striking the sacred river means this is not a mere request. Gathering all the temple heads and their Seer Priests here in the Great Hall would be wise. That way, if they are here consulting with Pharaoh, they cannot be on their own, pushing their private, self-inflating interpretation of the events. At least with them all together, we can monitor the debate and be assured that every god will have their proper say."

He paused, debating how much to reveal with Ramses sitting in the room.

"There is more here than the star striking the Nile," Seti said. "I am hearing about a growing list of portents and omens from the temples throughout the city."

"You look concerned, great one," Paser said.

Seti hesitated, weighing how much to reveal. But Ramses would one day be Pharaoh. He should know.

"I had a dream, an omen during the night." Turning to Ramses, he said, "It greatly upset your mother. In it, a leopard attacked you, and while you were defending yourself, a viper unexpectedly advanced on you from behind. You were saved by a young Hebrew who intercepted the serpent's strike with his staff."

A series of conflicting emotions ran across his son's face, and Paser quietly uttered a vulgarity. "There is more," Seti continued, "but that is all you need to understand right now. Both your mother and I believe that this is a warning that your life will be in danger one day, but we want the priests to help give us a full interpretation."

Turning to Paser, Seti said, "I believe it is wise to bring the Chief Priests and their Seer Priests to meet with us here. You can assist me in overseeing their deliberations."

"I am at your command, my Pharaoh."

"Send messengers to all of the temples and call the Chief Priests, along with their Seer Priests, to come immediately to the palace."

Seti paused. Sostris, the Chief Priest of his sisters' goddess, had a reputation for dream interpretations. Perhaps I should speak with him privately. However, I should be careful about consulting with him alone. That might create problems for Sostris with the other priests, especially those of Amun-Ra or Ptah. He should arrive late. That way, they could meet without making it obvious.

"Instruct the messenger you send to the Temple of Satis to go first to the Chief Engineer at the Great Lock and see if there is anything new to report. Then he can go to the Temple of Satis."

Paser was puzzled and asked, "Won't that cause him to arrive late? Will he take that as a slight?"

"Yes, he might, but I want a private meeting with him when he arrives. Hopefully, his late arrival will prevent Sostris from having problems later. He has been a valuable asset to our family and has a reputation for interpreting dreams. I don't want the other powerful priests, especially Nephura, to become jealous or suspicious of him. Better for Sostris if the other priesthoods continued to look down on the Chief Priest of Satis and dismiss him as favored only because of my sister, but essentially unimportant and not a threat."

Just then, Sekmet, the Chief of Police, who also held the office of Chief Scribe of Investigations and Secrets, entered the hall.

"We need to get started," Seti told his vizier. "I will obtain Sekmet's report and consult with him regarding the necessary security measures for the city and the surrounding area. You can make preparations for the meeting with the priests."

"I will begin immediately," Paser said, standing up and motioning to his scribe. "We will return as soon as possible."

Seti waved Sekmet forward.

"Sit here," he said, pointing to the vacated chair to his left. "Have something to eat."

The Chief of Police bowed with a flourish, moved around the table, and sat down. His face beamed. It was evident to Seti that the man could not believe his good fortune. After all, he was sitting next to Pharaoh and sharing food with him.

"Is there anything in particular I can have brought for you?" Seti said.

"My Pharaoh is most gracious. Some black tea would be most helpful. It has been a long morning."

Seti raised his hand, and a servant appeared. He ordered the tea and summoned the Royal Scribe. Glancing over, he saw Sekmet nibbling cautiously on one of the date cakes that Paser liked so much. His tension at being so close to his Pharaoh was palpable. Trying to make the man comfortable enough to function effectively, he said, "Those are my vizier's favorite."

"I can see why, my Pharaoh. They are delicious."

Leaning toward Ramses, who watched the exchange with an inquisitive look on his face, Seti whispered, "Pay attention to this discussion, my son. It's not easy to control the emotions of a city when the gods speak so powerfully."

"Yes, father," Ramses nodded.

Turning to Sekmet, he said, "It is a rare gift when a father has such excellent teaching opportunities for his son."

"I agree, my Pharaoh. Do you want to hear what we've learned so far?"

"Let's wait for my scribe. I want to begin keeping a detailed record of everything that happens today."

"A wise decision," Sekmet replied.

The black tea arrived, and Sekmet, who seemed to become more comfortable sitting next to his Pharaoh, raised the cup in acknowledgment of his hospitality. Seti had watched this man for many years as he came and went from the court of Haremhab. He appeared exceptionally competent and honest, and his loyalty to Egypt was beyond question. He believed in the sacredness of his duty, and Seti felt Egypt was fortunate to have him.

The Royal Scribe arrived and, with only a quick, small bow, sat down in front of them on the cushion that Osri had occupied. After arranging his tools and setting his writing platform across his open lap, he prepared a sheet of papyrus. With the ink ready and pen in hand, he looked up at Seti and waited.

Leaning over to Ramses, Seti said quietly, "There are times a written record helps keep the facts from wandering. A pharaoh has to decide what to carve in stone, what to record on papyrus, and what to leave to men's memories."

"So, father, papyrus opens the door, but only stone talks to the future?"

Seti smiled approvingly at his son's insight and said, "Give your report, Chief Scribe of Investigations and Secrets."

Sekmet began his account, which contained little new information. Seti thought about the courses of action open to him. He wondered what else the gods had in store for them today. This was no traditional battlefield.

But Seti's warrior's instinct warned him—the true battle was only beginning.

The Temple of Satis

Asati longed to rush to the temple, but courtly decorum demanded otherwise—she had to prepare before making her public appearance. No woman of the court of Pharaoh would dare go beyond her private areas until her toilet was in proper order, which included a suitably presented wig, meticulous facial makeup, and appropriate clothing and jewelry. She could not deny this necessity even with her impatience inflamed by finding the child.

The princess hurried her servants through the preparations and then rushed her escort and bearers out of the compound. Asati wanted to cross the river quickly to reach the Temple of Satis. Semri ordered the bearers to use the palanquin, as it was covered and would provide the princess with privacy as they moved through the excited crowds. When they went through the gate leading from the estate, the sun had risen only a short distance in the morning sky.

Asati leaned close to the curtain and called out, "Semri."

"Yes, my princess," he said, coming alongside.

"I know the Ferry Master was notified, but send one of the guards ahead to ensure he is alerted that we are coming."

She knew the Ferry Master was anxiously awaiting their arrival and probably had someone watching the road, but she did not want to leave anything to chance.

"As you command, my princess."

Semri waited for the rear guard to catch up to him.

"Nazim, run ahead and alert the Ferry Master that we are coming. The princess wants to ensure no delay crossing the river."

With a quick nod and a quiet grunt, his friend trotted off, passing the lumbering palanquin. Semri followed him to his place at the front of the procession.

After she heard the two men trot past the curtain, Asati settled back into the cushions. It did not take long, however, for the urgency and excitement to give way to the rhythmic pace of the bearers. Her underlying weariness, stemming from the lack of sleep and the emotionally draining excitement, gradually overcame her determination, and before she knew it, she was asleep.

Satis, Asati's patron goddess, ruled over the First Cataract of the Nile, far to the south near Nubia. Once a lesser figure in the pantheon, her influence had grown—especially since Asati's family rose to power. Since the ascent of Asati's family to the throne of Egypt, people began to see the goddess as the protector and supporter of the annual life-giving inundation of the Nile, upon which all of Egypt depended for its sustenance and survival.

Despite its deeply embedded traditions, the Egyptians' beliefs were also highly flexible. As long as no single god or goddess tried to claim exclusive rights, as the solar deity Aten had done under the efforts of the Pharaoh Who is Not Named, the priests and people of Egypt adjusted to the gradual ebb and flow of popularity and significance within the pantheon of their deities.

While every one of the numerous divinities had temples scattered throughout the Two Lands, none claimed absolute preeminence. Instead, their priests strove for power and prestige. Since the fall of the unnamed one, the priests of Amun-Ra had become the primary religious force in Egypt. Their center of power was in Thebes, a journey of almost ten days by river to the south. In response to their influence, recent pharaohs had relocated the capital to Memphis in the north, where it remained. While this meant there was no counterweight to the priesthood's southern influence, it demonstrated that Pharaoh ruled independently of their direct influence, a significant statement in its own right.

Only the solitary Hebrew God, the invisible, nameless one, stood alone. He did not matter. The deity of shepherds, servants, and slaves was insignificant compared to the powerful divinities of Egypt.

Asati was born after her father had returned from a successful campaign against bandits based in the southern Kurkor Oasis. She was an unexpected gift since Pramesse and his wife thought they were beyond the time of childbearing.

Traveling home from his military campaign, Pramesse had stopped at the estate of an old army friend, Mut-Khendra. The Pharaoh Haremhab had given him the provincial governorship of what was formerly the First Nome of Egypt. It was a princely reward offered to a former general in recognition of years of faithful service. This trip had been Pramesse's first chance to see his friend since Mut-Kendra had taken over the governorship two years earlier.

He lived on the luxuriant estate of a former official of the despised and forgotten pharaoh. Located on Sahal, a lush island in the middle of the Nile, it was a short distance upstream from Nubt, the region's administrative center. One of the island's chief features was a small but beautiful temple dedicated to Satis. This obscure goddess was the protector of the First Cataract, a day's journey upstream, and guardian of the southern border of Egypt. Her most important function, however, was unleashing the annual inundation, so her name signified the outpouring of the life-giving waters that created the yearly Nile flood, the lifeblood of the Two Lands.

In the short time he had resided on the island, Mut-Khendra had become a loyal follower of the goddess. Wanting to share his newfound devotion, he took Pramesse to a festival at the temple, a ceremony of blessing for the coming inundation.

Pramesse, like many soldiers, was not a devout man. But standing in the temple, he felt something—a presence, a pull, as if the goddess herself had spoken to him. That evening, Mut-Khendra gave a banquet in his honor, and Pramesse suggested he invite Sostris, the First Priest of the temple. In the midst of the meal, a thunderstorm struck. It rained and thundered for almost a full notch on the water clock, a rare and propitious event.

Sostris saw it as a good omen, especially since it occurred on the day of the festival. Because the feast was in honor of Pramesse, he declared that it boded well for his future. Then, to everyone's surprise, he uttered a prophecy.

"You will become as the life-giving waters that bring forth the inundation, and greatness for Egypt will spring from your seed."

Asati's father, awed by the priest's words, responded, "My wife is about to give birth any day. If the child is a girl, I will bring her to the temple and dedicate her to Satis."

Twenty-seven days later, or as Sostris would later point out, the sacred three, times the sacred three, times the sacred three, Pramesse's wife gave birth to a baby girl. After the full force of the inundation had passed, they undertook the ten-day journey up the Nile. His new daughter, Asati, was dedicated to the goddess at the Temple of Satis. Since that day, the fortunes of Satis and her First Priest had risen with the fortunes of the house of Pramesse.

Upon his ascension to the throne, Asati's father took the name Ramses, which meant "born of the sun" or "born of Ra." Despite his short reign, he exerted considerable effort uniting the Upper and Lower Kingdoms, the two traditional divisions of Egypt, under his new dynasty. He was aided by the most significant inundation in anyone's memory, occurring in conjunction with his ascension to the throne. This endeared him to the people and assured them that the gods would bless this new dynasty. The priests, however, were another matter.

Pramesse had humble beginnings. He was a scribe and the son of a soldier. Though he eventually became Vizier to the childless Pharaoh Haremhab and Chief Commander of the Armies of the Two Lands, he had little more than his Pharaoh's designation, himself a soldier's son, to secure his throne. To placate the powerful priesthood of Amun-Ra and obtain their support for his ascension, Pramesse agreed to reissue Haremhab's edict against the newborn Hebrew males and see to its rigid enforcement.

Already old at the beginning of his reign, Ramses died of a sudden fever toward the end of his second inundation. Though he had designated his son Seti as heir and future Pharaoh, his unfortunate death weakened Asati's brother's ascension. He needed the support of the priesthoods of Egypt. Named after the god Set, the brother and enemy of the popular god Osiris, the god was never universally liked. In recent generations, Set's esteem had dwindled so low that the only place they still practiced his worship was in the northern delta, far from the religious power center at Thebes.

When Seti became Pharaoh three inundations ago, he had to work harder than his father to secure favorable allegiances. The priests of the prominent gods, especially those of Amun-Ra, all expected favors from the new Pharaoh. As a result, he had no choice but to continue enforcing the edict against the Hebrew male births. While he privately disagreed, Seti did give Egypt what it needed: a strong Pharaoh supported by the most powerful priesthood in Egypt.

Asati knew her brother believed that the Hebrew death decree went against Ma'at, the overarching principle of truth, justice, and the cosmic order that made Egypt beloved of the gods. However, he knew that his strength as Pharaoh this early in his reign was not enough to contend directly against the priests of Amun-Ra. That priesthood, especially its representative and First Priest in Memphis, Nephura, actively sought the destruction of the Hebrews. On this issue, Seti had only one steadfast ally: Sostris and the priests of Satis. However, they were few in number, and their influence was weak.

Now, Asati was turning to those same priests for help.

The litter bearers stopped a short distance from the people waiting for the ferry and lowered the conveyance to the ground. The jolt startled

Asati awake. The distant murmur of the crowd drifted through the curtain. Stretching her stiff limbs, she steadied herself and then stepped out.

The Ferry Master, accompanied by Semri, stood alongside her litter.

"We have the ferry ready for you, your Highness. You can leave immediately."

"I will remember your service to the house of Pharaoh," Asati replied.

Any irritation the beaming Ferry Master might have felt at having to hold the ferry disappeared. He called to his rivermen to clear a path through the crowd.

The crossing was brief, but despite Semri's best efforts, the crowds on the western shore slowed their progress.

The delay aggravated Asati, but she fought to calm herself and keep her usually acerbic tongue in check. There was no need to create a scene, and excited people were notoriously unpredictable. The crowds were almost a mob. The populace was milling around, still excited over the falling star, listening to hawkers claim to have relics from the event or trying to catch a glimpse of what was happening farther south, where the heavenly body had struck the sacred river. At last, with Semri's soldierly perseverance clearing the way, they arrived at the Great Southern Gate and passed inside the city's walls.

When her litter arrived at the temple of Satis, the number of people waiting to enter surprised Asati. Usually, the petitioners were few. Sostris, the First Priest of the goddess, and two of his older priests were waiting for her. The First Priest bowed as the princess used Semri's sure hand to assist her from the litter.

"Come in peace in the name of Satis, my Princess. Your messenger said you've had an eventful night."

Asati nodded, turned to Semri, and said, "Send the guards and bearers to rest in the shade and have water and food brought to them. The heat will soon begin to conquer the morning air, and it is no use tiring them further. This is their second trip this morning, and I don't know how long I'll be."

"We will be ready when you are, my Princess," he replied, his eyes fixed on the crowd.

Her brother had assigned Semri, who, despite being young, was one of his most capable and battle-hardened field officers, to oversee the security of the Great Estate. His main task, given by Seti himself, was always to ensure the princess's safety. After surveying the area, Semri decided there was no immediate issue. He told his men and the bearers to rest.

As Semri took a protective yet non-aggressive stance beside the princess, Asati turned to the First Priest and said, "Yes, the night has brought many things that need explanation, but the morning, noble one, has been even more important. Significant events have followed a strange night. I don't know where to begin…the child or the dreams and omens."

Sostris tried to hide his astonishment at her words. She did not say, "I am with child," but simply "the child." That was a strange and unexpected development occurring on an already extraordinary day. He decided to avoid a direct response. He wanted the princess's revelation to go undiscussed while they were in public. There were many ears out here in the open, and there would be time to discover what this new disclosure meant after the offerings.

"The gods are very active today, my Princess, with the star falling and everything else happening. We have also had dreams and omens."

Sostris saw the princess start to say something, but he stopped her by saying, "As for your immediate concerns, we will do our best to find answers to all your questions. Sacrifices have been prepared on your behalf, and the goddess is ready to receive you. Please be patient."

Sending the priests ahead, Sostris moved alongside Asati, leaned close to her ear, and whispered, "I suggest that we do not discuss anything about this child here in public. We should wait until after the offerings."

He took Asati's elbow, and as the crowd parted to let her pass, he guided her up through the entrance into the forecourt, the Court of Appearance. As they went through the gates, leaving Semri in their wake, Sostris felt a shudder pass through the princess. Perhaps she was starting to grasp the enormity of what was happening.

The Ceremony of Petition was usually simple, as it was repeated regularly for each supplicant; however, Sostris wanted to make the goddess as receptive as possible to the Pharaoh's sister. He also knew that an extended ritual, accompanied by its sweeping ceremony, would help put Asati at ease. Now, with her new revelation, he was thankful that he had overprepared.

Everything they had organized for the princess went into motion. On opposite sides of the great hall, two small groups of priests joined in response to the chant of the *kher heb* priest, who intoned the goddess' most elaborate hymn of petition. A troupe of Khenerit, clad in sheer linen, was led by a priest wafting sacred incense. The women danced in slow, measured steps down the center aisle, striking their raised sistra in timed response to the slowly ascending chorus.

Asati followed behind the dancers, Sostris still at her side, watching the delicately choreographed movements of the Khenerit as they rhythmically shook their sacred instruments. With each reverberation, she felt the hypnotic pull of their ritual dance, drawing her to the goddess. The morning's anxieties began to evaporate as the music, movement, and holy incense flooded her senses, making her feel light-headed. Suddenly, everything went dark as Sostris reached out and caught her as she fell.

> Asati was back on the shore of the great sea, but this time, the baby lay quietly cradled in her arms. The coarse blanket of the Hebrews, which had been floating in the water, was now wrapped snugly around him. The storm still raged, the wind howling against her. While the waves did not touch her, the sand held her fast, as if fate itself had anchored her in place.
>
> Suddenly, a shaft of light pierced through the turbulent clouds, striking her in the face and flooding her with brightness. With the light came warmth and a rich passion that spread out from the brightness, infusing her with a sense of strength that cascaded through her body. This slowly gave way to a profound sense of purpose, which first enveloped her and then took root deep within her breast. Like pieces of a puzzle slowly falling into place, she knew she had to keep this child safe from the tempest churning before her. This was her purpose, her destiny.

Holding the unconscious princess as the ritual continued without them, Sostris considered the possibility that she was having a vision. Two priests rushed over and took Asati from him.

"Take her to the Audience Room. Do not leave her alone."

As they carried the princess away, Sostris noticed a small ostrich feather lying on the floor. It was the familiar symbol of Ma'at, the spirit of moral order and truth. He was sure it had not been there when she had begun to fall; they had swept and washed the floor in preparation for the ceremony.

He reached down and took the feather, slipping it into his garment. Until he could talk with the princess and inquire of the goddess, he had no idea how to interpret its meaning.

Growing Problems

Nephura's private scrolls lay scattered across the floor, their ancient ink whispering of past omens and forgotten warnings. While his servant finished preparing for the inevitable summons from Pharaoh, he thoroughly searched his private records. The only related texts he could find were about stars that had struck the southern and western deserts. These rare celestial visitations left behind sacred yellow-green stones—prized by pharaohs and priests alike as divine relics. Treasured since the dawn of history, they were gifts from the gods. One text said that the Pharaoh Tutankhamun had been buried with a consecrated necklace made entirely of these holy stones.

However, this star had not struck the desert; it had hit the blessed river at the edge of Memphis and coated the city's southern wall with mud and debris. No one had reported finding any sacred stones. Priests from every temple had scoured the site since sunrise and returned with nothing but dirty clothes and the immediate need for a bath. The uniqueness of this event would make it extremely difficult to guide any interpretation in a way that favored his plans, as if that was the desire of Amun-Ra.

Nephura's gaze locked on the water clock, each drop stretching time—like a blade drawn slowly across flesh. The steady plinks against the basin gnawed at his focus like a vulture pecking at carrion. He reached over and inserted a wooden shaft into its slot, which caught the drops as they left the reservoir and spread them down its length into the water, quieting the offending noise.

Irritation coiled tight, a serpent crushing his ribs. Where were his priests? Several divisions on the water clock had passed since he had ordered Mioa to send them on their clandestine missions. He needed their reports to plan his strategy. Until they provided him with more information, there was little else he could do to prepare himself for Pharaoh's summons. His toilet was complete, and his robes and other necessary items were laid out; the bearers stood by, waiting. It was only a matter of time before the call to the palace would arrive. He had two choices: to enter last and make a grand entrance, which spoke to his importance, or arrive first and have each priest come to him, which would enable him to gather information and refine his strategy before the meeting started, but would also give importance to the summons and Pharaoh. If his priests failed to return, he would go first. He would not stand before Pharaoh, blind, exposed, and weak. Information was power—and power was his alone.

It was more important than status. He needed facts, observations, rumors, anything.

"I cannot face the palace blind in the face of the gods' significant encroachment. My control must hold," Nephura vowed.

Gathering the scattered papyri, he rolled them up, tied them shut, and put them into the carrying cloth. Taking it across the room, he returned the scrolls to their assigned places in the hidden compartment. As he shut the panel, he heard a knock at his door.

"My lord, two priests have returned with information."

Nephura ensured the panel was closed correctly, adequately concealing the hiding place. Smoothing out his robe, he went over and sat down on the raised seat positioned opposite the entrance. The high-legged chair and footstool were elevated on a small dais so that he would be at eye level or above with any person standing in front of him. It maintained his commanding presence as if Nephura's reputation and demeanor were insufficient.

"Enter!"

Amunsa opened the door and motioned the first of the two waiting priests into the room.

This young priest, named Ameny, had never entered Nephura's inner sanctum before, and his nervousness made walking into the room difficult. As the door shut behind him, the young priest bowed low. He probably expected to give his report to Mioa, not to the First Priest himself.

"Calm yourself."

The young man took a deep breath and became slightly less rigid. However, as he tried to relax, his body began to tremble. Nephura remembered that Mioa had good things to say about this one.

"I assume that because Amunsa sent you in first, you have the more significant information."

"Yes, my lord. I have vital information," he replied.

When he did not continue, Nephura grew irritated but controlled his voice. He wanted the priest's information; however, he might never obtain it if he further upset the young priest. "There is nothing to fear. Tell me what you've learned."

Ameny had planned the substance of his report on his way back to the temple. He expected to provide a brief synopsis to Mioa and then immediately go out to gather additional information. Someone had to find and then shadow the two servants of the princess. Reporting directly to the Chief Priest was unexpected and made him nervous, especially since he was the harbinger of such bad news. Once he regained enough control to speak, his words came out too fast, and the Chief Priest's shoulders began to rise. He stopped, took another deep breath while begging Amun-Ra for a merciful intervention, and willed himself to slow down. When he started again, his speech was more measured and under control, but he could still feel the deep trembling that continually tried to assert itself. He began detailing the information gleaned from the riverman, starting with the guard sent as a messenger from the princess to the Temple of Satis, and then described Princess Asati's dreams and portents.

Nephura was stone. If he possessed feelings, they lay buried beneath his cold calculations. His only response was, "Is there anything else?" He had saved the most upsetting revelation for last, knowing that nothing else would likely be heard if he spoke about the child first. Every member of the priesthood of Amun-Ra despised the Hebrews; it was ingrained into their earliest training. But everyone knew Nephura hated these foreign intruders with an uncommon, and some said uncontrollable, passion. If the Chief Priest had his way, he would use his own hands to feed every Hebrew in Egypt to the crocodiles.

As Ameny related the additional information from the two maidservants who were going to get things for the nursery, he told him about the Hebrew baby boy found floating on the Nile and, finally, the princess's assumption that he was a gift from the gods. The Chief Priest's eyes narrowed and darkened. The muscles at the back of his jaw began to bulge, and without warning, a bitter curse shredded through his clenched teeth.

Nephura's rage flared—black, seething, clawing for release. A Hebrew called a gift of the gods. Blasphemy! He almost couldn't think as he fought to put the dark beast back into its cage. Grasping at an ancient incantation for control, he forced his breath to steady, willing his fury into submission. The pounding in his chest and the ringing in his ears began to subside. When his fury degraded to mere anger, reaching a tolerable level, he said, "Is there anything else?" The words were almost a hiss.

"Yes, my lord. I arranged with the riverman to pass on any additional information he might hear. There is a lot of loose talk by those who ride the ferry, and they seem to forget the rowers are there. It could prove to be a valuable source of information."

With the darkness temporarily controlled as the spell finished its work, Nephura felt almost calm. He looked over this young priest. He was common-looking, with a forgettable face, which would be an asset for someone who took on special assignments. It was apparent from how he presented the information that he was intelligent, and the way he handled his nervousness indicated that he could exercise control. His initiative in recruiting the riverman demonstrated he knew how to seize and act on an opportunity, another critical skill. He and Mioa had been searching for an apprentice. He would have to keep an eye on this one.

"You have done well. However, you will keep this information to yourself. Tell Mioa, but discuss it with no one else —no one else! When he returns, do whatever he says. Now go and send in the other priest."

The young priest bowed, let out a sigh of relief, then turned and opened the door. Amunsa was waiting impatiently on the other side. The other priest was no longer there. However, Mioa had arrived, and immediately, the two men brushed past Ameny. As he passed, Mioa told the young priest, "Get something to eat. I have work for you, and it will be a long day."

Nephura's servant closed the door, and they bowed hastily. With a flip of his hand, he wasted no time ordering them to speak.

"My Lord," Amunsa said, "I sent the other priest away. He didn't know anything important. Much is happening. The messenger you expected from Pharaoh arrived as you predicted. He is calling for an assembly of all the Chief Priests and their Seer Priests in the Great Hall. There have been portents and signs from the temples of Satis, Ptah, and many others."

Looking at his servant, Nephura said, "Go and tell the Seer Priest to prepare. I will join him shortly."

After Amunsa had left the room, closing the door behind him, Nephura looked directly at Mioa, raising his hand to cut him off. "Time is short, and there is something important we need to set in motion."

With practiced guile, Nephura devised an improvised yet ingenious plan to neutralize this unexpected Hebrew threat. He left the specific details to his trusted priest to work out, but they settled on how Mioa would report the success of this clandestine mission.

"Provide me a brief summary of anything I need to know?"

Mioa quickly explained the significance of the signs and portents at the city's temples. He began with Asati mentioning a Hebrew child, verifying the young priest's report. He then noted her collapse at the Temple of

Satis, followed by the queen collapsing on the steps of the Temple of Ptah. He closed with Pharaoh's strange dream and its upsetting Hebrew connection.

"It is good to know these complications, but they don't matter," Nephura said, his upset now entirely under control. "Everything turns on the success of our plan. Do not fail me, Mioa."

"Have I ever done so, my Lord?" His words hung in the air as he bowed and left the room.

Nephura donned his finest robes, smoothing every fold with meticulous care. Power was a perception—he would face Pharaoh with his appearance flawlessly prepared. He needed to be at his best before Pharaoh and the other priests. Time was short. Too many things were happening at once, and the magnitude of the occurrences made every perception, every decision, and every word crucial. Events in Egypt usually moved at a measured pace, giving him time to plan his moves carefully. He prided himself on keeping his undertakings hidden from view, but successful secrecy required adequate preparation and controlled action. This challenge, however, required immediate action, which had to be taken during the most disruptive and turbulent period the Chief Priest had ever encountered. He felt exposed, as if on a raging battlefield, unsure of where the next attack would come from.

Nephura crushed uncertainty beneath sheer will. He would act—before power bled from his grasp. That would not happen! No, never. This plan had to succeed.

More Omens and Portents

After completing the offerings and prayers to the goddess, Sostris left the House of Morning and discovered that Asati remained deeply entrenched in her vision. Two of his priests came through the gate, looking anxious. He motioned them over.

"What have you found?"

Satyu spoke first. "Noble one, I visited the Temple of Hapi. The priests were in great excitement. Early this morning, one of their hippopotami gave birth to twins—an extremely rare event. They consider it a powerful omen, though its meaning is still debated. Some believe this inundation will bring two divine gifts."

Without answering, Sostris turned to the young wa'eb, Satemra, an orphan who had spent his entire life in the temple. He was visibly disturbed and seemed hesitant to speak.

Reining in his impatience, Sostris said gently, "What is wrong, my son?"

"You sent me to Amun-Ra's temple, noble one, since I am unknown there. While waiting for the gates to open, I overheard an argument between a vendor setting up his stall and a petitioner who had slept outside the entrance, hoping to be first inside. The petitioner had confided a secret, but the vendor saw an opportunity to use it for his own gain. They quarreled over whose need was greater."

"What did the man hear?"

"During the morning ritual, a vulture appeared above the god's shrine. It flew out of the naos, defiling the sacred space—and the priests beneath it, including the great Nephura himself. Then, it vanished through an open door. The temple was thrown into turmoil. The Chief Priest demanded silence, threatening a curse upon any who spoke of it. But the market was already stirring, and whispers had begun. The secret would not stay hidden for long."

Sostris was stunned. This was no ordinary omen—it endangered the unpopular yet powerful First Priest of Amun-Ra in Memphis. And a cornered Nephura was dangerous. No one in the city, other than Pharaoh himself, held more power than Nephura. In some ways, the Chief Priest of Amun-Ra was even more dangerous than Pharaoh, who had the power of life and death. What if Nephura tried to blame Satis for what happened? A vulture, one of Satis's symbols, could represent her presence. That may well threaten their temple and undo all their gains since the rise of the new dynasty.

Keeping this concern to himself, he placed a calming hand on the young priest's shoulder. "You have done a valuable service for our temple, my son. I see you have questions. However, for now, you must keep this to yourself. Go, get something to eat, and then help prepare for the midday offerings."

As Satemra bowed and reluctantly left, Sostris turned to Satyu. "Try to calm him down and make sure he doesn't speak about this to anyone. We will meet later. We need time to discuss these events among ourselves, and we should prepare additional offerings to the goddess."

"I will look after him and see to the offerings," he said and hurried after the retreating boy.

As he turned these reports over in his mind, Sostris thought about the other things that had occurred throughout the morning. The events surrounding the princess appeared connected to what was happening at the other temples. The ostrich feather he found under the princess now took on greater significance. If it did represent Ma'at, as he was beginning to believe, then it symbolized all that was good and noble in the heart of Egypt. It had to be a crucial omen, and each new omen pointed to a larger design—one the gods clearly wished him to grasp. But to what end? The patterns were emerging, yet all carried risk for Satis and her priests.

Sostris reined in his speculations. First, he had to deal with the princess. Hurrying to the Audience Room, he found her lying unconscious on the couch. The priest watching over her stood up as he entered.

"She has not moved since we brought her in here."

As Sostris approached, Asati began to groan softly. "I do not want to wake her. I believe she is under the influence of a sacred vision."

"My lord, we also thought the god was speaking to her. It would be sacrilege to disturb her."

"I agree. Go and find Semri. I want to talk to him about something she said when she arrived."

Bowing, the priest left in search of the head of the princess's guard.

Finding a stool, Sostris placed it in front of the doorway and sat down, waiting for her to regain consciousness.

Asati had been a significant blessing to Satis and her priests. When she was old enough, her father had been true to his word. Pramesse sent her upriver to the temple so Sostris could instruct her in the cult of her patron. It was an easy duty. All of the priests genuinely liked her, as had many at the court of Haremhab. She was one of the former pharaoh's favorites, and he had arranged her marriage to one of Egypt's first families. Her husband owned the Great Estate across the river to the south, and his family's loyalty to the priests of Amun-Ra had strengthened Pramesse's position in Haremhab's court. Asati's initiation into the mysteries of the goddess had kept Sostris close to the household of Pramesse. The princess's devotion helped Satis rise in importance within the family of the man who would become Pharaoh Ramses.

When Haremhab designated Pramesse as pharaoh after him, everything changed for those favored by the new royal family. Now buried in the Valley of the Kings, Ramses never forgot Satis or Sostris' prophecy. One of the new pharaoh's first projects was to build the Temple of Satis in the capital. It had taken Sostris a considerable amount of time, over twenty inundations, to bring his priesthood to its current position. Under his leadership, they had been patient, not greedy.

It helped that every possibility had worked to Satis's advantage as she began to rise to greater heights in the minds of the people. Many of the new faithful were starting to honor her as the First Mistress of the gods. After the auspicious inundation that marked the ascension of Pramesse to the throne, demonstrating to everyone that the new Pharaoh had the approval and blessing of the gods, each of the last three gifts of the Nile had been lower than before. In most places, the previous two inundations did not flood the whole expanse of the fields, leaving a portion of the land dry and untilled. The last two harvests were insufficient to sustain Egypt's people. Pharaoh had to draw down grain from the standing reserves, which were at the lowest level in a generation. As the difficulty increased, offerings to the goddess for a favorable inundation also rose dramatically. In the marketplace, the priests of Satis had begun to hear pleas to the goddess for the coming inundation.

"But that could change," he murmured. Today's omens could either elevate them to new heights—or plunge them to ruin.

The Hebrew Village

The return to her village was much quicker than her journey to the river, thanks to a shorter route and guards urging them forward. As Nari carried her brother, they made their way through the fields of the Great Estate on a well-traveled cart path, which, after a few turns, went in an almost direct line to the east. The wide elevated pathway made their walking easier.

Unlike most Egyptians, this woman treated her kindly rather than showing the usual contempt for Joseph's people. Unable to stifle her inquisitive nature, she looked for an opportunity to learn more about this curious woman. Miriam moved alongside Nari and began asking questions.

"You are different from the other Egyptians I have met," she said.

"How is that?" Nari asked, a puzzled look crossing her face.

"Most treat me like something scraped off the bottom of their sandals."

Nari laughed quietly, and Miriam noticed her wry smile as she said, "Not everyone, child, believes the brothers of Joseph are an evil blight on the land of Egypt. Some know better than to listen to everything they hear. Many priests do not speak for the gods they claim to serve."

Her cryptic response only increased Miriam's desire to know more about her. She cautiously asked, "Have you been with the princess for a long time?"

"All her life, little one," Nari said.

"That is a long time. How did you come to serve in the great house?"

"Yes, child, there's no harm. My family entered the service of the princess's household a few years before she was born. When she arrived, I became her nursemaid; now, I am her chief maidservant."

Gathering her courage, Miriam delicately redirected her probing to the real area of her concern. "You must know her very well. May I ask why she seems to want this child so much?"

"You certainly have a lot of questions," Nari said. "Don't you know? I thought all of Egypt knew. I suppose what might be common gossip around the courts and marketplaces of Memphis and Perunifer is not discussed in the villages of the Hebrews. For five floods since her marriage, I have watched her plead—using potions, magic, and countless prayers—all to no avail. Until him." She looked wistfully down at Moses. "So, she sees this child as a gift the gods gave to remove her reproach."

"Thank you, thank you, God," Miriam silently prayed.

The woman's answer was beyond hope. Miriam had to fight back her excitement, fearing she would draw more suspicion about her brother.

I must calm down. This journey is joyful, but I cannot show it.

One of the guards drifted back and spoke with Nari. She turned to Miriam and said, "The guards want to get us home before the heat rises. How much longer is it?"

"Not far. Do you want me to carry him for a while?" Miriam said, hoping for a chance to hold him again. She noticed the Egyptian cradled him like her own, not a burden she had to bear.

"I am fine, child," Nari said as she shifted Moses to her other arm and increased her pace. Struggling to keep up, Miriam saw a strange delight in this Egyptian woman's eyes as she carried her brother, and he seemed comfortable in her arms. He had not complained once since they had left the river.

Unlike most Hebrew living areas, Miriam's village was within walking distance of Memphis, which was necessary for her father's daily trips to work in the shipyards at Perunifer. He was a skilled carpenter. Most of her people were scattered among the work sites throughout the Pharaoh's construction projects in the delta. The dispersion of her people made their large population easier to manage, but it also meant they were everywhere.

"Here we are," Miriam said, cresting the last rise before her village.

Her feet itched to run, excited to share the fantastic news with her mother. Fortunately, there were almost no men in the village. They, along with some of the women, were working in the despised brick pits. Every construction site in Egypt had them. The Egyptian builders had become dependent on their Hebrew brickmakers because of their skill and sturdy constitutions. Working the pits drained the life from a person, and the Egyptians despised it. They had long relied on the Hebrews doing the hardest, dirtiest labor.

Miriam knew the village's resentment could be dangerous. She needed to speak to her mother alone. As they approached the outer dwellings, she called to the guards, "Stop here!" She turned to Nari and said, "Please wait here while I go and find a wet nurse."

"Why don't you want me to come?"

"I don't want anyone to offend you...or worse. There are angry people in this village. As you can see," Miriam said, pointing to a small group beginning to gather, "someone has already noticed our approach. Some of the families in the village have lost children, but I may have to ask more than one. It would be difficult if you were there."

"Such wisdom for one so young," Nari said. "You have the heart of a diplomat. Do as you think best. We will be content to wait here."

Surprised at the easy approval, Miriam ran off to find her real objective: her mother. News of the Egyptian guards escorting a woman with a baby spread through the village as fast as Miriam could run.

Miriam found her mother sitting against the back wall of their house in the shade of a lean-to roof. Jochebed was tired but was weaving a basket from the rushes she had cut that morning. Miriam's younger brother Aaron was playing with his armies, which were made of small stones and bits of wood, in the dirt next to her. Aaron had been fortunate. He had been born before the Pharaoh's father had begun rigidly enforcing the edict, and when the slaughter began, they only killed the newborns. He would be among Egypt's last surviving Hebrew men unless something changed.

As Miriam raced up, half out of breath, she saw no one else was nearby. Before she could restrain herself, her words flooded, "Momma, it's a miracle; you won't believe it. I saw it and can hardly believe it."

Startled by her daughter's appearance and the onrush of her excitement, Jochebed reached up and grabbed her by the arm. "Slow down, Miriam. Tell me what happened. Did someone find your brother?" Her words were flooded with emotion, and her concern was written on her face.

Miriam took a deep breath, trying to gather her thoughts and calm herself. Then, looking into her mother's anguished eyes, she said as calmly as she could, "I watched as you told me to, but I didn't have to wait very long. The Pharaoh's sister, Princess Asati, came to the river to bathe and found him immediately."

She saw a sudden look of fear sweep across her mother's face, and the grip on her arm began to hurt. "Don't worry, momma! It's all right! The princess has no children and thinks my brother is a gift from her Nile god. Oh, momma, she wants to keep him. She even gave him a name, Moses. It means 'taken out of the water' or something like that. At first, I didn't believe it. But that is not all. She saw me by the river and sent me here with her servant and my brother to find a wet nurse for him. So, I came straight to you. Momma, can you believe it? You will get to nurse him, and she will pay us!"

Jochebed suddenly felt lightheaded. Letting go of Miriam, she fell back against the wall, her mind tangled with thoughts and her heart pounding. If this was true, it was a miracle beyond all her and Amram's hopes.

"God be praised!" she said, reaching forward and grasping Miriam's hand. With that, all of the doubt, fear, and agony that had bound her life since she discovered she was pregnant escaped its bindings and poured out of her heart in a series of wrenching sobs. Rocking back and forth, she kissed her daughter's hand repeatedly as the emotions surged, crested, and then gradually ebbed away. Looking up into the clear morning sky, she offered a prayer of thanks to the God of Abraham for protecting her son. Jochebed had never imagined that she would ever see him again, let alone nurse him. She asked, "Where are they?"

"They are waiting on the road outside the village. There...there are two soldiers with them," Miriam said.

"Take me to them. We'll leave Aaron with our friend Merba. She watched him this morning and won't mind doing it again. But you cannot let the Egyptians know I am your mother. It would arouse suspicion and cause too many questions."

"Okay. Did I do well, Momma?"

"You did very well, Miriam. Your father will be so proud of you."

Miriam took Aaron by the hand. As they left the house, a shadow crossed their path. Looking up, she saw two falcons circling above the village.

Jochebed had to stop her feet from dancing in sheer pleasure. Her tiredness vanished, replaced by joy. She knew God had heard her prayers. Her words had not fallen on deaf ears, and the realization filled her with an unshakable joy. She allowed herself a moment to let her heart sing. Then, on the way to her friend's house, she steeled herself, preparing to play the part of an indifferent wet nurse.

Veiled Missions

Ameny picked at his meal as Mioa beckoned from the doorway. Though the food was excellent, the weight of his encounter with the First Priest dulled his hunger. Gathering his plate and spoon, he dumped the remaining food in the alms basin set aside for the poor and placed the dish and spoon in the washtub. After following Mioa into the temple garden, they arrived at a private seating area out of the ascending sun, where the priest told him to sit.

"You've pleased me, boy, don't falter now."

His cheeks reddened as the praise washed over him, displacing his former upset. Ameny sought every nuance in the senior priest's words. Finally, he might have a chance to do something interesting, something other than prepare offerings. This morning had been exciting, even with his frightening experience reporting to the First Priest. He vowed to do better when he got another chance to go before Nephura.

"I have another mission for you. You said two of the Princess's servants were going to Perunifer to get items for the nursery. Discover what they are purchasing and from which merchants. Do you know any young priests that you can trust to help you?"

Two immediately came to mind. Ameny replied, "Yes."

"Good. They can assist you, but you have to be discreet. They must know as little as possible about why you seek this. You must tell them only what they need to know to obtain the desired details. After you report what you discover, all of you will forget everything about this. Ensure that none of you ask any questions or discuss this matter with anyone else, not even among yourselves. I don't care what happens in the coming days. This order comes directly from the First Priest. Is that absolutely clear?"

Ameny felt a knot tighten in his gut as he understood the implications behind those words and the danger they carried. Knowledge was power—and a danger. To rise in Nephura's service, he had to know enough to be useful but never enough to become a threat. He had no desire to serve in a small temple at some desolate outpost in the western desert or possibly something worse. Ameny recalled the five priests sent west—whispers said more than desert awaited them. That kind of speculation, however, was more than dangerous and best disregarded. Some priests believed that Nephura could read their minds, so what he did with his problem priests, as long as it did not happen to them, was dismissed and purposefully forgotten.

"V-very clear, my lord."

As Ameny started to leave, he remembered the boatman and stopped. He turned back to Mioa, who looked at him and asked, "Is there something else?"

"Yes, my lord. I arranged with the ferry boatman, the one who provided me with this information, to come here and ask if he had heard anything else of interest. His name is Wasur, and I told him he would be amply rewarded."

Mioa did not immediately respond. His features gave no hint of what he was thinking. He merely said, "I'll take care of it," and with a flick of his hand, told him to leave.

Ameny went to find his two friends and then abruptly changed his mind. No, he would pick two priests he disliked. They would be flattered, but if reassigned—or worse—he wouldn't mourn them. To protect himself, he would have to make his usefulness too valuable to merit any reckoning.

Mioa studied the young priest as he left. This one might have real talent, and if he lived up to expectations and could be trusted, he would bear nurturing and careful watching. Even though he might prove useful, I will have to deal with those who assist him before the afternoon is gone. Later for that. Nephura's plan pressured everything. He couldn't wait for additional information. He had to contact the necessary resources, which would take long enough as it was. The Chief Priest's strategy was bold—and dangerous. Delay was not an option.

Awakening

Sostris eyed the unconscious princess, stunned by her revelation of a child. Hearing a muffled cough, he saw one of his priests and Semri outside the doorway.

Motioning them to be quiet, Sostris got up, pushed the seat aside, and left the room. He sent the priest away, and when he was out of earshot, he said to Semri, "Tell me about the child."

"I am concerned about the princess, my lord."

"There is no need to worry. We believe she is under the influence of a sacred vision." After a slight pause, Sostris went again to his concern. "I need to know about the child."

Asati's chief guard was reluctant to speak.

"I need to know everything so that we will know how to help the princess."

"Shouldn't you wait and let her tell you herself?"

"Usually, I would agree, but I don't know how long that will be before I can talk with her. The more we know, the better we can prepare to assist her."

Semri sighed. "You've known her since childhood, and you are the First Priest of Satis, her patron."

"As you said, I have been with the princess a long time. Who can you trust to help her if you cannot trust me?"

Semri stared at him. The warrior seemed to be measuring him, trying to reassure himself. Then he sighed and said, "It will eventually become common knowledge anyway. Maybe this is the place to start."

Sostris gave him a reassuring nod.

"The princess had dreams throughout the night. Because of that, and despite the star striking the river, she went to the sacred waters just before sunrise to bathe and make offerings to Hapi. While there, she found a basket wedged in the rushes along the bank. She had it brought to her, and when she opened it, she saw a baby inside, a Hebrew male child. Despite his lineage, she believes, like many other childless women before her, that because he was found on the Nile, he is a gift from the gods. She believes he is the answer to her night dreams and the prayers and offerings she made this morning."

"Did you say a Hebrew male child?" Sostris said, hiding his shock.

"That's what I said. I thought she would come and tell you, and you would talk her out of keeping him. You would make her see that she was mistaken."

"I am not sure that's wise," Sostris said, surprised by the path his opinion was taking.

"Well, if this truly is a gift from the gods, then it is a cruel reward for her devotion. Pharaoh's family is subject to the law like everyone else in the Two Lands, and this child, whether from the gods or not, is still under the edict and sentenced to die."

Sostris had to sit down. This information changed everything. If she came seeking the goddess's support for this Hebrew child, it would put them in an impossible situation. They would be in direct conflict with the law's enforcement and in opposition to the most powerful priesthood in Egypt, Amun-Ra, not to mention going against its chief proponent, their First Priest in Memphis, Nephura.

Events were moving Satis's priesthood into dangerous territory. However, despite the peril, he could not dismiss the signs, ticking them off in his mind. They all aligned despite the danger looming around this child. He needed time to prepare a course of action.

"Who knows about this?"

"By now, all of the household and my guards."

"Do you think anyone will talk?"

"Only a few people have left the compound. Two maidservants went to Perunifer to buy items for the nursery. That will begin to raise questions, especially as deliveries start later today. Then there are the bearers and four of my guards, who are here, resting in the shade. They know better than to say anything. However, once it starts, the story will fly through the city and Perunifer."

"Then I should tell you about a significant omen." When the princess fainted at the beginning of the procession, I caught her. When she was carried out, I found an ostrich feather on the floor under where she had fallen."

"That is the symbol of Ma'at."

"Yes, and it cannot be ignored. If Ma'at herself placed it, then the decree does not merely stand in defiance of divine order—it is a corruption of it. The gods may be turning their hand against anyone who supports it. But what does that mean for us? If the feather is a sign, it is the most dangerous one I have ever seen. If it is not... No, there are too many signs converging, too many forces pressing toward a single point."

"How..." Semri began and then stopped.

Sostris watched the arguments play across Semri's face as the seasoned soldier slowly came to the only possible conclusion.

"Are you suggesting the gods are using the princess to confront Pharaoh's decree and its corruption of Ma'at?"

"I do not want to rush to a conclusion that could imperil us all. I am waiting on more information, including what the goddess is saying to the princess right now, but yes, everything points to that possibility," and letting out a sigh, concluded, "So far, nothing contradicts it."

"Would any of the other temples agree with this stance? Are the voices of the gods clear enough to sway the priests of Amun-Ra? What about Nephura?"

"If this is the will of the gods, then the signs will become clear to everyone—except for those who refuse to see. Nephura would not yield easily. His power was too deeply tied to the decree. He had bent the will of Pharaoh before; he would do it again if given the chance." Sostris had no illusions—if Nephura stood against them, there would be no compromise, only war. "We have no choice but to let the day develop as the gods intend. Despite all that has already happened, there may be more to come. Right now, we must be patient. We have to trust the gods to make their will known."

"No matter what the gods demand," Semri added, "I do not trust Nephura. This is becoming dangerous, and just as important, we have not considered what Amunthura, her husband, will do when he comes home."

"I agree, but first, we must look at the immediate problems. We will increase our offerings and prayers to the goddess, calling for wisdom in our decisions and protection for the princess and this child. That is where you come in. This move by the gods has been in the making for a long time. It is no accident that you and your army brothers are guardians of the princess. She could ask for no better protectors. "

"That may be true, but we need to return the princess to the estate and ensure both she and the child are safe. We are woefully unprepared."

"Semri, I know we're not alone. Not everyone agrees, and many believe that the edict goes too far and contravenes the law of Ma'at. The goddess of truth and justice touches the heart of the Two Lands. She is part of the fabric of creation itself. The killings jeopardized her long reign in the life of Egypt by breaking the divine order that sustains us all. Despite having no temple in Memphis, she undergirds every god and their priesthood."

Semri scowled. "Killing these babies offends Ma'at—the poor floods prove it."

Sostris heard a soft groan come from over his shoulder. Looking back into the room, he saw the princess beginning to stir.

Turning to Semri, he said, "She's returning to us. You need to leave me alone with her."

The head of Asati's guard looked undecided. After a short hesitation, he let out a sigh of resignation and said, "I will consider the preparations I need to make. But we must leave as soon as possible."

"I will do what I can," Sostris said as Semri turned and walked across the courtyard toward the bearers and his men.

As Sostris entered the room, he softly called out Asati's name, hoping that would help to orient her as she returned from her spiritual journey.

A sea roared as destiny surged through her. Asati heard someone calling her name from behind. Surprised that her feet were now free from the sand, she turned to see Sostris, framed in translucent brightness, beckoning to her in the distance.

The luminous image calling her name flickered like ripples in the water. The warmth that had enveloped her began to dwindle. The scent of salt and brine clung to the air, as if unwilling to be erased. Then the wind shifted, hot and dry, smothering all traces of the vision. The sea fractured—its endless expanse shrinking, curling, becoming the temple's walls. And then, only the anxious face of Sostris remained.

As her head slowly stopped spinning and the soft buzzing in her ears faded, Asati realized that she had experienced a genuine vision, a true portent. This was much more powerful than the dreams of the previous night. During the entire time, she had been an initiate in the cult of Satis; this was her first sacred vision.

"Are you all right, my princess? You have been away for some time," Sostris said as he approached.

Asati slowly sat up. While her stomach felt queasy, her mind lingered on the child she had been holding. She could still feel the weight and warmth of his presence pressing on her arms. She sat up and remained quiet while she regained her bearings. Finally, looking at the questions displayed openly on the priest's face, she said, "I had a vision."

"That is what we thought, my princess. We brought you here so you would not be disturbed. We did not wish to interrupt the will of the goddess. Can you tell us about it?"

Asati noticed that Sostris was using the official we. He only did this to emphasize his role as First Priest. It was clear he thought that her vision was a revelation from the goddess. However, a lingering doubt fed by a persistent whisper in the back of her mind suggested there might be another source. She had seen no goddess, no Nile, but the sea. If it was not Satis, then who?

The hair on her neck and arms prickled, increasing her growing apprehension.

"What is happening to me?" she said under her breath.

"Did you say something, my princess?"

She looked at Sostris and shook her head. He brought the stool to the opposite side of her and sat down. Although she had known this priest all her life, she suddenly felt that she needed to be cautious about what she revealed to him. This surprised and unnerved her. Why now, at the time of her greatest need, did she feel as if she could not trust him? Does he ever truly speak from the heart? As she thought back, he seemed measured and calculating, and always, when in public, wore a mask that hid his true intentions. She began to question everything she knew about him, trying to remember anything that might help her to understand. She was left with a quandary, if not Sostris, whom could she trust? This impulse perplexed her and added to her already heightened anxiety. She decided that until she understood the cause of this premonition, she would only give him the barest details and not reveal her concerns about the goddess as the source of her vision.

Quickly and without elaboration, Asati told Sostris only the essentials of her night dream. Then she explained how a few hours later while bathing and making an offering to the gods, she had found the Hebrew baby in a basket along the Nile. In addition, two falcons had flown from the direction of Memphis, circled three times over her head, and then flew back in the direction of the city. All the while, she studied his face for any hint of his true feelings. She closed with the high points of the vision that started when she had collapsed in the temple. She purposely left out her sense of destiny, and in both the dream and the vision, the water was the sea, not the Nile. It was not until she told him about his shining presence at the end of her vision that she saw any reaction on his face. A sudden twinkle appeared in his eyes, and the slightest hint of a smile started to form on his lips, but it quickly vanished.

Why hadn't I ever noticed his practiced control before? Had he always been this way? Maybe I hadn't seen it before because I had never been wary of him until now. Could this growing danger have sharpened my senses?

"It is good you came to us. The gods have had much to say today."

Even though the princess was staring at him, Sostris was sure her scrutiny would reveal nothing of his deliberations. To succeed in court, he masked his true abilities. He always presented the appropriate image. Underneath his controlled appearance, however, his agile mind worked adeptly through the intricacies of power and privilege. Although he frequently attended the numerous parties and social gatherings in the capital, he never played the popular game of hounds and jackals, except to lose. He lost graciously but not too quickly, which enhanced his practiced image of benign incompetence. This diverted any responsibility for occasional failures onto him and allowed the goddess to take credit for all his successes. It was what everyone came to expect from him. Pharaoh had always been perceptive, but whether Seti truly saw through his careful presentation remained unclear. Sostris preferred it that way. Some truths were best left unknown.

"What do you think this all means?" Asati asked. "Is this child a gift from the gods?" Her words almost broke apart as she said them.

"That is the question we are trying to answer."

Like most First Priests, Sostris walked a narrow line. His belief in the real power and purpose of the gods fought with the natural cynicism that plagued those forced to deal with the demands of leadership, politics, and court intrigue. Powerful forces were at work here, and while the signs and portents might be pointing to a specific course of action, their efforts would be futile unless they found a way to deal with the decree. Pharaoh's family is subject to the law like everyone else. But if the gods were intervening, even directing events, the former rationale for destroying newborn Hebrew males would lose its authority. The problem, however, was getting everyone who had a say in the matter to agree.

Looking directly at Asati, Sostris felt a shiver go down his spine as the scales tipped in her favor. Despite all of the problems it caused, it was becoming evident that the gods were leaving only one course open to them.

"So?" Asati asked, her voice quiet, uncertain.

Sostris held her gaze. He had spent his life interpreting the gods' will, but never before had he felt it rest so heavily upon his own shoulders.

What if they were wrong? What if this were no gift, but a test? His hands flexed against his knees.

"With trepidation," he said, voice steady. "We agree. With the help of the Nile god, Satis may have sent him. We believe her purpose, as well as that of the rest of the gods, is rescinding the edict. One thing is missing: how do they intend to solve this grave problem?"

Asati remained quiet, only nodding her head, while Sostris saw her eyes continue to scan his face as he spoke.

"Our first concern is the decree. Having the child under your protection is only a temporary solution. If this is indeed the will of the gods, then the edict itself stands against divine order. Therefore, we must protect the child while we find a way to rectify the situation. Even with the portents pointing toward rescission, the gods must make their will undeniable—so that even men who still resist it cannot deny it. Pharaoh alone could rescind the edict—but Nephura had ensured that the priesthood, the courts, and the city itself depended on its enforcement. Pharaoh's decree was law, but Nephura's will shaped belief. The gods could shake the earth and bend the river, but so long as Nephura controlled the argument, words alone would not be enough."

Sostris knew that all too well, which is why they needed to tread carefully.

"For now, go home, take care of the child, and keep these things to yourself. We will intercede with the goddess for guidance. Events are moving rapidly, and the falling star has pushed the future in a direction no one can control. We must trust the gods to prevail."

"Won't there be gossip about the child in the markets before the day is over?"

"Yes, but for now, it will only be a rumor. It is only one concern amongst everything else that has happened today. We need time to formulate a plan. Additional sacrifices to the goddess are already being prepared. We will seek to enlist the aid of the priests of Hapi, who had a favorable omen when a hippo gave birth to twins, a rare and propitious event. Other things are happening throughout the city, but we do not know the extent of these portents or their favorability. Our priests are still returning from gathering information."

"Does that matter?"

"It matters a great deal. We need to know how many gods are involved and what side they are on."

Sostris remembered the incident at the temple of Amun-Ra, and despite the possibility that it might turn to their advantage, an involuntary shudder rippled down his spine.

"Please, my Princess, go home and take care of the child. He may be in danger. We have already talked with Semri, and he is making plans. We will send you a message as soon as we have more information. If anything happens to you or at your estate, anything at all, send someone to us immediately."

Asati rose and moved past Sostris to the door. At the threshold, she paused, looked back at the priest, and said, "When my husband returns from the fortress of Buhan, he may be more difficult than the edict, any priest, or all of the gods."

"A complication we cannot afford to underestimate," Sostris admitted. "But for now, the immediate threat demands our attention."

Asati sighed, then turned and left the room.

Sostris went into the temple garden. Several small coteries of priests were engaged in animated conversations. Sostris signaled them to a collection of shaded seats near his private area, where he often held larger audiences. He could see the thinly veiled alarm written in their concern.

Semri saw Asati wave to him as she approached.

"I want you to send a trusted messenger to my brother, to Pharaoh. He needs to know about the child and that I had a vision in the temple confirming him as a gift from the gods. Tell him we are concerned about the edict and need to know what he wants us to do."

"Is that all, my princess?" Semri asked, wondering why she had not mentioned the ostrich feather. Maybe Sostris never told her. Well, it was too important. Seti needed to know everything.

"Yes, for now. I need to get home. I want to be there when Nari comes back with Moses."

Semri bowed, and after assisting Asati into the palanquin, he summoned Nazim. He explained the message to give to Pharaoh and sent him off. After assembling the remaining guards and posting them around the palanquin, the bearers lifted their load and began their journey home. He used the travel time to plan the protection the princess and the child would require. He had to decide who he could trust to be near them.

A Wife's Counsel

As Tuya left Ptah's courtyard, revelations churned, driving her in too many directions and confusing her. Seti needed answers before today's gathering of First Priests, yet she was unsure what she would say. Memories raced past, leaving little time to think. She needed to work through the implications of her dreams to understand how they fit into everything else that was happening. In addition, she was still embarrassed. It was unseemly for the wife of Pharaoh to faint in public, even if it was attributed to being overshadowed by the great Ptah.

When she passed out, Kamwaset, the First Priest of Ptah, caught her and carried her into his private Audience Room. While the priests thought she was having a divine vision, she was reliving her earlier dream. It felt familiar, and she knew what was coming before it happened. She thanked the great god Ptah. He had been gracious to her; this time, she remembered everything.

Though he restored her memory, it was unsettling, blending hope and dread.

When it began, she was standing with Seti and Ramses on the palace roof, enjoying the cool evening air. Off to the east, storm clouds suddenly appeared in the tranquil sky. The dark clouds tumbled on themselves, agitated with lightning. The storm began to push westward toward Memphis, and lightning struck the ground repeatedly as the tempest got close enough for them to feel the wind against their faces. The three of them instinctively moved closer together, with Ramses protected between Seti and herself. They were standing a few feet back from the eastern parapet when a massive bolt of lightning leaped out from the still-distant clouds and struck the edge of the wall in front of them, sending them flying backward in a hail of mud and brick. When she recovered enough to look at the destruction, Ramses stood alone near the damaged wall.

Before Tuya could recover from the shock, another dream asserted itself. She watched two men, one in the full flower of his manhood and a younger one just leaving his boyhood behind, training with swords. The man was Ramses. Tuya could see her son reflected in his mature features. He was tall and noble-looking, and he laughed as the two of them circled one another, practicing various thrusts, counter-thrusts, and parries. She could not tell who his sparring partner was. He was well-muscled and had a darker complexion with curly black hair. Despite being younger, he was almost the physical equal of her son as they parried back and forth, the sword blows ringing out as their weapons struck one another. They seemed to enjoy each other's company and the simulated combat. Then, tired from their exertion, they clasped arms and, with their laughter dying, faded into the distance.

In her third and final dream, she saw a baby she did not recognize, sleeping on a wool blanket surrounded by two snakes. The blanket had a pattern and colors similar to those commonly used by the Hebrews. A few feet away, Seti held a mongoose, which he tossed onto the blanket next to the child. In a quick and vicious attack, the catlike animal made quick work of the serpents. After dispatching the danger, the mongoose laid down next to the child. A smile crossed Seti's face as he turned and disappeared, and her dream was over.

Though Ptah restored her memory, Tuya struggled to decipher his message. Were the dreams warnings or assurances? The gods seemed intent on showing her that Ramses' destiny was intertwined with that of this Hebrew child.

Returning home, the bearers, flanked by her guards, stopped in front of the palace and lowered the litter for her to exit. Tuya could see that there was activity everywhere. Preparations for the gathering of the First Priests were nearing completion, and she had returned before the meeting had begun. If she hurried, there might be enough time to speak with Seti before the court's demands took his full attention. She knew she had to tell him about her dreams. Though she did not understand what the gods were trying to say, she knew in her heart he needed this information to prepare for his deliberations.

Tuya sent the bearers away and, accompanied by her escort, headed into the palace. Osri noticed her amid the hall's bustle and came over.

"My Queen, how may I assist you?" he said with a slight bow. If he was irritated at the interruption, he hid it well.

"I need to talk with Pharaoh. It is imperative," Tuya replied, doing her best to maintain a calm dignity befitting the seriousness of the day's events.

"He is preparing for the assembly with my master and your son. Shall I bring him your message?"

His gracious effort to shield her husband from interruption did not offend her. It was his duty. "Tell my husband that the intercession of Ptah was successful, and I have remembered my dreams. He may want to know what I learned."

Osri bowed and, with a gesture of his hand, invited the queen to follow as he slowly began to cross the room. He knocked at the door of the chamber and then slipped inside. Tuya waited patiently. Though she was his queen, it would be inappropriate for her to interrupt Pharaoh while he was in counsel.

While she waited for Osri to return, Tuya continued to wrestle with the unsettling images. Ptah had helped her remember but not to understand. Some things about her dreams were straightforward and clear, while others were confusing, even disturbing. This frustration, coupled with the morning's other events and portents that had escalated throughout the day, was beginning to give her a headache and a stiff neck.

Osri appeared at the doorway, bowed slightly, and motioned for her to enter the chamber. As she came into the room, her husband stepped forward to greet her. Neither Paser nor Ramses were there.

"You have remembered," Seti said, his voice conveying a mix of concern and excitement as he reached out and took her hand.

"Yes. Ptah has been merciful, but I am confused despite his help."

Seti led her to a well-appointed divan, and they sat down together. He held her hands, raised them to his lips, and kissed her fingers gently.

His tender touch calmed some of the tension in her neck. Tuya relished the moment. As much as she wanted to be with him, she could not take up much of his time. "You are Pharaoh and needed, but I thought you also should hear about what I have seen."

"Don't worry about the time. Tell me what you remember, and we will sort it out. If we can't, we will soon have the assembled First Priests of Egypt to assist us."

Tuya shared her dreams, touching every sign, awaiting his response, but Seti sat quietly, holding her hands in his. Tuya's heart, meanwhile, beat faster, waiting for her husband to say something.

Seti sat quietly, a flicker of worry briefly darkening his face before he gently squeezed her hands and responded.

"Ptah has been merciful. There is news you may not have heard that sheds important light on your dreams. My sister sent me a troubling message. It seems the gods gave her an unexpected gift—a baby boy, whom she found in the sacred waters after her morning bath."

Tuya's chest tightened, and her heart rebelled. She did not want to hear what she sensed he was about to reveal.

"And yes, he is a Hebrew child, which means things have become very complicated indeed. However, the gods have given you back the knowledge of your dreams, which will help us find our path through this difficult day."

"Do you understand what they mean, my husband?" Tuya said, sliding her fingers around so that she could now hold his hands in hers. She raised them to her lips, her heart confused but still trusting in Seti's calm strength.

He smiled reassuringly and said, "It's possible that the Hebrew in your dreams, and mine, is the same one my sister found. If he is, he will need protection, as your last dream showed. The mongoose could be Semri, whom I have every confidence in. However, the gods seem to be counseling patience. It appears that they are suggesting that Ramses and this Hebrew child share a common destiny. We must trust the gods to reveal their intentions. I trust them to make everything clear as the day wears on."

Seti stood up, took Tuya into his arms, and gave her a reassuring hug.

"You didn't sleep well last night. Go; take your rest while Ramses learns a lesson on how the gods affect the affairs of court and temple." Seti saw her hesitation and added, "You have nothing to fear. Remember, the gods let us see our son fully grown, and this Hebrew saved him. Now, I must prepare for the assembly."

Tuya looked into his reassuring eyes and then, leaning forward, kissed him softly. With his warmth still lingering on her lips, she turned and walked away, leaving her husband to be the Pharaoh he was destined to be. She did not look back as she headed to their private quarters, comforted by Seti's calm certainty yet still unable to shake the lingering shadows of unresolved dreams.

Seti called for Osri. When the scribe entered the chamber, he said, "Go get papyrus and sealing wax, and send in Nazim. I need him to take back a dispatch to Semri, the head of my sister's guard." As Osri hurried away, Seti mulled over the warning he would send to Semri, a true mongoose whose cat-like quickness made him a fearsome warrior.

The Wet Nurse Engaged

Jochebed had to act quickly to explain her milk. She decided on a recent miscarriage, kept private by the family, in case anyone in the village wondered how she could act as a wet nurse. Her heart ached at having to pretend such a loss, but protecting her child demanded sacrifices she never imagined. The edict forced her people to hide their pregnancies anyway, and no one would question it. When they arrived at her cousin's house, she sent Miriam ahead to tell the Egyptian woman that she was on her way.

Merba, fresh from childbirth, had the clean wrappings and ointment Jochebed needed for the child, and getting them from her would avert suspicion. She could watch Aaron until Miriam returned.

Nari, Asati's servant, looked up as Miriam came through the crowd that had begun gathering at the village's edge. "Have you been successful in your search?"

"Yes. I found a woman who had recently miscarried but still had milk. Since it wasn't the decree that took her child, she is not as bitter as most. She went to get fresh wrappings and ointment. I asked her to hurry."

The villagers, uncomfortable with an Egyptian presence, murmured resentfully, yet they parted for a Hebrew woman walking determinedly toward Nari.

"There may be hard feelings when this woman returns," Nari thought.

The woman stopped in front of her and bowed her head slightly, more out of need than respect. She assessed Nari sharply.

"I was told you seek a wet nurse and are willing to pay," she said, barely hiding the curtness in her voice.

Nari chose not to take offense. The woman looked strong-hearted and resolute, brushing off the grumbling as she passed through her neighbors, but she acted noncommittal in her presentation. She looked at the child, and though her eyes were cautious, they were filled with undeniable tenderness. There was straightforwardness about her that Nari could appreciate, even admire.

Yes, you will do nicely.

"Your name?" Nari asked.

"I am called Jochebed, a descendant of Levi, brother to Joseph, whom you called Zaphnath-paaneah."

It was a strong answer, full of ancestral and tribal pride.

"A worthy ancestor, but we can discuss that later. I have been sent to engage a nurse for the son of Princess Asati, sister of Pharaoh. If you want the work, you must accompany me to the Great Estate so that my mistress can decide if you are suitable."

"When will I be able to return?"

"I do not know. Will you come or not?"

The two women stared at one another for several heartbeats. Then Jochebed bowed slightly. "Give me the child," she said, extending her arms with quiet urgency. "He should eat. We can talk on the way."

Nari felt a flood of relief that this problem might be quickly settled. She carefully handed Moses to the woman, then turned to Miriam and said, "I will place an order with the granary officer at the princess's estate for two kihars of wheat. What name shall I record?"

Miriam hesitated but then said, "Amram. He is my father. He is a carpenter in the royal shipyard."

"You have done us a great service, child. We may meet again someday; until then, may your God be with you."

Leaving Miriam standing open-mouthed at the generosity and unexpected blessing, Nari turned and signaled Jochebed and the two soldiers to set out for the estate.

As they walked toward the estate, Nari glanced at the Hebrew woman. Something about her quiet strength felt momentous, as though the gods guided her steps. Indeed, divine winds were blowing across the sands of Egypt. She wondered briefly what role this child—and this woman— might yet play.

War in Heaven

When Sostris shared Princess Asati's startling revelations—the Hebrew child, her vivid dream, the temple vision, and their conclusions— commotion erupted, then slowly quieted. He was patient, but he couldn't wait too long, as he expected a summons to the palace was on its way. He trusted his priests. When the room finally quieted, he asked each of the priests who had been sent out to give his report.

In all his years, Sostris had never seen or even heard of a day like this. Every temple in Memphis reported signs. Divine power was unmistakably at work, centering on the princess. Yet they needed more time to grasp its implications.

Is it possible that one little child, a Hebrew baby boy, is at the center of such a great tempest?

When the reports were finished, a stunned silence fell over the gathering. The torrent of signs and omens was beyond comprehension; there was no precedent. This was not the misty, ambiguous approach the gods usually used. It was as if years of godly effort had been unleashed in a single day, not with a whisper but a shout.

Then Satirah, the eldest priest and Sostris's chief confidant, spoke. "Despite how unlikely it seemed before all this started, all of the portents could be interpreted favorably for the child, no matter how much opposition that may create."

The others murmured their reluctant approval. Despite where the signs led them, validating Sostris's interpretation, no one looked forward to confronting the edict. This perilous path led directly to a face-off with Nephura, the powerful First Priest of Amon Ra. One misstep could crush us.

Sostris went on. "The omen that concerns me the most is the vulture at the Temple of Amun-Ra. Nephura will do everything in his power to prevent it from affecting the edict. However, the fouling of the temple's morning ritual clearly rebuked him."

Sostris raised his hand and quieted the gathering. "We must be careful. Even if the meaning of these events appears clear to us, I expect most of the other temples will resist agreement. While we can hope, I doubt many priests will embrace a course that brings them into conflict with the Temple of Amun-Ra. If too many oppose our view, we should seek to agree with Nephura and accept whatever interpretation he proposes, as it would be dangerous for us, despite the support of omens for the princess. We must also consider the Royal House and the position Pharaoh will take," Sostris paused, waiting for his words to have their effect, and then continued.

"Even though Asati is his sister, we have no idea where Seti, may he live forever, will stand on the matter. We must weigh each sign and portent on its own merit. That way, we can determine how the arguments fit together and how heavily the scale is weighted. Satyu, bring papyri so that we can record our deliberations."

Writing this down on papyrus sheets showed the historical significance that Sostris attached to these events and his desire to keep a clear record of their deliberations. Satyu left but quickly returned and sat on the ground next to Sostris, a portable desk cradled in his lap.

Sostris looked over the assembled priests, and despite their understandable apprehension, he could see that none of them wanted to miss a single word of the proceedings. He didn't rush but calmly queried each of those who had information to contribute. At his direction, they gave their destination, the portent they had discovered, any interpretations they had heard, and their thoughts and observations. Then, the assembly debated each omen and each conclusion, sometimes with heated exchanges.

When they finally reached the events that had happened at their temple, there was no agreement about the dreams that had awakened several priests during the night. They agreed that the falcons' presence, sacred to Amun-Ra, landing on the gates of Satis' temple was a clear demonstration of Ra's anointing and support. In addition, because the sacred falcons had also flown over the princess while she was at the river, that suggested the anointing and support of the god included Princess Asati and her problematic gift.

The desecration of the vulture, which miraculously appeared at the Temple of Amun-Ra, ignited the fiercest words. Despite the contention, Sostris never let the debate escape his firm oversight. In the end, they all agreed it was not an act taken against the god but instead against his priests, especially Nephura, and their support of an unrelenting enforcement of the edict and its violation of Ma'at.

A motion disturbed the edge of Sostris's vision; he looked over and saw a young wa'eb priest hurrying across the compound. He approached the First Priest and hastily bowed.

"What is it?" Sostris said as a hush spread over the assembled priests.

"Noble One, Pharaoh summons you urgently to court. Besides the morning star, there have been omens within the Royal House. Pharaoh calls all First and Seer Priests from every temple in Memphis to council."

"Prepare the large litter immediately." Looking to the assembled priests, he said, "You have heard. As I expected, Pharaoh summons us. Satemra, you mediate the continued discussion. Satyu, give me the papyri you have written so far. Use fresh sheets to record the remaining deliberations." Looking at Osahar, the Seer Priest, he said, "We must leave as soon as possible."

They went to their quarters and hurriedly prepared to appear in the court of Pharaoh. As Sostris changed his robes and readied himself for the gathering, he knew everything about his appearance would have to be in perfect order. He could leave no room for anyone to diminish his testimony, and the preparations would help him get his anxiety under control. He had no concerns about Osahar. He was the epitome of decorum, unlike most of the Seer Priests, who were usually excitable and often unpredictable.

Their ride went quickly. As they passed through the city streets, Sostris heard enough snatches of conversation to learn that the people were buzzing with rumors and speculation about this portent or that sign, and how the star had impacted the meaning, mirroring their stance. The common talk ran against the priests of Amun-Ra. Even though the

Hebrews were not popular with the citizens of Memphis, if you believed the rumors, the priests of Amun-Ra were even less so. They were arrogant, and it was evident, especially to the common people. While the people respected their god, they held his priests in disdain. These common opinions carried no actual weight, but it was good to see similar positions were held outside of their temple. Sostris saw it as a good omen.

Sostris and Osahar used the travel time to discuss potential concerns and determine a plan of action. They would do everything possible to remain in the background as long as the circumstances allowed. If everything were successful, it would give them time to assess the opinions of others before they exposed their arguments.

As they approached the palace, Sostris saw the litter bearers of other First Priests already lounging in the courtyard. He had not expected to arrive so late. From the relaxed appearance of the bearers, his summons must have arrived later than those sent to the other priests. Most would view this as a slight if not outright disfavor. He felt the knot in his stomach grow tighter as he and Osahar made their way up the steps past the guards. As he started through the high doorway, Osri stepped out from a side passage and stopped him.

"Pharaoh wishes to speak to you alone, noble one. Please follow me," Osri said, bowing slightly.

"Lead on," Sostris said, signaling Osahar to remain behind, his stomach knotting tightly as he stepped alone into the unknown.

Deception and Intrigue

Indecision and self-interest dominated the priests' deliberations. Pharaoh's decision to put Paser, his Vizier, in charge of the meeting was a gesture of high favor—but today, it felt more like a burden. While they had expected the assembled priests to have difficulty agreeing on the meaning of Pharaoh and his wife's dreams, when they examined the meaning of the star and related it to the signs and portents sent by their gods, they also found no agreement. It was apparent that the other priests were keeping a close eye on Nephura. They were cautious, waiting for him to reveal his position before daring to oppose or support him. Paser knew, despite his power and ruthlessness, that the First Priest of Amun-Ra in Memphis was careful not to overstep his bounds when outside his temple. The god's High Priest was in Thebes, located to the south. Nephura was second to the High Priest of Amun-Ra in Thebes, yet his hunger for greater influence was apparent to all.

For Paser, it couldn't be more precise. The gods were warning the priesthood of Amun-Ra. However, as the debate proceeded, the priests eyed Nephura so that the omens discussed always ended with a meaning that was either neutral or advantageous to the priests of Amun-Ra.

"They are more jackals than true priests," Paser muttered to himself, thinking of Nephura more than the rest.

He heard a cough off to his left. It was his scribe signaling him from the north alcove. He leaned over to Pharaoh's ear and said, "Sostris has arrived, my Pharaoh."

Seti stood and struck the stone floor of the dais with the butt of his staff, silencing the room.

"Continue your deliberations in the presence of my son, and let him see how well the priests of Egypt heed their gods."

Looking at Ramses, he lowered his voice so only his son and Paser could hear him. "Watch and learn, my son. See who steps forward when Pharaoh leaves the room. Small things can expose important information."

"I will listen and observe, father," Ramses replied, his eyes flicking to Nephura.

Seti looked at Paser, gave him a reassuring smile, and then left the dais, going out through the north alcove to his private Audience Chamber. Paser looked at each of the priests in turn, reminding them of their duty to Pharaoh and that, though young, the prince was heir to the throne. This would be a valuable experience for Ramses, a rare meeting of events that would allow the vizier to give the young prince something their normal lessons never could. There was no substitute for experiencing the real thing.

After a respectful silence, Paser said, "You may continue your debate."

Pharaoh and Sostris

As his Pharaoh entered the room, Sostris bowed with exaggerated reverence. This chamber was reserved for private conferences and was situated off the north and cooler side of the main hall. Heavy tapestries depicting Pharaoh's triumphs hung along the walls, thick rugs softening the stone floor beneath their feet. These added to the room's richness, but more importantly, they muffled sound for secrecy and limited the effectiveness of prying ears.

The tapestries depict scenes from Seti's conquest of the Shasu, who had threatened the trade routes from Medigo in the north down through the Sinai Desert. A successful soldier for many years, the new Pharaoh was battle-tested and proved victorious in the first full season of his reign. The tapestries made an impressive backdrop for the Pharaoh's confidential discussions, imbuing confidence in his ability to rule.

Seti seated himself and called for wine. After the steward brought the wine and two cups, the Pharaoh sent him away, leaving him alone with the First Priest.

"How is your new temple? Have they completed the final touches?" Seti said.

"Yes, they have completed the work, O Divine One. Satis is most pleased with the efforts of the house of Pharaoh on her behalf."

"Good. I wanted to honor my father's commitment to the goddess," Seti said, and then was quiet. After a pause, his Pharaoh looked at him and said, "An interesting day, isn't it?"

Sostris knew Seti well, having spent considerable time with him over the past twenty inundations, long before his father, Ramses, had ascended to supreme power. He understood his Pharaoh was prone to severe understatement and translated his remark as, "Heaven-shaking events are happening, are they not?"

Sostris replied, "Some have said so. How may I be of service to my Pharaoh?"

"I hear my sister bathed this morning in a section of the Nile to the south of Memphis, not far from where the star struck the river. It is also said that she received a gift from the gods." After a slight pause, Seti added, "Do you have an opinion?"

Noticing how much the Pharaoh left out of his statement, Sostris weighed his words carefully and said, "We have studied the subject, Divine One. We have also inquired of the goddess about the event." He removed the papyrus from his scribe case and started to speak, but Pharaoh suddenly held up his hand and motioned him closer.

When he was near enough, Seti whispered, "The walls may have ears today." He turned his head and motioned to the edge of a shadow barely visible on the alcove floor leading into a side room. Then, in a normal voice, he said, "I need some air. I will walk in my garden for a while as the priests deliberate. Bring the wine." Seti rose from his seat and left.

Why hadn't Pharaoh confronted the spy? Seti rarely ignored such offenses unless they served a greater purpose. Was the shadow's owner more useful undiscovered?

Sostris returned the papyrus to his robe, picked up the tray holding the wine and two goblets, and followed Seti through a short corridor that led out into the palace's large walled garden. They headed toward an extensive area of shade near the palace wall. The height of the palace blocked some of the sun, which was further aided by the great linen awnings that extended from the walls. That, along with the trees and a small canal-fed stream that ran through the middle of the garden, made this one of the coolest places in all of Memphis. He was thankful as the heat of the day was beginning to assert itself.

While he was relieved and honored that Pharaoh wanted to confide in him about such important matters, Sostris was concerned about where this might lead. His absence from the assembly openly exposed him, and he did not want to give the priests of Amun-Ra an excuse to oppose him or Satis. As they passed the two guards stationed at the garden's entrance, Seti told them he did not want to be disturbed.

His Pharaoh motioned him to a seat overlooking a small fishpond. Sostris was thankful for the coolness as he sat under the broad canopy of a large Nehet tree. No one could approach within earshot without being seen, and they had complete privacy, a rare circumstance in the court of the Pharaoh.

"Pour us some wine," Seti said.

"Should I taste it for my Pharaoh?" Sostris asked.

"A wise precaution, but I think unnecessary. Do so if it pleases you."

As Sostris raised the cup to his lips, his heart skipped a beat. He thought how unfortunate it would be to die right now when so many signs pointed toward historic events lying just ahead. However, the strong red wine went down without incident, and he passed the cup to his Pharaoh with a bow. Seti nodded toward the container, and Sostris poured a second cup for himself.

Egypt desperately needed stability after the chaos caused by the Pharaoh Who is Not Named. Seti's father, Ramses, had ruled just over a year before dying unexpectedly. Seti was strong and capable, but he was older than ideal for such turbulent times.

After sitting together quietly, Seti finally said, "I want to hear about my sister's dream."

Surprised that he had not first asked about the child, Sostris told him about Asati's night dream, added the details from her vision in the Temple of Satis, and explained how he had found the ostrich feather. He did not elaborate or attempt to interpret anything; instead, he let the images speak for themselves.

Without reacting to Sostris's description, Seti said, "Did you also have omens?"

"Yes, my Pharaoh, we did."

Sostris, careful to sound neutral while trying to gauge his Pharaoh's sentiment, related the morning's events at the temple.

"One of the young wa'eb priests, while going to the sacred river to get water for the morning procedures, saw the falling star as it descended from the eastern sky. It hit the Nile a short distance away, right in front of him."

"That would have been a sight to see," Seti said. "Was he injured?"

"No, my Pharaoh. The gods protected him from harm, and he brought a jar of the sacred water blessed by the star back to the temple. It was a wonderful gift."

"The gods have favored your temple and bestowed honor upon your goddess. Go on."

"As the young man returned, he saw two falcons land on either side of the temple gates. I sent someone to watch them. After the goddess had been awakened and brought out to her audience station, they flew off to the southeast. The princess later told me that they circled three times over her morning bath before flying back towards the city, where they landed on our temple gates again and stayed for over an hour."

Seti sat silently, his mind analyzing the scenario like a commander preparing for battle. Each omen a soldier, each interpretation a weapon—Sostris's information provided him a new flank to consider. If the Hebrew child offered strength to Ramses rather than rivalry, perhaps opposing Nephura's powerful priesthood could be justified. Yet caution remained critical; one miscalculation could cost him dearly.

After what seemed like an interminable length of time, Seti said, "I also had a dream. While it seems straightforward to me, my assembled priests couldn't find an interpretation if the gods had written it out and handed them the papyrus."

Is he comparing his dream to his sister's? He is right in sensing that these dreams may be the most important considerations at this point. Dynasties rose and fell based on the dreams gods revealed to their Pharaohs. Egypt's future might hinge on him if this child proved as significant as the omens implied.

"Upsetting dreams also awakened my wife, but she couldn't remember anything. Her dreams often fly away like cranes on forgetful wings. But Ptah was merciful and helped her recall all three memories. I have not shared these with the assembled priests, and I am not sure if I will—at least at the moment."

Sostris felt a chill run through his core, settle deep in his bowels, and then begin twisting them into a knot. He reminded himself that it was a great honor for Pharaoh to entrust him with his confidence, even if it might later put him at odds with Nephura. However, being trusted by Pharaoh meant offering an opinion—and yes, that opinion might soon put him openly at odds with Nephura. It was perilous, possibly fatal, yet refusing Pharaoh was unthinkable. Despite that and the churning that continued to twist his insides, he fought to sound calm as he bowed and said, "May I humbly hear what my Pharaoh and my Queen have dreamt?"

The Perunifer Market

Sephra couldn't remember enjoying herself this much. Although Setia lacked bargaining skills, her presence was pleasant, making the morning's task more enjoyable. Still, the real delight came from finally bringing Princess Asati's nursery vision to life. That made this trip special. For a long time, because they were so close in age and shared many of the same interests, the princess had used her as a place to test her nursery ideas. They had discussed all of the options: the furniture, the colors, the fabrics, everything about the room and its contents. They talked about it so much that it was easy for Sephra to picture everything they needed. All she had to do was find the items that matched her vision, and so far, she had succeeded.

The port of Perunifer's marketplace teemed between the river and the city's walls. It could take more than a day to visit all of the shops and stalls, which contained the best that Egypt had to offer, as well as exotic goods from all over the outside world. Merchants vied for the best locations along the crowded streets to sell their goods in one of Egypt's finest markets. Memphis and its port drew an endless stream of foreign visitors, merchants, and traders to her famed white walls and easy river access. You can find ships from every country with a harbor, as well as goods brought in by caravans from the east and west. As a result, if it were to be found anywhere in Egypt, it would be sold in the sprawling market of Perunifer.

Nearby, unnoticed by the women, Ameny—a young priest from the Temple of Amun-Ra—watched intently from the shadows.

As the two women moved from merchant to merchant, the most challenging part of Sephra's task was finding a suitable, serviceable bed for the wet nurse. The princess had been adamant about its quality. Her problem was that this piece would be a new addition to the nursery, which had not been part of their discussions about furnishing the room. And, since it was for a Hebrew woman, who was more robust than most Egyptian women, it had to be a sturdy bed. That was one thing the princess had made very clear; she wanted her wet nurse to sleep well so she would produce good milk.

Her frustration had almost gotten the best of her when she decided to try the stall of a Nubian tradesman. Nubians were larger than most Egyptians, and the merchant had two unassembled beds that looked promising. When he heard the bed would be for the household of the princess, the merchant set up the finer of the two beds, even going out to his storage area to get his best woolen mattress so they might see everything together.

It was a beautiful bed. The tightly woven center support was strong but not too firm. The woolen mattress was covered with two layers of fine, dense linen. The Blackwood bed had gazelle legs and Nile carvings. Yes, this was an excellent bed, almost too so. At first, Sephra was afraid it might be better than the princess's bed, which would not do. Ultimately, she relied on the fact that Asati had told her to find the best bed she could, and this was it.

Sephra purchased the bed and arranged to have it, along with the mattress and an extra set of linen coverings, taken to the Great Estate that afternoon.

"Now all we need is a cradle."

"May I make a suggestion?" the Nubian merchant asked.

Sephra nodded, and he told her about a friend, a Syrian furniture maker, who specialized in cradles. He was sure the man would have something they could use.

As Sephra and Setia headed off in the direction he suggested, they did not notice the young priest who had stopped to talk with the merchant or the other two priests who followed discreetly behind them.

The Syrian cradle maker was not far away, and the Nubian had been right to send them to his stall. His cradles were exquisite. Finely joined Syrian oak, sweet-smelling cedar, and serviceable ash filled the stall. Sitting in the back, one cradle caught Sephra's eye. Rather than sitting on the floor and rocking on curved feet like all the others, this cradle swung from a top bar on two sets of legs that allowed the cradle to swing under it. It reminded her of the pendulum stick the estate mason used to check the plumb of the walls he was building. The ease with which it moved surprised her. It did not depend on a smooth floor but on its mountings, which allowed the cradle to rock gently back and forth. The baby would also be higher off the floor than in the others. That would make putting the child in and taking him out of the cradle easier.

"No one seems to like that one," the Syrian said.

"It is beautifully made. What is the wood? I have never seen such a deep red before."

"It is carob wood, taken from southern Syria. I made that cradle for my own child, a son, but he died along with my wife right after childbirth. It was never used. I have always hoped someone would buy it for their son. You can see that I made it to sit off the floor. That was so my wife could easily rock it from her bed. You will notice that the top of the cradle is above the height of most beds."

Sephra hesitated, thought about it, and then said, "Do you have a regular cradle made from this same carob wood?"

"Yes, I do," he said, reaching behind a stack of oak cradles. He pulled out a cradle that appeared to have been made from the same tree, so close was the color and grain of the wood.

Sephra glanced at Setia, who nodded approval. "We'll take both."

"Once she tries it," the merchant said, pointing to the first one, "she will favor it. Will you need bedding?"

"Yes, I will," Sephra replied.

"May I suggest two? It is wise to have an extra set of clean bedding available for those inevitable times," the merchant offered. "I have some very comfortable ones, double-covered in linen." Opening a large lidded basket lined with fabric, he lifted out some very nice samples. "Is this what you had in mind?"

Sephra took the corner of the mattress in her hand, feeling the fine weave and soft feather stuffing. Her probing fingers confirmed that the tightly woven double cover prevented the quills from sticking through, a problem with most feather mattresses. Her mistress would demand nothing less.

"Feel these Setia. They are well-made," she said.

"You're right. We will need two of them."

"How will you get them home?" the merchant asked.

"You have no one to deliver them?"

"No. I am alone, and my wares are small. The husband usually takes the cradle with him or comes back for it later."

"They are for the Princess Asati."

The man rubbed his hand across his cheek and chin and said, "I am honored to serve the family of Pharaoh. I will find someone to deliver them."

"We need them right away," Sephra insisted.

"It will be done as you ask."

Ameny, having heard the entire exchange from outside the entrance, watched as the two women left the cradle maker's stall. As soon as they had moved far enough away, he approached the two priests who were assisting him. After a short discussion, he had one of them wait while the other continued to follow the two women. He was unsure if they had finished shopping or would get something else. He left the remaining priest outside to watch in case someone tried to enter and went into the stall. It would be helpful to have someone gain entrance to the Great Estate to investigate the situation, and he had an idea.

Pretending to buy a cradle for his sister, Ameny explained that he had some friends who would pick it up for him and deliver it. When the merchant asked him where his sister lived, he replied that she resided in the small village east of the Great Estate of Princess Asati.

"I couldn't help but overhear that you need to make a delivery to the Great Estate. Perhaps my friends could make that delivery for you, for a small fee, while they drop off the cradle to my sister?" He tried not to appear too eager, only mildly helpful.

The Syrian considered his suggestion and said, "That might be an acceptable solution. Now, which cradle were you interested in?"

"Something solid and simple," Ameny said.

"I would suggest this one," he said, picking up an ash cradle from the stack.

As Ameny paid him, the merchant added, "I will let your friends know if I need their services when they arrive."

"As you wish," the young priest replied and left. Outside, he found his companion and instructed him to find a nearby place and wait.

"Keep watch on this stall. It may be a while, but I expect two men to come and, after a short discussion, leave with three cradles. However, they may be disappointed and leave with only one. I need you to return to the temple as soon as you know which of these events happens."

The young priest found a place to wait that offered some shade. With everything in place, Ameny turned and left, hastily heading back to the temple. There was no time to waste—Ameny felt the gods were stirring something dangerous, and he needed to reach the temple quickly.

Royal Omens

"I awoke in the middle of the night from a strange dream," Seti said. "Even now, it remains vivid, as if I am still watching it unfold."

Pharaoh's gaze pierced him as if probing for a reaction. He felt utterly exposed. There was only one thing he could do. Sostris called on his last reserves of calm and practiced detachment.

After a short pause, Seti said, "It was early morning, in the soft light just before sunrise. I saw two young men hunting birds on a papyrus skiff in the marshes of the lower Nile. One was older, wearing the small cobra-headed crown of Pharaoh. The younger, darker, and curly-haired had recently removed his sidelock, marking his entry into manhood. He navigated their craft through the marsh with a long pole topped by a curved crook reminiscent of those used by Hebrew shepherds—though I did not reveal that detail to the assembled priests."

Sostris's pulse quickened, instantly sensing the danger hidden in the detail about the staff.

"The elder's hunt had been successful, and the front of the skiff was filled with many birds, while the younger one had only a few kills. They went east to dry ground just as dawn broke. Once they landed, the younger one bowed and, out of respect, gave his kills to his royal elder. As they were preparing to leave, a leopard appeared, blocking their path. The elder, who was larger and carrying a spear, advanced against the threat with his weapon, prepared to defend their catch. But, as he was advancing, a snake, hidden in the grass off the path's edge, rose and attacked him from the rear. The younger swung his pole, catching the snake mid-strike, and swiftly twisted the shaft, tangling the serpent in the crook. Then, spinning the pole around, he flung it deep into the marsh behind them. After voicing his thanks, the elder charged the leopard, driving him away."

Seti looked directly at Sostris and asked, "What is your opinion of my dream?"

Sostris's mind raced, helplessness gripping him as his thoughts chased one blind trail after another. Seti's dream hinted at a possibility more incredible than he could have hoped for, but he could see no way to tie everything together. Just as he was about to admit to his Pharaoh that he had nothing to offer about his omen, an avenue that would suddenly and unexpectedly blend the day's events became clear to him.

"Is there anything further you can tell me about the younger man?"

After a slight pause, Seti said, "Physically, the younger one could be a Hebrew."

"*Satis be praised*," Sostris thought as Seti's plain admission began to bring everything together in his mind.

"If the elder is your son Ramses, could the younger be this Hebrew child the gods appear to have given your sister?"

"Continue," said Seti.

"The Hebrew child may be an expression of Nu, the primeval water out of which creation was birthed, like this child who was birthed out of the sacred Nile, sent by the gods to protect your son."

Before Seti could respond, Sostris continued, "It is written, 'I am the god Nu, and those who commit sin shall not destroy me.' Have not some counseled..." Sostris paused, considering whether this might be a step too far. Still, his heart swelled with certainty, urging him to continue. "Some believe the priests of Amun-Ra's attempt to destroy the Hebrews has become a sin against Ma'at itself. What if the gods have sent this child as an expression of Nu who cannot be destroyed to stand against those who would commit this sin?"

Seti did not respond or show any change in his countenance. Sostris felt fear grip his gut. When Seti finally replied, he said, "Even if that were true, how would that relate to my dream?"

Sostris fought a surge of panic, struggling to compose a convincing reply. Suddenly, with startling clarity, the solution spread out before him like a great feast. He took a deep breath and said, "If I may, my Pharaoh?"

"Go ahead."

"Let us take the dream in sequence. First, you have one young man whose royal crown could represent your son, Ramses, and another, younger one, who could represent this Hebrew child. The staff could be a Hebrew shepherd's crook. You said the Hebrew shows submission and respect to the elder and royal young man. He readily adds his triumphs to that of his lord. That would argue that Ramses has nothing to fear from this child, who will willingly submit to him. Second, the same passage from the Book of the Dead also says, 'I fetter and destroy the hidden serpents which are about my footsteps in going to the Lord of the Two Arms.' Could the gods have sent this Hebrew to save your son from an unexpected attack? Would not the 'Lord of the Two Arms,' the arms of upper and lower Egypt, be Ramses? You know that no warrior can fight successfully on two fronts. He needs someone to protect his rear. Could the gods have sent this Hebrew to do that very thing?"

"Who, then, are the leopard and the snake?"

Here, Sostris needed to tread on dangerous ground. "Could the leopard be the Hittites, coming to wage war with Egypt? You have already engaged them in your first year. As to the snake, you did not describe its markings, my Pharaoh."

Seti let the question pass. As he searched the countenance of the First Priest, he could see no hint of evasion or deception in Sostris's look or demeanor. He had called this one priest to his council because, while he had a deep-seated distrust of the manipulations of the priests of Egypt, he grudgingly shared his father's respect for this First Priest of Satis. His directness and honesty had been apparent through the years, and what he said made sense and fit with his own thinking.

After a long silence, Seti shifted slightly. "My wife also had dreams last night. Until now, no one else has heard it, but it may reinforce your interpretation."

This admission caught Sostris off guard. If Pharaoh took him even further into his confidence, it would be an exceptional honor, but more than that, he hoped it would give further support to the princess, the child, and the direction he believed the gods were taking them. It was becoming clear that they could not avoid confrontation with the priests of Amun-Ra, especially Nephura. However, if the omens were strong enough, they would overwhelm any objections and become his temple's defense of their position.

"She had three dreams, but only one relates to our current discussion."

Seti told him about the dream in which Ramses sparred with a younger man, suggesting he could be the same Hebrew from his dream.

Sostris immediately saw the link between the two dreams. The young man in both dreams must be the same, and there was little doubt he was the grown child found in the Nile by Pharaoh's sister. The conjunction of the dreams and this event was not a coincidence. This was another sign from the gods.

Trying to contain his enthusiasm, Sostris said, "Everything seems to say that the gods have brought all of this together for a future purpose. The younger person in both dreams is probably the child the gods gifted to your sister this morning. How else would a Hebrew be hunting and sparring with the son of Pharaoh unless he had been brought into the royal family?"

He searched Seti's face for the slightest reaction, but the Pharaoh's expression remained impenetrable. Sostris went on, "The reason the gods seem to have chosen a Hebrew for their purpose is a mystery, but everything points to that being their intention."

After a short pause, he simply said, "Your interpretation is noted." He appreciated the priest's candor but would speculate no further in Sostris's presence. He had already placed this priest in a difficult position. Or, more accurately, the gods had placed him there. One careless word by this priest, and Nephura would seize the opportunity to crush his entire priesthood.

Motioning to Osri, who was standing in the shade by the entrance to the garden and well out of hearing, he said, "My Vizier's scribe will take you through a side entrance to the front of the Hall of Audiences. You will enter as if you have just arrived. This discussion was private and our words are between us alone."

"Yes, my Pharaoh," Sostris said, his mind racing with the implications of this meeting. He bowed and followed the scribe out of the garden.

Seti waited a reasonable amount of time to allow Sostris to settle into the gathering before leaving. Sostris had confirmed his understanding of what the gods were doing. If the Hebrew child truly was an expression of Nu, it explained the day's omens. His son's future hung in the balance, and Nephura, who could be the viper, would crush anyone who opposed him—even a royal heir. Today's deliberations would determine Ramses' fate and make plain to everyone exactly what the gods demanded.

Putting the Plan in Motion

After Ameny had returned and told Mioa, Nephura's confidant, what he had learned and done, the priest was startled to discover how well

Ameny's cradle ruse meshed with his lord's vendetta against the Hebrew child. He had Ameny return and bring back the young priest he had left to watch the stall. After Mioa made the necessary preparations—knowing one mistake could cost him everything—he quickly left the temple. Careful to avoid anyone who might recognize him, he was dressed as an ordinary merchant. He exited the city through a seldom-used gate and entered Perunifer, going to a private bathhouse. There, he altered his appearance enough to pass as a common riverman, at least from a casual inspection. After checking his disguise and ensuring no one saw him, he left by a secluded exit.

He carefully made his way to a group of warehouses near the docks, and just inside the rear of one of the buildings, he ascended the stairs. On a small landing at the top, Mioa slid a gold stele marked with the Amun-Ra symbol into a slot in the faded red door. After hearing it fall onto the floor, he rapped three times, then turned and, without waiting, went down the stairs and exited the building. He walked a short distance from the wharf and found the covered food stall, their usual meeting place. Despite the crowds filling the port of Perunifer in response to the falling star, it was nearly deserted, which he took as a good omen. Going to the darkest part in the far corner, he sat at a table against the wall. When the boy came and asked what he wanted, using the low Egyptian commonly spoken throughout the port, he ordered a beer with an extra cup.

He wore the loincloth of a common riverman, though upon closer inspection, his smooth skin would betray his true station despite his efforts at disguise. An unruly wig with matted and disheveled hair covered his shaven head. When the boy returned with the pitcher of beer and two cups, Mioa gave him a small piece of copper and told him that he did not want to be disturbed. He took one cup and turned it upside down in front of him. He took the second cup, filled it with beer, and placed it in front of the empty seat across from him. Then he sat back and waited.

He did not have to wait long. A short, stocky man wearing a coarse linen loincloth entered the stall and casually approached the empty seat. Sitting down, he silently drained the beer and carefully placed the cup upside down in front of him.

Without looking at Mioa, the man quietly said, "May Amun-Ra achieve the success he seeks."

Mioa, staring straight ahead, answered, "As long as his servants do his will."

The man poured another beer, emptying the pitcher. Without a word, Mioa slid a small folded piece of papyrus toward him. The man covered it with the empty pitcher, nodding once.

"We are all good servants of the god," the man responded as Mioa got up and, without looking back, walked out of the stall.

The priest turned away from the wharf and immediately headed to the back entrance of the private bathhouse. There, he washed his grime-smeared skin and checked himself. After a thorough cleansing, he redressed himself as a merchant.

This had to work, or Nephura's wrath could fall on me.

Ammuti finished the remaining beer, slipped the papyrus into his loincloth, and left the stall. After a short walk, he turned toward the wharf and climbed the same dark stairs Mioa had previously used. When he reached the top landing, he took out a thin bronze knife. Placing it in a small crack high on the doorjamb, he flicked the mechanism that unlatched the door.

As he closed the door behind him, a reedy voice emerged from the shadows on the far side of the room. "That was quick."

"They must be in a hurry. He was especially careful this time. I have a feeling this one is important."

"Aren't they all?"

"This one is urgent," he added, pulling the papyrus out from his loincloth and handing it to Sutekha.

The tall, thin man rose from his seat and moved fluidly across the room. There was something serpentine in Sutekha's movements as he opened 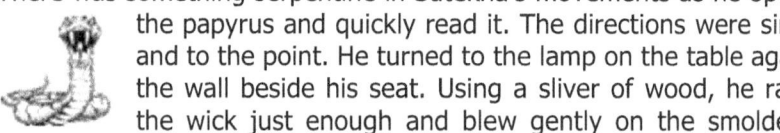 the papyrus and quickly read it. The directions were simple and to the point. He turned to the lamp on the table against the wall beside his seat. Using a sliver of wood, he raised the wick just enough and blew gently on the smoldering ember. It eventually responded, and using the small flame, he burned the piece of papyrus, dropping the flaming message into a bowl next to the lamp.

As it turned to ash, he grunted and said, "Hurry and find Omar. Get three of those special small vipers he breeds and tell him to make a special offering to Apophis for our success. I will meet you in the market at the Syrian cradle maker's shop. We are going to be deliverymen."

Ammuti smirked uneasily. "*He savors this far too much—let's hope it's worth the risk,*" he thought uneasily as he left.

Sutekha went to the far corner and removed a loose brick from the wall. Reaching into the cavity, he removed a leather pouch containing several small vials, a unique ring, and various tools. Returning to his seat, he used the wood sliver to raise the wick on the lamp a little further, creating a larger flame.

Spreading the contents of the pouch out on the small table, he took the ring and opened the cleverly hinged top using his fingernail. As he lifted the dome-shaped cover, it exposed a small needle-like prick rising above the surface of the ring. Sutekha picked up the amber vial and carefully opened it, then took a small reed and slid it down the neck. He lifted the reed from the vial, wet with the deadly liquid, forming a small drop, which he touched to the small prick on the ring. Closing the amber container, he opened the black vial and repeated the procedure with a new piece of reed. When put together, these two deadly poisons would kill a man in the span of ten heartbeats. This dangerous secret, once mixed, lasted only a few hours before dissipating. It was the perfect assassin's weapon. Its brief potency was irrelevant; it was lethally efficient, precisely what an assassin required—deadly and fleeting. He blew on the needle prick, drying the poison. Then, he carefully shut the hinged top of the ring and slid it onto the second finger of his left hand.

Taking his iron knife from its leather sheath hidden inside his loincloth, Sutekha coated the blade's edge with a small amount of the liquid from the black vile alone. By itself, it numbed the muscles, making the victim an easy prey for an attacker. It was a perfect weapon when you wanted to exalt your superiority over your foe as you took their life from them. He blew on the blade's edge, drying the poison, and then carefully put it back in its sheath, sliding it back inside his loincloth.

Replacing the two vials and the tools in the leather pouch, he burned the two reeds and the poison they contained in the lamp's flame and then extinguished it. He crossed the room, put the pouch back into its hiding place, and replaced the brick. After smudging the edges of the hiding place, Sutekha surveyed the room and, after noting that everything was in order, slipped out and closed the door behind him. When the lock clicked shut, he released the handle, descending the dark stairway, vanishing into the crowded anonymity of Perunifer, where the port's chaos concealed even the darkest deeds.

Subtle Positioning

Nephura was growing tired as the proceedings droned on. To keep the discussions running around in circles, he constantly maneuvered them away from putting the priesthood of Amun-Ra in a bad light. It was subtle but laborious work. He had to be careful that no one would single him out as the source of the morning's confusion.

As the First Priest of Hapi expounded on his twin newborn hippos and their significance to the day's events, Nephura saw Sostris, the First Priest of Satis, enter the great hall along with his Seer Priest. Finally, the priest who worried him most had appeared—surprisingly late.

His ties to Seti will mean nothing when my plan succeeds.

Despite Sostris's image of benign incompetence and the relative obscurity of his goddess, he could be a problem. He had ties to the royal household, which gave him the ear of Pharaoh, so that must be where Sostris had been. Since Pharaoh's sister had gone to the Temple of Satis, Seti must be trying to gather as much information as possible about the Hebrew baby...aargh!...even thinking about the vile child enraged him. That Pharaoh's sister had claimed him as her own was nearly unbearable. He struggled to regain composure. He forced his thoughts back to Pharaoh. Like an accomplished soldier, Seti would want to be prepared before his sister's duplicity became public knowledge and a matter of debate among the assembled priests. That revelation would turn the debate in a direction Nephura wanted to avoid at all costs. His plan, if successful, would settle the matter once and for all. It would also put the royal family and the First Priest of Satis at a disadvantage, but he needed time for his efforts to succeed.

Nephura wondered what they had discussed. He understood very little about Seti, who, for a Pharaoh, was remarkably private; there was only his military background to suggest how he might act. He always seemed to understate his opinions, and something about how he had explained the specifics of his dream raised the warning hackles on Nephura's neck.

He needed his plan to succeed before the deliberation broadened and began creating uncontrollable difficulties. There had to be a way to slow down the debate. He decided to seize the initiative. Waiting for a lull in the incessant chatter, he said, "May I suggest we put our discussion aside for a while and have something to eat?"

Paser turned in his seat to face him. He raised his hand for quiet and, after making everyone wait until the room was completely silent, said in a measured tone, "I agree. With all that has happened today, we need to be at our best. We will pause our deliberations and take a moment to refresh ourselves. A little food will help sharpen our thinking." Looking to Osri, who had just entered the room, he signaled for food and drink.

Almost immediately, servants began to appear, carrying low tables which they placed in groups around the great hall. Others spread rugs and cushions around the tables. The priests began moving to the tables and were starting to recline when they heard a staff strike the stone floor with three resounding thuds.

Paser, his staff still resonating, called out to the assembly, "Life, health, and strength be to the Pharaoh of the Two Lands, the great and noble Seti; may he live forever."

The priests scrambled to their feet as Seti entered the great hall and, without pausing, moved to his place on the royal dais. The servants, loaded down with food, paused in mid-step. Everyone waited for Pharaoh to speak.

Standing on his dais, towering above the assembly, Seti's strong soldier's voice echoed decisively throughout the hall.

"It is good that we refresh ourselves. A short rest and ample food should prepare us to hear what the gods are trying to say to us. Sit. Eat."

After a respectful pause, while Seti sat down, the assembled priests began reclining around the low tables. The servants wasted no time spreading out a small feast.

Nephura saw that Seti and Paser had planned well for this assembly. However, they were not serving any wine or even the ever-present beer with the food. Only water and juices graced the tables and were served in pitchers by the servants who passed among the priests, filling their cups. He had hoped that the befuddling sting of Pharaoh's good wine might stretch things out even more, but they were being very careful to limit anything that might distract anyone from Pharaoh's purpose.

His thoughts turned to his efforts outside the Hall of Audiences. The men he had engaged fed on the danger and uncertainty of their next breath, and he knew that excitement well. There was an exquisite rush that accompanied carrying out a perilous plot. When things got dangerous, your heart would begin to hammer in your chest, and you could hear the blood surging in your ears, rising and falling in time to the pounding in your chest. It was in those situations that Nephura felt fully alive. Everything became sharp and clear. Then, time almost stopped, and he felt invincible, as if he were among the gods and his adversaries were mere mortals, unable to withstand him.

However enjoyable it was to walk that precarious edge, it was risky to give those emotions their full expression, especially now. Despite his recent successes, he knew he could not afford to underestimate his adversaries. It was like in Hounds and Jackals, which he had not lost in a long time; one always had to think several moves ahead to be prepared for whatever twist the game might take. That foresight required knowing those who opposed you extremely well, often discerning the decisions they would make almost before they did.

As Seti looked over the Hall of Audiences, his practiced eye saw the combatants aligning themselves. Nephura was the last priest to sit down. The Chief Priest of Amun-Ra was careful to sit close enough to Sostris to hear whatever the First Priest of Satis might say, but not so close as to show an obvious interest.

Leaning over to his son, Seti asked, "What have you learned so far?"

Ramses leaned forward so that only his father could hear his words. "I have noticed several things, father. From my time at Temple School, I knew priests enjoyed hearing themselves speak, but today proves it is true. They seem to be vying to see who can hold the floor the longest before someone else tries to take over the debate and everyone's attention."

"You are right, but they have to be careful since pharaohs expect real answers, not the sleight of hand their words often perform for their followers. What else did you learn?"

Seti saw a look of concern spread across Ramses' face. "What's wrong, my young prince?" he asked, letting the emphasis on his royal standing help to ground him.

"Is it permitted, father, to question the motives of the First Priests? In our studies, those who hold such exalted positions are highly revered and inspire awe, or even fear."

"As a future Pharaoh, you must be ready to question everything about everyone. The problem does not lie in having questions, Ramses; it lies in not being faithful to the answers, no matter where they might lead you. Honest priests serve best. I am not discussing all men's ordinary failings regarding pride and the desire to matter. Good men desire those things. I am speaking about evil disguised as good, whose robes may be white but whose heart is black and blighted."

Seti paused momentarily and then asked, "So, whose motives do you question?"

Ramses leaned very close to his father's ear. "I think that Nephura, Chief Priest of the Temple of Amun-Ra, confuses the discussion. As I listen, he seems to say the right thing to steer the discussion in circles. It is the same trick we sometimes try on our teachers, but we are nothing compared to him; we usually get caught. He skillfully passed the debate to someone who rambled without substance, but then the Chief Priest responded as if the speaker had given a great insight. I do not trust him."

Seti was about to respond when Ramses continued, "Father, another thing concerns me. I have never heard so many priests sound so unsure, and these are the Chief Priests. My studies taught confidence, not this confusion. Seeing them so muddled is even more upsetting than seeing the manipulations of the First Priest of Amun-Ra."

Seti sighed and said, "An important observation, Ramses—a necessary yet difficult lesson. The failings of priests do not diminish the truth of the gods they serve. You will learn that the failure of those who serve does not always reflect on the truth of their masters, whether gods, men, or Egypt herself. You need to learn to separate the failures of those in service from what and why they serve. For now, you must trust to your own counsel; we will discuss this later. Nevertheless, Ramses, you are right not to trust Nephura or any of the priests of Amun-Ra."

Seti could see that learning this had disturbed his son. But his upset was necessary. Boys become men when they realize even those whom they admire have feet of clay. He hoped he would never cause his son the same disappointment.

New Additions to the Household

Asati paced back and forth across her garden, her impatience growing as she waited for Nari to return. After returning from the temple, she came to this peaceful setting, hoping to draw inspiration from the restful surroundings. But her excitement and concern prevented its calming effect. Turning to the maidservant waiting quietly nearby, she said, "Has anyone returned—Sephra, the messenger, Nari?"

The servant shook her head.

"Go up to the roof and see if you can see anyone coming. Come back when you see something."

With a quick bow, the servant departed, leaving her alone.

"I should have gone to see my brother myself," she said to no one in particular. "I was already in the city."

Going to a shaded bench in her garden, Asati felt the heat of the day finally asserting itself. She disliked these times of solitude. Rather than the quiet peace others found, for her, seclusion had become an empty desert sucking the last of her hopes into its barren sands. Like a life-giving oasis, a child in the household would bring that change. A baby was full of exuberant vitality and required ceaseless attention. This child, however, needed her constant protection because, for now, she was his only means of survival. Looking to the days ahead, she hoped caring for him would bring her a new and welcome purpose. She had drifted for too long, like the sand in the western desert, moving aimlessly without any real direction. Yes, she had allowed this one concern to rule her life for far too long.

"Maybe I need him as much as he needs me," Asati said aloud. Immediately, she felt a familiar resistance begin its inexorable ascent as if this realization threatened her hard-won freedom. Since childhood, she prided herself on her independence—but what had that gotten her? Having been strong-willed since birth, she heeded only Egypt, represented by her father and now her brother. However, when she was denied the expected child, she began the long struggle with priests, prayers, and potions to fulfill her husband's proper demands for a son, a prince to carry on his name and, through her lineage, to instill the blood of pharaohs in his offspring. Her deep reserves of determined will had sustained her through the difficult last five years, but she was wearing down. The gods had not even offered a miscarriage to sustain her dwindling hope; instead, they left her with nothing. The growing sense of barrenness had begun stripping her determination, eating away at her self-reliance. Now, what little she had left had to contend with the powerful instincts this child was setting loose. As she tried to honestly face the issues bearing down on her, she knew Moses didn't resolve the problems of her barrenness as she had glibly hoped when her early morning prayers seemed answered. No, this gift of the gods brought dangerous new concerns mixed with strange new yearnings she did not yet understand.

Hearing a cough in the distance, Asati looked up and saw two maidservants carrying food and drink, followed at a respectful distance by Semri. As the smell of the freshly cooked fish reached her, her stomach began churning, and she realized she had not eaten anything since the afternoon meal the day before. She had skipped dinner and retired early. Her sadness and exhaustion had quickly overcome her, drawing her into sleep. Then it all started. Until last night, sleep had always been her place of refuge and comfort, but not last night. And, as tired as she felt, she had no idea what the night would bring.

Motioning the servants forward, she allowed her attention to focus on the mundane concerns of life. "Set down the food and leave me alone," she ordered. They put a small table next to where she sat, laid out the food and drink, and then quickly departed. Semri, however, stood back, a short distance away.

She was about to call him over when he looked down at his feet. She changed her mind. He appeared only interested in watching over her. He wasn't bringing her a message. Well, if that was what he wanted, it was all right with her; his presence did give her a small measure of comfort. She turned back to the food; its aroma had awakened her appetite.

"Wake up, my princess. I have returned with a nursemaid and the child."

The words seemed to come from far away, almost on the edge of her hearing. At first, she thought she was dreaming, and Nari's words and the morning's incidents were all figments of a strange lingering dream. However, as the midday light penetrated her closed eyes, everything rushed back in, and Asati realized she had fallen asleep. Exhausted from her lack of rest the night before and the extreme intensity of the morning's events, she had drained her depleted reserves. After eating the food her maidservants had brought and feeling safe with Semri watching in the distance, she had curled up on the bench in the shade and, thankfully, drifted into her customary dreamless sleep. A glance through half-closed eyes showed two women standing in front of her, and her protector was still standing quietly at his post.

As the morning began replaying across the surface of her memory, her heart began to climb into her throat, and she sat up, jerking herself fully awake. Giving her head a moment to clear, she lifted her hand to her forehead, shading the glare from her sleepy eyes. Looking past Nari to the object of her desire, she found him nestled in the arms of a strongly built Hebrew woman who appeared to be studying her intently.

"Are you all right, my princess?" Nari asked.

"I am fine," Asati said as she stood and straightened herself, trying to present an image befitting her station before this barbarian woman. As for the Hebrew, she sought Asati's gaze and stared deeply into her eyes before looking to the ground, as was proper respect to the sister of Pharaoh.

A soft cooing sound from the child caused all eyes to shift to the child as he stirred gently, stretching his tiny arms skyward.

"It seems the child is waking. He fell asleep while being nursed on the walk here, my princess," Nari said.

"Did I not give him a name?" Asati said, looking sternly at Nari. "Is his name not Moses, he who is born of the water as a gift from the gods?"

"Yes, it is, my princess," Nari replied.

"Then bring Moses here, Nari. I want to hold my son," Asati said, almost not believing the reality of her words.

Nari bowed slightly and took the child from the Hebrew, who seemed reluctant to give him up, her fingers lingering briefly on the fabric wrapping him. He was awake, rubbing his eyes as she placed him gently in Asati's arms.

Then, as he had done when she had found him, he reached up and touched her chin. Warmth spread out from his contact, infusing her entire body, touching the deep emptiness at the center of her barrenness. All thoughts of the danger he represented fled, and despite her efforts to restrain her emotions, tears began to well up in her eyes. With all of the determination she could muster, she fought down the feelings. First things first. She had to question this Hebrew woman.

"Nursemaid, how are you called?" Asati said.

"I am called Jochebed, wife of Amram, a carpenter in Pharaoh's shipyards," the Hebrew replied without looking up.

Upon hearing the name of the nursemaid's husband, apprehension fluttered to life in Nari. Something the young Hebrew girl had said began connecting several threads of perception she had gleaned during the morning. However, she decided, for the moment, to keep these rapidly increasing insights to herself until she could make better sense of the implications.

"Explain why I should trust you—especially with the safety of my son."

"God protects this house, noble one. You have nothing to fear from me," she said, with a note of tenderness in her voice, countering the princess' abrupt tone.

Asati almost asked which god, but realized the woman meant her invisible Hebrew shepherd God. Looking past that, she saw obvious strength in the woman, which some might interpret as dangerous, though strangely, it made Asati feel secure. She used the woman's statement as if it were a contract: "Since you believe your God protects my household, then I will expect you to act accordingly."

"The child needs fear no one while in my care, noble one," Jochebed replied, bowing slightly but adding, with a determined note in her voice, "May I ask how I shall be paid?"

Asati noted the veiled reference to other dangers but refused the implications. Focusing on the issue at hand, she said, "My chief maidservant, Nari, will give your family authorization for two kihars of wheat each week that you remain in my service. You will sleep in the room with the child, take your meals with my servants, and your family may visit you here when circumstances allow. Any other needs you may have, you can present to Nari."

"It is more than generous, noble one. I will care for the child as long as he needs me and you desire my service."

Looking at Nari, Asati said, "Oversee the preparations for the nursery and see that the wet nurse is settled. Sephra should return soon, and the furniture and other necessities should begin arriving. Get together whatever else you think is necessary. I will remain here. I want to be alone with my son for a while." Though she said it, the words sounded strange on her lips.

Asati noticed a look of concern flash across her servant's face, but Nari only said, "I will see to it, my princess. " Then she turned and shepherded the wet nurse away. She was not alone. Semri maintained his post, though he was talking to the guard who had been sent to her brother.

"Nari is not sure I'm ready for you," Asati said to Moses as he lay in her arms, quietly looking into her face. She sat down in the shade. It got them out of the midday sun, but the real problem was not so easily solved. "She may be right, but here you are, Moses, whether or not I or Egypt is ready for what the gods have decided."

Amram's Lament

The carpenters laid down their tools as several servants carried around baskets of bread and dried fish. Each man got two pieces of bread and two fish for their mid-day meal. Amram filled his cup from the water container hanging from the beam and then went to the basket and took his share. The food was part of his pay, which was better than most because of his skill as a joiner. The workforce contained men from many countries, but besides Amram, there were only two other Hebrews. He went over to the corner where he always ate his meals.

He had a knack with wood. Even as a young man, he could see the shapes needed to make the joints before he scratched the surface of the wood with the bronze-tipped scribe. He could have worked for a furniture maker; his skill was that precise, but the fine work needed for the inlays and fittings used for beds, chairs, tables, and cabinets was too tedious for his restless spirit. Instead, he enjoyed working with large pieces of wood, making the structural joints that went together to fashion the keel and cross frames for the sea-going ships being built for Seti's new fleet.

Egypt had no real forests, and the acacia and sycamore trees that grew throughout the kingdom provided only relatively short pieces of straight wood, though sometimes getting up to five cubits in length. To be useful in anything but furniture, this wood required mortise-and-tenon joints splicing it together. But at the shipyard, Amram got to work with Syrian pine and Lebanese cedar. They were used for the structural timbers and planking that built Pharaoh's ships and had to be imported at great expense. Mistakes were costly, but Amram never made mistakes, making him such a valuable craftsman. His skill was further enhanced by his love for the wood. He enjoyed the feel and smell of it as his chisels and saws embraced the aromatic fibers and coaxed them into the needed shape.

Today, however, the wood gave him no consolation. His concern for his wife and daughter and the unknown fate of his infant son filled his mind. The falling star and the rumors of signs and portents filtering through the shipyards excited everyone else but held no allure for him. Even the young Nubian, who was his helper and rarely spoke, had voiced his opinions to anyone who would listen. The port and the whole shipyard were infected with excitement because of the star. Work had begun late because of the eager crowds that slowed everything and made moving anywhere through the port difficult.

"Even falling stars can't cheer you, eh?" Phinehas, another Hebrew, said as he came over and sat down. "You may be the only person in Memphis and Perunifer who is not stirred up."

"It is a private matter," Amram said, and after a short pause, added, "Tell me what you have heard."

"They are saying that Pharaoh has called a council of priests to discuss the star, a strange dream he had during the night, and the rumored signs and portents happening throughout the city." He lowered his voice and put his hand along the side of his mouth. "One of the scribes said that those crazy priests who worship the hippos saw the birth of twins this morning. Now, that would have been a sight to see."

"The crazy priests or the hippos?"

"Now, that is more like the Amram I know. Look, Beerta has come back. That Syrian hears everything," Phinehas waved him over.

As Beerta sat down next to them, Phinehas said, "I heard you went into the port on a task for the shipwright."

Swallowing a mouthful of bread, Beerta replied, "I did."

"Well, tell us, man, what did you hear? Why are you so quiet?"

"Maybe you won't like what I have to tell you."

"How will we know unless you say it?"

"Leave him be," Amram said, putting his hand on Phinehas' arm.

"It's all right, my friend," Beerta replied. "But, you may not like the latest rumor going through the port."

"Just tell us," Phinehas pleaded.

"I heard that the sister of Pharaoh found a child while bathing in the Nile this morning."

Amram almost choked on the piece of bread he was chewing.

"And?" Phinehas blurted out, not noticing.

"It was a boy. I heard that both she and the priests at the Temple of Satis believe that he is a gift from the gods. However, here is the part that you may not like. Some are saying he is a Hebrew, one of your people."

"No...and you say she kept him?" Phinehas asked. "She did not turn him over to the butchers of Sobek?" at whose mention he turned and spat on the dirt floor beside him.

"That's what I heard," Beerta said. "You know the rumors that she is barren, don't you? Anyway, her servants have been all over the market this morning buying things for the nursery, but that is not the problem. Though she is the sister of Pharaoh, she cannot protect him for long. Even the royal household is subject to the demands of the law."

Amram, his head bowed with his hands cradling the top of his head, fought to rein in his emotions. This news brought both hope and despair, each fighting for dominance. His son, by the favor of God, had found someone who wanted him, an important someone, but his ancestry was already public, and it marked him for death. His heart ached as he silently prayed to the God of his fathers, begging the one who had saved Joseph to intercede for his son. God's hand, not Pharaoh's, held him now.

They were all quiet. Then, having gained a measure of control, Amram lifted his head and asked, "What will they do?"

"That is the quandary. Some believe all these strange events are tied together and say the gods have taken a stand against the edict. It has been losing support for some time. Maybe the gods do agree that it goes against the law of Ma'at. I would guess that is what Pharaoh and his priests are debating about right now."

"More likely, they are stuffing themselves," said Phinehas, popping the last piece of fish in his mouth. "Who would have thought," he said, half mumbling as he swallowed, "that an Egyptian, a princess no less, would believe that any Hebrew was a gift from their gods," the sarcasm dripped off his words.

"Not me," said Beerta. "What do you think, Amram?"

Wanting to hide his barely controllable upset, Amram said roughly, "I think we should get back to work." With that, he stood up, placed his cup on the peg he used to keep it from getting dirty, and turned to leave.

"He's out of sorts today," Amram heard Phinehas say to the Syrian.

"Hebrews," Beerta said, mumbling. "Even when they are your friends, they are hard to understand."

Amram sighed and sat down on the unfinished beam.

He's right. Most of the time, even I don't understand my brethren.

Before picking up his hammer and chisel, he quickly prayed that the God of his fathers would protect him and turned to his work. His hands quickly found their rhythm, and the needs of the wood slowly replaced his concern for his son. He was in God's hands now.

Deliverymen

Sutekha found his accomplice waiting outside the Syrian cradle maker shop. They had to wait until two customers had left. The rush of shoppers in the alleyways between the stalls had diminished as the day's heat had risen, and many people had sought a cool refuge for their midday meal in whatever shade they could find.

Moving the large leather pouch strapped to his waist to one side, Ammuti crossed the open space and entered the shop. Glancing around and making sure no one noticed him, Sutekha walked casually along the shop entrances and entered after his companion. The shopkeeper was filling the space left by the cradles that the last customers had purchased.

"I will be with you shortly," the merchant said, restacking the cradles.

The two men were several cubits apart in the middle of the shop. The cradle maker turned around, his hand still on the stack of cradles, and looked from one to the other. "Are you together?"

The tall man answered, "Yes. We are here to pick up the cradle for the young priest. He also mentioned that you might need us to make a delivery...at the Great Estate. It is on our way."

As he took his hand from the cradles, the merchant felt a chill travel down his back at the sight of the two men. It was not their hardness that unnerved him. Many laborers in Egypt, especially the men who frequented the port, were hardworking. This was something else. Good merchants developed the skill of reading people. They learned quickly to see beyond the obvious; it was essential to their success. There was something not right, possibly dangerous, about these two.

Moving slowly across the stacks of wares, pushing aside his unease, he decided to let them take the cradles and bedding the princess's servants had purchased. He wanted them out of his shop quickly and, if possible, without incident. "That would be helpful," he replied, measuring his tone. "What payment do you want?"

"Since we are already going in that direction, one copper should do," the tall one said.

Reaching his worktable, he pointed to the two cradles, each containing a mattress and two sets of bedding. "These two are for the Great Estate." The taller one had moved closer, to his left, while the other went to his right, to the entrance, so it wasn't easy to see them both at the same time.

"Why are there two?" the tall man asked.

"The larger one is a special piece, as you can see. The princess's servant also wanted a traditional cradle in case her mistress didn't like the bigger one. They will return the one they don't want. Here, let me help you."

"That won't be necessary," the tall man said as the merchant felt a sharp, biting pain in the back of his neck.

Raising his hand too late in defense, the cradle maker could feel a burning fire spreading from the pain. Turning around, he saw the tall man dropping a small viper into a basket near the workbench, while the stocky one shut the shop's door.

Knowing he had been bitten, the merchant opened his mouth to cry out, but his throat was already constricting. The tall man stepped forward and slapped him on his backside, where his thigh met his buttocks. Confused, he barely felt the sharp prick, but he was suddenly weak in the knees. Reaching out, he grabbed a stack of cradles to steady himself. They shifted, and as he fell, he pulled them over, sending several of the cradles tumbling on top of his prostrate body.

Sutekha looked down at the merchant, whose breathing was becoming labored.

"The snake is deadly enough, especially on the neck, but its poison is too slow, and you might have been able to give us away. No one will notice my little prick on your backside. Still, everyone will think the bite is what killed you, a sad accident, or the judgment of the gods. It will make for a good debate."

Struggling, the cradle maker gasped out a last demand to the gods for justice and was still.

"Nephura's will be done," the tall one said.

Carefully closing the top on his ring, the tall man stepped around the body and the fallen cradles, reached out, and removed the top mattress from the taller cradle. Taking out his knife, he found the seam on the underside of the long edge and slit a span of stitches near the center. Holding the slit open, his companion carefully removed the two remaining vipers, one at a time, from the leather pouch and slipped them into the opening. As the snakes slithered beneath the covering, he closed the fabric, folded the mattress to prevent their escape, and put it back into the crib. He then took the second mattress and wedged it into place, using it to keep the first one folded and safely imprisoning its deadly cargo for their journey to the Great Estate.

His companion picked up the smaller cradle and stuffed it with the remaining bedding. After he opened the door, making sure no one saw them, they casually left the shop, two common deliverymen heading on their way.

The Nursery

Nari was relieved that Jochebed's rough reception had not upset her. The Hebrew nursemaid did not react to the questioning looks or callous indifference sent her way as she was introduced to those who served the Great Estate. Nari decided to wait until later to discuss her suspicions about who she was with the wet nurse. She would speak privately later, once the household had settled. Too much was happening right now. Besides, her intuition told her the woman would be good for the child's care, provided no one found out what she suspected, since that would disrupt everything.

They were near the main gate when Sephra and Setia came through, which was closely followed by the first delivery for the nursery. Semri, who had come from inspecting the house and nursery, ordered the guards to stop the deliveryman so they could examine his goods. While the man waited, the guards and Semri checked through his boxes and sacks.

As Sephra and Setia approached, Nari introduced them to Jochebed. As Semri released the bearer and his goods, Nari told Sephra to take the wet nurse and the man to the nursery. She asked Setia to wait while she guided the others upstairs.

As the two women and the bearer headed toward the house, Semri asked, "What do you think of her? Will she be a problem?"

"No," Nari replied. "She genuinely likes the child and seems protective of him. I am sure she will do fine. Tell me, Semri, why the extreme precautions?"

Before he could answer, Semri was interrupted as several additional bearers and an artisan arrived at the gate. After the guards searched them, Semri further inspected them, then told Setia to escort them to the nursery and return.

He then turned to Nari and quietly said, "I received a warning from Pharaoh that the child's life was in immediate danger. He has charged me with his protection."

"Well, I can think of no one better. I pray it is only a wise precaution. I need to go and check on the preparations in the nursery."

"Please keep a watchful eye."

"I will," Nari said as she started toward the house. She passed the first bearer, leaving as she entered the house. At the top of the stairs, she could already hear Sephra directing the setup and storage of the items. She enjoyed giving directions, and while there was a great degree of flexibility in the Great Estate's household duties, Sephra tended to take on more authority than her position warranted. While the princess tacitly fostered such actions with her strong-willed independence, including today when she put Sephra in charge of getting the items for the nursery, Nari knew that it would be dangerous for her to get in the habit of exceeding her place, especially when the household steward returned with Prince Amunthura. Despite her motherly affection for this orphan, whom she had taken in when barely an inundation old, Nari recognized that a firmer hand was needed to protect her young charge from her aggressive tendencies.

When Nari entered the room, Sephra did not notice her; she was focused on directing the assembly of the changing table and the storage shelves for the various jars that lay in baskets on the floor. Not until Nari coughed pointedly did the young maidservant turn and see her standing there. She began to speak, somewhat flustered by the unexpected appearance.

"Things arrived so quickly that I thought..."

Nari held up a hand, stopping her mid-sentence, though she was happy that Sephra knew she was overstepping her duties.

"It's fine. There's much to do, and your help is appreciated. I only came up to show the new wet nurse the location of her duties. Please continue the preparations, but remember your place when this excitement has settled down."

As Nari spoke her conditional approval, she saw Sephra relax, and the anxiousness that had gripped her seemed to drain away. Nari knew she understood her guardian's ever-present concern. Sephra was two years younger than the princess and had been with Nari as long as she could remember, moving with her onto the Great Estate when Asati married the prince. Having grown up with the princess, her familiarity sometimes made her too forward, too easy to cross the lines that governed social standing and duties in Egyptian society and households. Nari knew Sephra knew she had to be careful. The prince and his steward were not as lenient as she and the princess were about such things.

Jochebed was standing against the far wall, out of the way, watching. Pointing to the Hebrew woman, Nari told Sephra," I will leave her with you since this will be the place of her duties. She needs to know about these preparations, what everything is for, and where the items she will need will be located. She can help you organize things, and you can see that she is settled into the room. I will go and attend to the princess. If you need anything, you can find me in the garden."

Sephra bowed slightly in response to the receding figure. She was pleased that Nari had let her continue setting up the room, but the chief maidservant, usually so organized and in control of the household, seemed torn in too many directions. Some of her difficulties resulted from the absence of her male counterpart, Nakhti, the estate's steward. He had left fifteen days before, using the Nile to travel south to the fortress at Buhan. The prince, Asati's husband, had sent for him, wanting the preparations for his return home to be organized appropriately. Amunthura was about to complete his service period at the fortress, which ended after the next new moon. The prince seldom went anywhere without his comforts, so there were many things to organize and ship home.

Turning back to the nursery preparation, Sephra noticed that Setia and two new men had appeared at the doorway, carrying the disassembled pieces for the beautiful new bed. She also saw that the wet nurse had moved out of the way and was now standing calmly against the near wall, her arms folded across her chest.

Sephra pointed to the open space along the far wall and said, "The bed should go there."

The two men nodded and, moving the pieces to the end of the room, began assembling the bed.

"Will there be anything else, mistress?" asked the man who had assembled the changing table and installed the cabinet and shelves for the jars, filling several large baskets on the floor.

"Are you sure these are well-mounted?" Sephra said, pointing to the shelves on the wall above the changing table. "They will not collapse when they are filled with these jars?"

"They will not fall, mistress. The oak pins to which they are fastened are firmly embedded in the wall. I know my craft, as well as for whom we are working. You have nothing to fear."

"Then that will be all. Stop in the kitchen on the way out and get something to eat," Sephra replied. The man bowed, thanked her, and left the room. He was immediately followed by the two men assembling the bed.

"We will need to make several trips to finish the bed, mistress," one said, bowing slightly before they both moved into the hallway.

Without responding, Sephra nodded at the retreating men and turned to the wet nurse.

"You are called Jochebed?"

"Yes," she replied, not curtly, just quietly and to the point.

Sephra decided it was best to treat the woman with as much dignity as possible, despite her being a Hebrew. If she performed adequately, this woman would be in the household for a long time, and the better they got along, the easier things would be for both of them. It was common knowledge that a good wet nurse could make everything surrounding a new baby so much easier and less disruptive for the household. That would be especially important considering the uproar surrounding this child.

Getting the nursemaid's attention, Sephra said, "Come and help me go through these baskets. As I put things away, we can discuss each item and its use. Afterward, you can tell me anything you think needs to be added."

As the Hebrew came over, Sephra lifted the first basket and placed it on the changing table beside her.

Jochebed bit her tongue, realizing the young woman did not mean to belittle her. She assumed her Hebrew background and poverty meant she knew nothing about the luxuries of an Egyptian household. Now that she was part of this household, she needed to be careful. To stay with Moses over the next eight to nine months, she could not give anyone a reason to discharge her.

"I will do my best to understand your instructions," Jochebed said with as much humility as she could muster.

The Long Debate

Despite the break for food, they made no progress when they restarted their deliberations. One priest from a minor temple was droning on, disputing a minute point of little consequence.

Ramses leaned over toward his father and said, "Father, do they always take so long to agree, even on insignificant things?"

Seti was amused at his son's growing impatience and used Ramses' question to teach him an important lesson.

"Ruling well is *always* a test of your patience, Ramses. This is a hard lesson, but one you have to learn. There are times when being a good pharaoh requires forcing a debate to a conclusion; this usually occurs during emergencies when there is no time for further argument and a decision needs to be made. However, when dealing with the priests of Egypt and the actions of her gods, it is never wise to rush anything, no matter how frustrated you may become with the time it takes them to accomplish anything. Priests are men who, like all men, will have their own motives. Though a rare few will pursue the truth wherever it leads them, most will try to interpret the signs in a way that puts their god and themselves in the best possible position. Some may try to influence how the omens apply to them as well as the outcome of the entire proceedings. Knowing that Ramses, never forget that despite the manipulations of their priests, the gods are working out their purposes."

Seti paused briefly, noticing Ramses' furrowed brow. "Does this seem strange to you?"

Ramses hesitated, then nodded. "How can I distinguish between genuine signs and mere manipulations?"

Seti smiled approvingly. "That is precisely the wisdom a good Pharaoh must master. A Pharaoh must always be open to the gods' voices, no matter how strangely they may choose to speak or what demands they may make. You will learn that even a strong-willed, self-controlling priest like Nephura cannot completely resist the gods. Given time, they will find ways to express themselves. Somewhere, even within his carefully constructed arguments, you will hear their voice, if only to expose his efforts at manipulation."

Looking squarely at Ramses, he said, "If you learn nothing else from today's debate, remember this, my son: while men may make their plans and execute their designs, the gods eventually exert their will on the course of events. It is the duty of Pharaoh to discern the will of the gods and to support that outcome."

Ramses looked apologetically at his father and said, "I am sorry for being so impatient, father. It is difficult to listen to their arguments when they repeatedly cover the same ground. I hope this does not sound disrespectful, but they remind me of some of the puppies in our kennel. Once they start chasing their tails, they do not stop until they get tired."

Seti had to stifle an urge to laugh at his son's words. He could almost see the assembled groups of priests transformed into a bunch of furry balls, all spinning round and round and going nowhere as they feverishly tried to catch the tails of their arguments.

While this amusing image helped lighten the mood, which was becoming wearisome, he needed to keep Ramses focused if he was to learn this important lesson. Tedium was one of the chief enemies any ruler had to overcome, and this assembly proved to be very good training. As Seti started to speak, he saw his son's face turn serious, so he stopped and waited.

"I know it's important to pay attention, Father, even when things become dull and boring. I will try to be more patient, and maybe I will see how the gods accomplish their will despite what appears to be happening."

"That will be an important lesson for you, my son," Seti said, thanking the gods for granting Ramses humility and such valuable lessons at an early age. It was a blessing that would serve his son well in the years to come.

As he turned his attention back to the continuing debate, Seti had to contain his pleasure. The younger Ramses was when he learned these lessons; the deeper they would be ingrained into his heart. It was too easy for a royal heir growing up in the court of Pharaoh to lose his sense of balance. With everyone trying to curry his favor and spoil him, he was always in danger of losing the essential humility every student needed to learn. Seti was thankful this had not happened to Ramses, but most of all, he appreciated this chance to teach his son such essential lessons.

As he scanned the assembled priests, Seti saw that the debate had become more heat than light. It seemed the priests were coalescing into two groups. No one wanted to appear to be in opposition to Nephura and the priesthood of Amun-Ra. However, many in the assembly had begun to distance themselves from his self-serving interpretations. From his vantage point at the head of the assembly, Seti could see the delicate separation beginning to express itself in the physical arrangement of the priests. The weight of the bodies was steadily shifting away from Nephura.

Despite that observation, which even the First Priest of Amun-Ra ought to have noticed, Seti saw that Nephura was almost distracted. As the day wore on and the discussion of the signs and portents slowly caused the edict to enter the debate, this usually arrogant and forceful man had failed to mount the usual vigorous defense of his long-held position on the destruction of the Hebrews.

Where was the biting rhetoric that came so quickly to Nephura's tongue? Was something going on here?

It was true that Nephura had offered a few of his well-worn and tedious arguments. They were the same harangues Seti had heard for years, but something was missing; there was something he was not seeing. The more Nephura argued, the more it seemed he purposefully delayed the proceedings. As Seti watched the practiced gestures and listened to Nephura's confident tone, the priest failed to convey his arguments with his usual intensity. Instead, he took every chance to divert the discussion onto minor points. He constantly dragged out the interpretation. These diversions were like small animal burrows; no matter how much you dug into them, you never seemed to find the creature. What Nephura was doing guaranteed that the debate would stretch into the late afternoon.

As he watched the debate bounce back and forth, Seti realized what was happening. The priest's eyes flicked toward the entrance, almost expectant. Seti narrowed his eyes, following Nephura's distracted gaze toward the entrance. Who—or what—was the High Priest waiting for?

Assassins

When Asati first moved into the great house as a bride, this room had been set aside as a nursery, filled with hope. But after years of emptiness, it had become nothing more than storage space.

No longer. The sudden transformation was complete. The room radiated promise once again, ready to welcome her new son. Everything was different. New paint adorned the walls, and new furniture and accessories, acquired in a sudden frenzy of activity, were everywhere. So many people had come and gone, bringing one thing or another, that it had become difficult to keep track of who had done what. Only Semri, who checked everything before it came upstairs, seemed to have a grasp on what was going on.

After Jochebed and Sephra finished emptying the baskets and storing the items on the shelves and in the cabinet, Nari returned and took Jochebed back to the garden. The child was asleep in Asati's arms.

"May I give him to the nursemaid, my princess?" Nari said as they approached.

Asati looked up, reluctant to let go of her new son. Though she was tired, he did not weigh heavily on her arms. Indeed, she had begun to enjoy his warmth nestling against her chest. However, she noticed that something new had become part of his presence.

"I think he needs changing."

As Nari reached out and took the sleeping baby from her, Asati felt a strange mixture of loss and relief. The conflicting emotions puzzled her.

"You are right, my princess," Nari said, "He does need changing. It is time the nursery was put to its proper use."

After handing the baby, whose wrappings were now obviously full, to Jochebed, the wet nurse bowed and left. As they watched the woman disappear into the house, Nari looked at Asati and said, "You need to get some rest, my princess."

"I'll do that, but I'd like to sit here for a while. He still feels fresh in my arms, and I want to hold onto that for a little longer. I will be up shortly."

Nari bowed slightly and said, "I will see to his first changing in the Nursery."

Jochebed's Return

Jochebed left the garden, knowing her son's safety was not assured. She entered the house through the kitchen, walking past Semri, who was on his way out, and went up the rear stairs. She passed two men she had not seen before as she went along the hallway to the nursery. The eyes of one of them drew out all of her protective instincts when the tall man's snake-like gaze lingered on the child, leaving her chilled even after he passed. Despite her reaction, she shook off the feeling since he had left, but her unease refused to fade completely as she entered the nursery.

As she looked around, Jochebed realized that the princess and Nari had allowed Sephra to overfill the room. The young maidservant was gone, so Jochebed took a moment to look at everything. Alongside a grand hanging cradle, plush and piled with bedding, a beautiful bed, along with a fine nursing chair, was stuffed into the corner. The bed was much larger than any she had ever seen, richly appointed with finely detailed river scenes set into the footboard. Its size almost overwhelmed the room, but Jochebed would not complain. At least she would sleep well. Along the wall, on the other side of the cradle, were two tables stocked with more wrappings and powders. A smaller second cradle was shoved underneath the left table. Shelves were mounted on the wall above the tables, and cabinets were set to either side, filled with oils, perfumes, and other luxuries. Multiple chamber pots with finely painted lids were under the right table, soon to be pristine no longer. This baby needed changing immediately.

The room was on the eastern wall of the house, so the hot afternoon sun did not create a problem. Instead, the rising sun, a proper greeting for a new baby, would welcome Moses to each new day. Jochebed was glad since the early afternoon heat had risen higher than usual. Sephra had told her some of the servants were speculating that the falling star had brought a hot, evil wind to Memphis. Jochebed's only concern was that though this room was cooler, it had less light in the afternoon. The two high window slits provided just barely enough illumination for her duties, but if necessary, there were ample oil lamps mounted on the walls. She laid Moses on the first table. As she removed his soiled wrappings, Nari entered the room.

Danger Discovered

The chief maidservant surveyed the nursery, and despite the overstuffed feel of the room, she was pleased that they had accomplished so much in such a short time. The place had been emptied, cleaned from top to bottom, and repainted. An artist had come this morning and painted a mural of the sacred river on the wall opposite the bed. Princess Asati had added her unique touches: the fine bed, the nursing chair, and two of everything that the baby might need, including the tables and the items spread out on them. "Just in case," she had said. No one argued with her. When Asati made up her mind, she brooked no disagreement.

The last two deliverymen, who had brought the strange hanging cradle, had just left the house.

After the nursemaid finished oiling Moses' newly cleaned skin, she bent down to remove the lid from one of the pots under the table and deposit the soiled wrappings. She suddenly began to waver as she replaced its lid while her other hand steadied the child. She grasped the edge of the table to steady herself.

"Is everything all right?"

"It's hunger," Jochebed replied. "It's been a long day, and there hasn't been time to eat. You have to eat regularly when you are nursing."

Not wanting the nursemaid's first day to create unnecessary problems, Nari said, "Why not let me finish his changing while you go to the kitchen and get some food?"

"That's very kind. I will do that."

Stepping around the wet nurse, Nari placed her hand on Moses to steady him on the table.

As Jochebed turned to go get something to eat, she suddenly felt faint, and her balance slipped away. She reached out for anything to catch herself. Her hand found the side rail of the hanging cradle. It immediately spun away from her hand and turned upside down, sending the covers and mattress tumbling out and sliding across the floor toward the bed. With her support gone, Jochebed fell to the floor, striking first her forearm and then her forehead on the tile.

Nari watched the events unfold like one of those strange dreams where everything moved slowly, like honey oozing out of a jar. The covers and mattress had spun away from the cradle and slid hard across the floor until they had hit the rear leg of the bed and stopped. As the thud of Jochebed hitting the floor resounded in the room, Nari saw movement under the fabric of the mattress. First one, then another small viper slithered out from an opening in the fabric along a split seam. Then, one of the snakes started slithering in their direction.

The ear-splitting shriek was out of her lips before she realized it. Clutching Moses with her left hand, she used her right hand to grab the jars of oil and perfume from the shelves and began to hurl them at the approaching snake, the scream echoing into the rest of the house and out the high windows.

Semri's Response

Semri, in the backyard, was talking with one of his guards when he heard the piercing wail erupt from upstairs. Running at full speed, he burst into the kitchen, past the startled servants, and charged up the back stairway three steps at a time. He bounced off the hallway wall and ran to the source of the bedlam, the new nursery.

Without breaking stride, he drew his sword and entered the doorway in a fighting crouch, ready to meet any foe. His trained eye quickly scanned the room. To his right, he saw Nari holding the child and screaming. She was apparently about to toss a jar at the nursemaid, who was groggily trying to get to her feet.

Nari looked at him, and her scream turned in mid-breath to "snake!" as the jar left her hand and crashed onto the floor next to the bed.

Glancing past the nursemaid to where the jar had struck, he saw two vipers next to the bedding from the upended crib, one already moving toward the two women. He had a mere breath to react. Taking a quick stride, bending his body low, he brought his sword down in a tight arc, striking the first snake right behind the head, severing it in two, sending a ringing shock up his arm as the blade reverberated off the stone floor. Immediately, the second viper struck at his exposed face. Only a miracle and his sharply honed reflexes saved him as he spun up and away, the fangs missing his cheek by a hairsbreadth. He came out of his spin, swinging his sword in an upward motion, which caught the viper in mid-air before it could finish pulling back from its strike, cutting it in two. Without stopping, he twisted his sword stroke back into a downward arc and struck the writhing front half of the viper squarely on the head, cleaving its skull.

As Semri regained his balance, he stepped back, took a deep breath, and scanned the room. An overwhelming smell of sticky sweetness assaulted him from the broken jars scattered around the now-dead vipers. The nursemaid was still struggling to steady herself. Nari had both arms wrapped protectively around the baby, held tightly to her chest. Looking at the chief maidservant, he asked, "Where did they come from?" Nari stared at him blankly, then, regaining her composure, related the events to him in a surprisingly calm and direct manner.

"Were the men who delivered the cribs the last ones in the room?"

"Yes. They were leaving through the kitchen door as I came in from the garden." Nari replied.

Jochebed, who had stood up, rubbed the large bump on her forehead and added, "I passed them in the hallway. One was short and stocky, had light skin, and wore a coarse linen loincloth. The other was as tall as you but thin, with a craggy face and dark skin. He wore a leather loincloth and had eyes like a snake."

"You are very observant," Semri said to the wet nurse. Turning to Nari, he said, "For now, take the child to Princess Asati's room and put the bar on the door. You should be safe there. I will send someone to guard you."

As he sheathed his sword and turned to leave, Nari reached out to him, her hand touching his arm. "Bless you, Semri. May God protect you and give you a strong arm, and swift feet. Come safely back to us."

Exiting the room, he ran down the hall and up the steps to the roof. The brilliance of the early afternoon sun briefly overcame his vision, but as he shaded his eyes with his hand, they quickly adjusted to the brightness. The day's heat was in full swing, and he did not expect anyone from the estate to be beyond the outer walls in the direction of the city. As he surveyed the landscape, he saw movement along the cart path to the river road. Two men were walking quickly, not obviously fleeing, but wasting no time. Making a quick mental calculation, he knew he would have difficulty catching them despite being an excellent runner, but he had no choice; he had to pursue the fleeing assassins.

Leaning over the edge of the wall that circled the roof, he called down to Nazim, who was standing near the main gate. "I must pursue the last two men who left the compound. Sound the alarm and send Worset to guard the child in the princess's bedroom."

Hurrying down the two sets of stairs, he was thankful for the trusted and skilled friends he had on his guard. As he came around the house into the front courtyard, he passed Worset, who, armed and heading into the house, only grunted as he went by. Nazim was standing at the front gate, a spear in his hand, which he held out for Semri as he ran past.

"Get two men with bindings and follow me as quickly as you can," Semri said, grabbing the spear and running out of the gate.

Seeking a Safe Space

Asati was sitting in the garden, lost in thought, when she was aroused by the commotion, screaming, and shouting from inside the house. At first, she was confused, and then she saw Semri running out of the compound's main gate. A strange premonition washed over her, and she knew that Moses was in danger. Her new maternal instincts flooded her senses with an overwhelming desire to protect her son. Jumping up, she ran toward the house.

Knowing she had to get to Moses, she rushed through the kitchen doorway, passed through the commotion, and ran up the rear stairs with a quick wave of dismissal to the flood of questions. As she reached the hallway, she turned and ran to the nursery's doorway. With her heart racing, she turned into the room and saw Jochebed and Nari holding each other, Moses protectively cradled between them. The Hebrew was saying repeatedly, "Thank you, Lord. Thank you, Lord."

On the floor, near the upturned cradle, were the *severed* remains of two snakes. Asati's mind reeled at the sight. Death had tried to touch him. Her body began to shake as she rushed over to Moses. Reaching the two women, she put her arms around them and looked down at her new son, calmly resting between them. He was the only one in the room not in turmoil, and as he had done twice before, he reached up and touched her face. As before, his contact had an almost magical effect on her, and her raging heart began to quiet down.

"Mistress," Nari said, "he is all right, but someone tried to kill him."

"God protected him," Jochebed said.

"And the strong and quick arm of Semri," Nari added.

"Give him to me," Asati said.

As she took Moses, out of the corner of her eye, she saw one of the guards, Worset, appear in the doorway, followed by several anxious servants crowding behind him in the hall.

Remembering what Semri had told them to do, Nari said, "We should go into your bedroom and bar the door."

Before the princess could respond, Worset said, "Mistress, Semri ordered me to stand guard at your bedroom door to protect the child. No one you do not trust should enter until Semri returns."

"It is a wise precaution, my princess," Nari said. "We should go to your room while the nursery is searched and cleaned along with the house and grounds. We do not need any more surprises."

"I agree," Asati said. After telling the servants to clean up the mess in the nursery, she followed Nari and Jochebed down the hall, with the guard taking up the rear. Once in her room, with the door closed, the bar set, and the guard stationed protectively inside, she put the child on her bed. The princess turned to Nari and Jochebed and said, "Tell me everything."

Semri's Pursuit

Semri had run out the gate and, within a few steps, had swerved to his left, going down the pathway into the first field rather than following the estate's elevated road to the north. He knew cutting across the lowland fields would be much faster than following the raised roadways. But he took a chance, and it might work as long as he could keep his footing on the uneven and broken ground without twisting an ankle. This gamble might be the only way he could catch the two men. It reminded him of the races the general who had raised him had regularly held. The commander believed that good warriors needed not only to be swift-footed but to catch a fleeing enemy; they had to be able to run over rugged terrain, even while carrying their weapons. Semri had always won the contests and was known as one of the swiftest warriors in Egypt. During those competitions, he had quickly learned the importance of well-made and well-fitted sandals, so he always ensured that his feet and those of his men were well-shod.

Despite being the captain of Asati's household guard, Semri was well-regarded among the warriors of Egypt. He was an exceptionally skilled fighter. He agreed to watch over the princess's safety at the behest of his Pharaoh. Although his primary duty was to protect Pharaoh's sister, he diligently maintained his training, regularly holding competitions with his men to keep their skills sharp. He always reminded them that the gods favor the swift and prepared. It felt good to stretch out his abilities with a real purpose guiding his efforts. Deftly picking the best path through the uneven earth, he stretched out his long stride until he settled into a fast but sustainable rhythm. As the great house receded behind him, he began to gain on the two figures in front of him. It took them a while to become aware of his pursuit. At first, they were startled, but then the men picked up their own pace, eventually breaking into a run as they tried to counter Semri's gains. While his initial assumption of guilt had been based on opportunity, they had the only real chance to hide the snakes in the bedding; the effort to evade him sealed their fate. However, while attempting to escape, they remained on the elevated paths, which forced them to zigzag North and West, making their path to the road running to the Nile's bank much longer than his more direct route.

One of the first things Semri did when he took over responsibility for protecting the Great Estate, despite grumblings from the field hands, was to change the elevated paths to their current staggered arrangement. It was a purposeful defensive measure. He had broken up the long straight run to the Nile into a series of three staggers. That way, no group of men or chariots could charge down the cart path at full speed into the estate. They would have to slow almost to a stop at five sharp-angled turns, making them vulnerable to attack. It was basic warcraft.

As the two men reached the river road that ran along the Nile's bank, they turned north. Semri was less than 15 strides behind them as he angled across the last field. He looked back and noticed two of his guards, along with Nazim, were already halfway across the stretch of fields, taking his same shortcut.

Semri was close enough to his quarry to hear their feet striking the hardened ground. The shorter of the two looked like he could not sustain the demanding pace and was beginning to fall behind. Without breaking stride, Semri leaped onto the road and path junction and began his pursuit along the river road. The shorter man had begun rubbing his left side, and his breathing started to labor.

It was only a matter of time. Semri knew he would catch the trailing runner. However, catching his companion might mean the tall, lean one would get away. Strategic questions raced through his mind. Was one more important than the other? Should he bypass this one and go after the other? Semri had no way to know. There was one thing he could do: he could commit everything possible about the two men to memory, including their appearance, clothing, and gait, anything that might later assist in their identification.

Then, unexpectedly, the lagging runner made his deliberations moot. He stopped and turned to face Semri, ready for a fight, a bronze knife in his right hand. That was a serious mistake, making Semri's decision for him. He rolled his arm, bringing the spear up, turning the point forward above his right shoulder as he bore down on the waiting figure. Gauging the target with a long-practiced eye, he hurled the weapon without breaking stride. The spear made a slight ringing sound as it spun off his fingertips and began its vibrating arc toward the crouched shape.

Semri had run only two strides when the spear struck the left shoulder of his target despite the man's attempt to dodge the oncoming missile. The impact spun him around, and he staggered off the road, falling off the raised path toward the Nile as Semri sped past him. He could hear that Nazim was not far behind and would deal with him. He wasn't going anywhere. The tall man lost a few steps of his lead when he turned around to see what had become of his companion. Semri was now less than 10 strides behind him, but they were now on the river road and quickly approaching the more populated areas opposite the city's southern edge. Even if he managed to escape among the buildings and boats that lined this side of the river, it might not matter. A tall, lean man in a leather loincloth, breathing heavily and sweating profusely, would not blend in easily. While the afternoon heat and the long fast run had also taken their toll on Semri, he could see his quarry was beginning to labor.

Then Semri had the second surprise of his pursuit. Just as his target reached the outer edge of the first buildings, he veered to the left, down the embankment, and dove into the Nile. He did not appear to be an accomplished swimmer, but he looked good enough to make it across the river and possibly disappear into the crowded port of Perunifer. If that happened, he might never find him.

Running along the road, Semri searched between the buildings and piers lining the river's edge for a boat, which he found on his third attempt. It was a common papyrus craft from which two men were unloading the last pieces of cargo they had ferried across from Perunifer. Semri emerged from between the buildings and ran onto the small dock, shouting at the startled rivermen. "I am Semri, the chief guard of Princess Asati, sister to Pharaoh. I am pursuing an assassin, and I need your boat."

Looking across the river, he saw that his quarry was already a third of the way across. Carefully but quickly slipping into the prow of the skiff, he faced the two men, who stared at him with their mouths agape. "Do you see that man swimming across the river?" Semri asked, pointing in the direction of the swimmer.

One of the men turned and looked across the river.

"I see him."

"I need to catch him before he gets to the port and escapes," Semri said, his hand on the hilt of his sword. The two men looked at each other. They hesitated despite his obvious commanding presence, so he added, "There will be a reward if I catch him."

"Then sit down before you fall out," the one closest to him said as one of the rivermen untied the craft from the dock. Both grabbed the oars that had been stowed while they unloaded their cargo.

Semri carefully turned around and knelt, facing forward in the prow, each hand grasping the roll of reeds on either side wall. He felt the skiff lurch as one side of the oars backwatered and started to turn the craft around. When their prow and Semri faced the center of the river, the two rivermen began their strong, practiced strokes, which began biting deeply into the water.

With each heaving stroke, the skiff steadily gathered speed until there was no doubt they would catch the swimmer before he reached the southern edge of the harbor. They aimed for an intersecting point just before a ship tied off at the first wharf.

The swimmer looked back and saw that their pursuing skiff would cut him off from the port's congestion, so he changed course and headed for a shaduf station directly across the river.

"He is turning toward a shaduf station south of the port. Change course a quarter turn to the south and follow him," Semri yelled back to the rowers. It took them a few strokes to comprehend his orders and change course. They were used to ferrying a heavily loaded skiff with energy-saving strokes. They had stepped well outside their typical rowing pattern to meet the demands of this swift pursuit.

By the time they had adjusted to the new course, it was obvious the swimmer would beat them to the shaduf station. Surprisingly, it was deserted. No one was lifting water from the Nile despite the heat. The authorities must be keeping everyone away from the area because of the falling star that had struck the river a short distance upstream. That would make it harder for his quarry to escape, as he would not have the normal flow of people to hide his flight and hinder Semri's pursuit.

The boat had gained on the swimmer, but they were still a good distance away from the shore when he reached the bank, scrambled from the water, and began climbing up the path beside the shaduf station. To Semri's good fortune, the man's footing gave way, and he slipped and fell. He assaulted the path again, only to fall back again. Partially dried mud and debris covered the normally hard-packed dirt, and it continually broke loose and slid down the incline, preventing him from making any headway up the embankment. Unable to gain a foothold, he turned and faced Semri, settling into an easy crouch.

The skiff ran aground in the sand about a body's length from the feet of the crouching figure on the elevated bank. Not taking his eyes off his quarry, Semri instructed the boatmen to keep the boat steady. The man grasped a simple but deadly iron knife that he turned low, away from his thigh, which he held with a loose, confident grip. He was no ordinary killer, but a well-trained and deadly assassin. Looking at his knife, Semri also suspected the possibility of poison.

He freed his sword, holding it in his right hand, angled low across his body. Then he rose slowly and deliberately, sliding his left foot forward while keeping his right knee anchored in the bottom of the boat. His left hand gripped the roll of reeds on the left side of the boat. He took no chances of upsetting the craft or falling out.

For several intense heartbeats, they stared at each other. The wet nurse had been right; he did have eyes like a snake. Beyond that, the man's gaze had a mesmerizing quality that seemed to pierce right through him. As Semri stared at him, he could feel the man's eyes reaching out and massaging something deep inside him, easing the tension and tempting him to relax. He had heard rumors about people who could control you with their eyes. Slowly, the relaxation began to give way to a feeling of tiredness, as if sleep was the most critical thing in the world.

Semri spat at the man as he forced his focus away from the man's eyes and onto the middle of his body. While the tiredness lessened, it still hung over him like an oppressive cloud, momentarily shaking his confidence. He took a deep breath and spoke to his adversary, "You think I can be controlled that easily?"

The assassin laughed derisively and remained facing him in a fighting crouch. There could be only one outcome to their confrontation. Still, if possible, he had to try to capture the man. It was obvious that he was the leader of the two and would know who had ordered the attempt on the baby's life.

"You have nowhere to go," Semri said, buying time as the unnatural tiredness began to dissipate. "Surrender and tell us who sent you, and Pharaoh may spare your life."

The man did not respond, but the slight twitch in his left cheek revealed the roiling turmoil underneath. He was trapped, and a trapped man was at his most dangerous. Even ensnared by the bank, the assassin had a slight advantage since he possessed the higher ground. Sometimes, when men believed the situation favored them, they were not as cautious as they should have been, and their confidence led to mistakes.

Semri braced himself as he noticed the slight tightening of the man's leg muscles, signaling the beginning of his attack. Then, unexpectedly, an arrow whizzed past his ear and, with a resounding thud, struck the leg of the shaduf station, passing less than one hand's span from the shoulder of the assassin. "*Nazim*," thought Semri as his startled opponent momentarily lost focus, disrupting his leap from the bank. Despite that, the man smoothly switched his knife to his left hand as he lunged and started it down in a tight arc. Semri's sword and honed reflexes responded with practiced quickness; slicing from his left, his sword flashed up and across his body to the right, striking the advancing wrist as the knifepoint approached his chest. As the powerful sword stroke advanced through the bone, it deflected the knife's edge by a mere hairsbreadth from his chest. As he finished the slice, he severed the wrist and sent the knife tumbling into the water; Semri's advancing left shoulder swung hard into the shrieking assailant's upper body, deflecting him into the river's edge along the right side of the boat. The assassin hit the water, blood gushing from his wounded stump. He immediately struggled to his feet in shallow water and began staggering toward the port through the rushes along the bank. From the corner of his eye, Semri noticed movement emerging from the tangle of foliage into the now bloody water behind the fleeing man. Before he could cry out a warning, the crocodile struck. The water thrashed violently until the beast and the man spun out into the deeper water and were swept away.

Semri scanned the water, but as quickly as the attack began, the surface calmed, leaving nothing except a streak of blood-stained water, which quickly disappeared as the steady flow of the river bore the evidence downstream. When he was sure the assassin would not resurface, he let out a curse. The Nile had claimed what might have been his only chance to learn who was behind the attack. His fists clenched briefly before he turned back to face the stunned rivermen.

With frustration evident in his voice, Semri said, "Take me back across the river, but farther upstream. I will show you where."

He sat down in the boat's prow while the two men, murmuring words of awe and respect, oared the craft free of the sand and backwatered the prow into the river. He directed them back across the river towards the place where Nazim was waving to him, his bow still in his hand. The two guards who had accompanied him were busy tying up the wounded man who lay sprawled out on the sloping bank. He was still moving, and with any luck, he would live long enough for Semri to question him.

As the rivermen's oars settled into their practiced rhythm, propelling them across the river, Semri remembered Nari's prayer on his behalf. He wondered to which god she had prayed. He would need to make a thank offering after he had dealt with the second assassin.

Aftermath

Nazim's guards carried the wounded man up the embankment and onto the path that ran to the estate.

"That was quite a shot, considering the distance, and even though your arrow missed, it threw off his concentration," Semri said. "He was no mere thug, and I suspect his blade was poisoned, so you probably saved my life."

"Who said I missed? You were in the way, so I only tried to distract him. Besides, you handled him well enough. I wanted to capture him. This one may not survive. He has lost a lot of blood and may not regain consciousness."

"Maybe we should stop, try to awaken him, and question him right here."

"I agree."

Nazim had the guards slow down and ease off the path into the field. Finding a relatively smooth spot, they laid the man on the ground. One of the guards took a water hide from his belt and handed it to Semri. After pulling the stopper, he splashed water on the man's face, ensuring some went up his nose. The man sputtered, his bound hands flailing at his face, and let out a deep groan.

"Who hired you to kill the child?" Semri demanded, placing his foot on the wounded shoulder. Adding to the pressure, he asked the question again.

The man cried out and, through clenched teeth, said raggedly, "I didn't do anything. I made a delivery."

Applying more pressure, Semri said, "Who ordered you to include two vipers as part of your delivery?"

"I don't know what you are talking about."

"Then why did you run and then try to attack me?"

"I was defending myself."

"That's a lie. Tell me the truth."

"I swear, I know nothing!" the assassin gasped, eyes darting wildly.

Semri leaned closer, pressing down harder. "Someone gave you those snakes. Someone told you where to put them. Speak now, and Pharaoh might grant you mercy."

The man's eyes flashed with sudden defiance. "Pharaoh's mercy means nothing compared to what awaits those who betray..."

"Betray who!"

He coughed. "My throat is dry. I need some water."

"Here." Semri leaned over and squirted a stream of water into the man's open mouth.

"Who are you afraid to betray?"

As the man swallowed the water, he maneuvered his bound hands to reach into a fold of his linen loincloth. Finding a small ball of paste, he shoved it into his mouth. Before they could stop him, he had swallowed most of it.

The assassin looked at his accusers, and a wry smile crossed his face. He seemed like a man who had won a bet. It did not take long for the poison to work. His body convulsed twice, and as white liquid leaked from his lips, he stopped breathing.

"I should have stripped him," Nazim groaned, kicking the bank beside him, sending the dirt flying.

"You couldn't have known," Semri said, touching his friend's shoulder. "These were accomplished, well-prepared assassins, not common murderers. We will have to see if we can find someone who recognizes him and work backward from there. I am going back to the estate. I want you to report to Pharaoh that his warning was timely and correct and that the child is safe due to the intervention of the gods."

"Good. I can run off some of my frustration. I will be back as soon as I can."

"Keep your eyes open. Whoever hired them may be watching," Semri said as Nazim handed him his bow and arrows. Taking Semri's spear, he turned and headed down the cart path toward the Nile and the ferry.

Keen Observers

Sitting on the farm-side dock, taking their rest, Wasur and his fellow rowers had watched with interest as the events unfolded upriver. The Nile's bend as it flowed past Memphis, along with the extension of the ferry dock into the river, provided them with a view of the first man's spearing and fall down the embankment, as well as the pursuit of his companion across the river. It had been some time since they had seen a crocodile get such a large meal. Anyone who desired to see such things could always go to the Temple of Sobek and observe the morning offerings of the Hebrew infants. On most days, several were tossed into the crocodile pens. When the offerings began, large crowds came to witness the sacrifice, but now it was usually only the priests and a few soldiers who attended the bloody spectacle.

As Wasur had watched the wounded man being carried up the riverbank, he remembered the two men who had used the ferry right after midday. They were carrying cradles and kept quietly to themselves. As he reflected on their passage, it looked as if they were trying to avoid attracting attention. They had gone south along the river, and at the time, he had thought they were one of the many deliverymen bringing newly purchased items to the Great Estate. A steady stream of goods had been riding the ferry across the river all morning and into the early afternoon. He was sure the two men carrying the cradles were the same men who had been pursued to the river. Wasur wondered what they could have done to cause such a violent ending to their task.

It was not long before a guard from the Great Estate appeared among those waiting for the ferry. The man carried a spear and paced back and forth as if he were anxious to get moving. Still, he kept to himself as much as possible, ignoring any questions from those on the dock about the events upriver.

Looking back across the water, Wasur saw that the ferry had started back. Getting up, he stretched his arms and legs, preparing to take his next turn as rower. He walked up the dock, past those waiting for the ferry, and stopped within earshot of the pacing guard. Stretching his back and trying to appear casual, he commented, "That was quite a commotion upriver."

The guard stopped pacing and looked at him but did not respond.

"It is not often you see a man speared and another eaten by a crocodile, all within a few minutes."

Almost under his breath, the guard muttered, "They deserved it."

He probably thought Wasur did not hear him, but the boatman's hearing was excellent. He waited a few minutes and added, "They must have angered the gods to deserve such a fate."

The guard did not respond. As Wasur looked toward the river, he saw the ferry pulling into the dock, so he casually walked back down the ramp and joined his fellow rowers. There were only a few people on the ferry, so it emptied quickly along with the tired team of rowers. Wasur and his companions took their places as the Ferry Master collected the fee from those crossing over to Perunifer.

On the way back across, the guard stayed to the rear, so no one was at his back. Since Wasur had taken the rear rowing position, he and the guard frequently crossed glances as he worked his oar. The ferry reached the other side, and as the guard walked past Wasur, he spit out the words as he said, "Anyone who attempts to murder the innocent deserves whatever fate the gods decree."

Wasur did not react. As they waited for the returning passengers to make payment and board the ferry, he saw Ameny coming out of an avenue of stalls across from the dock. Seeing an opportunity for another payday, he got up and passed the Ferry Master, saying, "I will be right back." Before the man could respond, Wasur had moved quickly up the dock and begun walking to a spot a few feet away from the priest.

Ameny saw the oarsman approaching, so he approached Wasur and asked, "Do you have something for me?"

Wasur held out his hand.

"Let's hear your information first."

"Did you see the commotion upriver?"

"No. What happened?"

"I have to get back to the ferry, but two men were pursued from the Great Estate. One was speared and captured. I am not sure if he is alive or dead. The other tried to escape by swimming across the river to the port. After a fight with a guard from the estate, he was caught by a crocodile and disappeared into the river. A short while later, another guard from the estate told me, 'Anyone who attempts to murder the innocent deserves whatever fate the gods decree.' After exiting the ferry, the guard headed for the city gate. I assume he is going to the palace to make a report."

Ameny's mind began to swim. The day was becoming even more dangerous than he had anticipated. Quickly reaching into his robe, he pulled out the first thing he found—a strip of silver—and handed it to the boatman, who hurried back to the ferry.

He knew how significant this information would be to Mioa, who needed the news immediately. However, having this knowledge, along with what else he knew, all of which could be tied to an attempt on someone's life, probably the Hebrew child, placed him in grave danger. He had just heard that the Syrian cradle maker had died from a snakebite. It was the talk of the market. Many believed that the gods had judged him. Ameny immediately connected the two events. It appeared to him that the same judgment of the gods had been tried at the Great Estate and failed, and the guard did say that a "murder" was attempted. Was this the work of Mioa and Nephura? Who else could it be?

He had to find a way to protect himself. As the young priest hurried through the early afternoon crowd toward the city gate, his heart pounded wildly against his chest.

Calming the Household

With Nazim off to Pharaoh, Semri left the two remaining guards to attend to the body and returned to the estate's compound. As he came through the gate, he immediately gave orders to the other four guards.

"After they bring back the body, shut and bar the gate. No one, except Nazim, enters or leaves without my permission. Have everyone except those in the princess's bedroom come out into the yard. Then, begin another search of the house and the entire compound. Make it thorough. Look for anything unusual. But, be very careful in case there are more surprises."

Suddenly, his contingent of eight men, once thought extravagant, now looked woefully small. Turning, he ran into the house, through the kitchen servants, and up the back stairs. Looking down both ends of the hallway, he observed everything was quiet. Moving carefully, his hand on his sword, he checked out the nursery. It was clean, and everything appeared in order; even the mattress and coverings were back in the cradle. The only remnant of the previous crisis was the strong, sweet smell of spices that hung in the air.

After checking the other rooms at this end of the hall, he went to the door of the princess's bedroom and gently knocked, saying, "Worset. It is Semri. Open the door."

He heard the bar being removed from the inside of the door, and it opened barely enough for him to see Worset, his sword drawn. After Worset was assured that it was Semri, he reached down and removed the wedge, blocking the door from opening.

Noticing his friend's foresight in setting the doorstop, he said, "Good idea," pointing to the wedge in his hand.

"You taught us well. We have searched the entire room, and there is nothing dangerous here."

As Semri surveyed the princess' bedroom, he saw the wet nurse asleep on the couch, her back to the far wall. Nari and Asati sat on the bed, the baby sleeping on a blanket between them. They looked at him, their eyes filled with questions.

"Princess, I have ordered everyone out of the house until it can be adequately searched for anything else that might be harmful. I have also sent Nazim to Pharaoh, advising him of the failed attempt on the child's life."

"Did you catch the assassins?" Asati asked her hand protectively on the child.

"Yes. I speared the shorter one when he tried to attack me. He survived the wound but took his own life with a poison hidden in his loincloth. Unfortunately, we were unable to complete our questioning of him. The other tried to escape by swimming across the river. I pursued him in a boat, and we had a short encounter before Sobek ended the matter."

"So, you could not find out who sent them?"

"No. But we do have one body, which we hope someone will recognize. However, until we can investigate, it would not be wise to speculate publicly on anything. Most importantly, everyone is safe, especially Your Highness and the child. The gods have been merciful."

Looking at Nari, he said, "Thank you for your prayer. When things calm down, you must tell me to which god I should make a sacrifice for the protection I received. These were no mere thugs dredged from the port of Perunifer. They were trained assassins, highly skilled and well-prepared."

Asati turned to Nari, motioning for her to watch Moses, and got up from the bed. Turning to Semri, she said quietly, "How did they do this so quickly? Almost no one knew about him."

"That is a mystery, but they must have been well known to whoever sent them, considering the speed with which this happened. I have closed the compound, so no one will enter who I have not authorized and who has not been completely searched by two men. We will not take any chances, Your Highness."

Shading the Light

Mioa cursed Ameny's report. No, this was not good. They'd never failed—until now—and catastrophe hit him in the gut. When the guard reaches Seti, Pharaoh will see an assassin's hand, not the gods'. He hoped the second man took his poison before they broke him.

He sent Ameny back to the ferry to dig deeper, warning him to stir no suspicion. Port whispers might reveal the second agent's fate. His gut still churned as he donned court robes, racing for Pharaoh's palace. Before he left, he ordered the two priests who had aided Ameny banished to the desert temple before his return—only Ameny knew the truth.

As his litter hurried to the palace, Mioa felt panic rising in his chest. If Pharaoh discovered the truth, everything they had built—their influence, status, and perhaps their lives—would collapse. The plan's failure gnawed at him like a wound that refused to heal. They'd gambled everything and lost. He cursed himself silently. They had underestimated Pharaoh's vigilance and Semri's response. It might have cost them everything.

Nephura's Failed Hope

Nephura tried to stifle his growing impatience. He was certain that at any moment, he would hear of the successful results of his plan. The constant maneuvering was becoming tedious. He could tell nothing from Seti's demeanor, though he was sure that once "the gods" had taken care of the Hebrew problem, Seti would be relieved that it was no longer an issue. However, at the moment, he was being driven into a corner, as almost all signs were being interpreted as supporting the child.

Usually, he could rein in his more aggressive tendencies, especially in public view, but with so much at stake, the delay was starting to grind on his resolve. Trying to guide the discussions of his fellow priests had been an exhausting dance, each step a calculated effort to steer the debate in favor of his position. He had woven his words carefully, employing techniques passed down through generations—tones and phrases crafted to pierce men's minds, bending their will without their awareness. He had not yet applied any spells, as their use would be more noticeable and even draining for him. He was saving them for a future emergency. However, after taking a break for food, the tone of the debate intensified considerably. He was forced to exert more effort to guide the proceedings. Now, it was approaching the hottest time of the day, and as the heat had slowly risen in the great hall, the spirit of contention had grown with it. The arguments were turning against him, and he was growing weary. When you are exhausted, you are more likely to make a mistake or overlook something essential.

Up to this point, as the representative of Amun-Ra to the court in Memphis, Nephura had been able to avoid making any official statements. While he had offered numerous clarifying questions to draw out and guide the positions of the other First Priests and made numerous leading suggestions, he had kept his real arguments to himself. Omens were always a double-edged sword; they can work for you or against you, depending on the interpretation, and sometimes, an unexpected convergence of events pushed them beyond your control. The key to this assembly, Nephura had known from the start, was gaining control over the debate. He had needed to subtly guide the meaning of the dreams along with the signs and portents to his desired result while not making his efforts to manipulate the outcome too obvious. It was true the star had made his efforts more difficult, but he had worked very hard to lay the groundwork for what he knew would come to fruition when his plan was confirmed. With the abhorrent obstacle removed, he could push for an interpretation that continued the edict until it reached its final goal, the complete elimination of the Hebrews. And when they were gone, their accursed invisible God would disappear along with them.

He watched Seti, his expression as enigmatic as the Sphinx itself. Could he have heard something? If my plan had failed, Seti would surely have reacted, and depending on how it failed, his reaction might have been forceful; he could even dismiss the assembly. But Seti had shown no reaction.

The plan won't fail; these men have never failed me in the past. They are very good at what they do.

Finally, with his patience exhausted and the proceedings reaching an impasse, Nephura stepped forward and said, "May I suggest a possible explanation."

Paser, after first looking at Seti, who nodded, stood up, turned to face Nephura, and, with measured tones, said, "We have been waiting patiently for a guiding word from the worthy Second Priest of Amun-Ra."

Nephura recognized the veiled sarcasm hidden beneath the overly courteous manner. The emphasis on Second Priest was meant to remind him of his place in the larger scheme of things. All the other assembled priests were First Priests of their god. Only he was a Second Priest, though he was First Priest of Amun-Ra in Memphis, assigned to the court of Pharaoh, and extremely powerful. The head of their priesthood stayed in Thebes, the center of their priestly authority.

So, Pharaoh would let his vizier bring the day's events to their climax. It was a wise course of action that demonstrated Seti's growing political shrewdness. It would allow Pharaoh to serve as a moderating voice of wisdom and restraint if things became too contentious. Nephura knew that there were many pitfalls awaiting his slightest misstep. He also knew he had to continue to walk the narrow path between apparent rejection by his god and the accusation of trying to manipulate the meaning of the events to his desired end. Neither result was acceptable; either could prove problematic to the continued preeminence of the priesthood of Amun-Ra in the court of Pharaoh. More was at stake here than a few omens, and hopefully, the Hebrew baby would no longer be troublesome.

As he was about to speak, Nephura noticed his Seer Priest signaling him. From ancient times, the priesthood of Amun-Ra had developed a secret and subtle sign language that enabled them to pass information back and forth without those around them realizing what was happening. The specific coded signs that the Seer Priest used, while their exact meaning was unknown to him, told Nephura that Mioa had arrived, that his plan had failed, his agents were dead, and Pharaoh would soon know about the attempt on the child's life.

This was catastrophic news. It took all his practiced control and remaining reserves to forestall any visible reaction. As he hesitated before the assembly, trying to decide which of the limited scenarios left to him he should use, he felt a fluttering in his heart.

As Nephura lifted his hand to his chest and failed to continue, Paser asked, "Is something wrong?"

"No," Nephura said, suddenly confused, "Nothing is wrong, but my heart has given me pause." As the words hung in the air, so out of character for a man who admitted no weaknesses, the light in the room suddenly dimmed. Outside, for the first time since the gathering had begun, a large dark cloud passed across the sun, sending the palace into a deepening shade.

Inside the hall, a murmur went through the assembled priests. The timing of Nephura's heart giving him pause, along with the sudden darkening of the room, suggested to everyone that the gods were sending the esteemed Second Priest a message, possibly a warning.

Someone in the back of the hall even voiced what everyone must be thinking, saying loud enough to be heard throughout the assembly: "It's a sign."

As Nephura fought through the unexpected confusion, he forcefully stifled any visible reaction to this apparent admonition by the gods. Sweeping his hand around the hall at the assembled priests, he said, in a voice that was noticeably weaker than before, "As my assembled brothers know, I only want to make sure that whatever I say about what the gods seem to be doing is done with great care and proper submission to their will."

Though this was stretching the truth to a breaking point, a barely audible murmur of assent rose in the hall as some of Nephura's most ardent supporters quietly expressed their support and agreement, helped by a gradual brightening in the room.

As the initial shock of his failed plan and this unexpected, though possible warning from the gods dissipated, Nephura knew he had a fleeting chance to gain control over the situation. But as the room fell silent, waiting for what he would say, it darkened again, casting a sudden pall over the proceedings.

Drawing on everything he knew to fight against the oppression filling the room, he again swept his arm in an expansive gesture to those in the hall and said, "It has become obvious that things have changed." He paused to let the words find their mark and then continued, "What was the right course in one situation and at one time, may not be the direction the gods desire for later times."

With the room silent and every eye fixed on him, he gathered himself against the weight pressing him down. Suddenly, everything brightened as the sun cleared the cloud, and an instant vividness filled the room, dissipating the gloom, removing the heaviness, and throwing Nephura off stride as murmurs filled the assembly. The signs were impossible to ignore.

Quickly recovering and taking advantage of the opening, though biting his tongue against the direction it forced him, Nephura continued, "The desires of the gods and their goals for Egypt often change as the needs of Egypt change, just as we all saw the illumination in this room change from light to darkness," and then with emphasis added, "And then...back into the light...twice."

Nephura looked around the room. Everyone was staring at him with rapt attention. There was a growing sense of expectation as they began, almost without realizing it, to lean toward him. He knew the gods had given him this chance to salvage the day, to recover from his failed attempt to force the direction of destiny, and to reclaim for the priesthood of Amun-Ra its rightful preeminence. As to the Hebrews, he would find another way to deal with them.

Under his breath, he wove his most powerful persuasion spell and secretly signaled his Seer Priest to do the same. It was a dangerous gambit, but the situation demanded it. As he spoke the sacred words, a heaviness descended on the hall and everything grew quiet. Then, using his special voice, the secret speech that the initiated priests of Amun-Ra saved for those rare times when their words had to carry extraordinary weight with their hearers but at the same time hide its influence, he began, "When the vile heretic, may his name be cursed and forever forgotten, was overthrown, Egypt suffered through a time of great difficulty. For many years, the gods we serve labored mightily with their priests to bring calm and stability back to this sacred land and its people."

Added to general nods of affirmation were a few quiet words of agreement.

Carefully pushing at the weight of his words, he continued, "However, there was in our midst, a strong and numerous people who did not bow to the gods of Egypt, who instead listened to their own imaginary and invisible god."

This was one of his well-worn accusations, and many ears had grown tired of hearing it, so he had to be careful; he walked a fine line that could break the spell. Despite the danger, he had to set the stage. He was encouraged when most of the assembly leaned farther forward in anticipation. He went on.

"The gods made it very clear that these stiff-necked people, these Hebrews, had to be disciplined, and the festering influence of their offensive god rooted out of the land so that the sacredness and vitality of Egypt could be restored. The gods of Egypt needed to regain their rightful place before the people of the Two Lands."

With that, the words of affirmation became more open and more vocal.

"Ramses, may he dwell forever in the light of Ra, agreed, and on the first moon of his reign, he reissued the edict of Haremhab against the firstborn Hebrew males. And then, like a true Pharaoh and a god among the gods, he had it dutifully enforced."

Nephura did not remind them that he was the reason Ramses had taken that course of action, gaining the Pharaoh's agreement to act in return for the priesthood of Amun-Ra's support for his ascension to the throne. Instead, extending his hand toward the dais, he said, "And then, our great Pharaoh Seti, may he live forever, continued in his father's counsel." He ended the acknowledgment with a formal bow.

More words of agreement rose from the assembly.

"The seed of the Hebrews was fed to Sobek," he said, nodding to Obekka, the First Priest of the crocodile-headed god, "and the might of Pharaoh and Egypt grew strong on the vitality of their sacrifices. The power of that first inundation showed all of Egypt that the gods were pleased with Ramses' actions."

As Nephura looked over the assembly, the effort at maintaining the spell and using the voice was beginning to wear him down, but he had to complete this part of his statement while his thrall still held.

"That was over four inundations ago. Sobek, and through him all of Egypt, has received the benefit of the proscribed offerings, and the divine Seti, the strong son of his father Ramses, may he reign forever with the gods, now rules over a renewed and restored Egypt."

An appeal to vanity seldom went astray. Obekka, though an unproven ally in the day's events, was also in a difficult position. The number of worshippers at Sobek's temple began to decline as sentiment throughout Egypt shifted. Even Obekka's priests had started to loathe the daily bloodshed at the Nile's edge as the low river, caused by three weak inundations in a row, no longer hid the crocodiles as they fought over the grotesque offerings.

Nephura gathered his remaining strength. As much as it galled him and went against everything he had fought for, no other path was left open to him. Despite that, he had to find a way to maintain the preeminence of the Priesthood of Amun-Ra and his position as First Priest in Memphis.

With an expansive gesture, he bit back the bile and spoke with all the power he could muster. "Sometimes the gods take away, and sometimes they give back. For the last four inundations, the gods have taken. Now, in their wisdom, the gods have decided to give back." After a dramatic pause, he said, "Early this morning, a falling star struck the west bank of the Nile. It hit next to the Great Lock, which is Memphis' protection during the inundation, but did not damage it. The gods were sending us a message, not seeking to do us harm. The west bank of the sacred river represents death, or the ending of times." He let that thought sink in. The room became eerily silent.

"When early this morning, Princess Asati was given the gift of a son, taken from the life-giving waters of the Nile, this too was a sign from the gods." He had to use all of his practiced ability to keep the bitterness out of his voice. "That this son was a Hebrew also showed the gods' intent. As evidence, he was taken from the east bank of the Nile, which represents life, or the beginning of times."

As the realization of what he had said spread around the room, there were a few gasps and growing murmurs. Some had not heard the story of this foundling child, as it had not been discussed in the open deliberations. Not allowing the impact to wane, Nephura pressed on.

"From the sacred waters that for four inundations had swallowed up the infant sons of the Hebrews, now an infant son is given back, not to a Hebrew, but to a princess of Egypt." Nephura waited for his dramatic words to find their mark. "What better way is there for the gods to announce their desire to end the sacrifices and show us that they have fulfilled their intended purpose?"

Amidst the murmurs and confusion, words of assent filtered through the hall.

With a nod from Seti, Paser raised his hands for quiet. It would be better for Pharaoh's Vizier to address the question Nephura had left hanging in the air. It would leave Pharaoh room to maneuver.

"Powerful words, but this is a radical shift in direction for the priesthood of Amun-Ra. Are you sure this is the interpretation you want to support?"

Before Nephura could respond, Paser went on.

"Or does this change of heart have anything to do with the report that early this morning, in your own temple, a vulture spread its droppings on the head of the god, your priests, even yourself, fouling the morning ceremony? Was this not an evil omen for you and the priesthood of Amun-Ra?"

Nephura already knew about the pilgrim and that his story had begun to spread, so the accusation was not a surprise. He was prepared. But it was clear that the spell had run its course. It had exhausted him, and it would take him time to recover. That meant he had only his wits and prepared arguments to carry the moment.

"That depends," Nephura replied.

"On what?" Paser retorted.

"On the droppings. They were watery and clear and contained no vulgarity."

Nephura knew no one could refute this statement. They had cleaned the statue and the Naos immediately. No one outside his immediate senior priesthood had seen the dirty truth. The pilgrim had only heard them talking about the droppings through the temple door. He had not seen anything.

"We believe the vulture represented Satis, the patroness of the princess," he said, turning and acknowledging Sostris. "The goddess was merely anointing Amun-Ra to announce the arrival of the child, which she had prepared for the princess. In doing this, she also alerted us, his priesthood, concerning her gift."

Sostris did not object despite the obvious problems with the argument. Nephura knew his argument was accomplishing everything the First Priest of Satis could hope for.

"We believe Amun-Ra accepted her offering, as the First Priest of Satis earlier argued when the great god demonstrated this honor by sending two of his sacred falcons to grace her temple gates. What he didn't say then was that they also flew to the river and circled over the princess as she took the gift from the sacred waters, after which they flew back to the Temple of Satis and graced her gates again for an additional hour."

Looking around the room, he asked, "Was that not a powerful omen?"

Murmurs of agreement answered his question.

Forcing the bile rising in his throat back down, Nephura knew his argument about the droppings was weak, but there was nowhere else to turn. He had to cast the vulture in a positive light, but at least the action of the falcons served his need, and he had subtly brought Asati's gift into the discussion. While that helped shift the focus, he was still in serious trouble. Not only had his plan failed, it had turned into a catastrophe. Everyone would soon know about the attempt. While nothing could be proved, his only hope to save face for himself and his priesthood depended on this tenuous argument at least being tolerated, and the focus shifted. He knew he had to distance himself from his failed plan and resolve this debate before the attempt became public knowledge. Then the point would be moot.

Paser pondered this self-serving interpretation. He looked at Seti, who showed no response. If his Pharaoh wanted a reason to rescind the edict, Nephura's words had given him what he needed. Paser bit his tongue.

It was wise of Seti to be silent. Now was not the time to confront the priesthood of Amun-Ra. The Royal House could gain much by letting Nephura save face as long as his solution did nothing to diminish either Pharaoh or his family. The more he thought about it, the more he realized that Nephura's direction helped everyone and defused most of the problems.

"I'm sure we all appreciate your insight on these events. However, to ensure we are all clear and there is no misunderstanding, are you referring to this as the First Priest of Amun-Ra in Memphis? Are you saying that the child Princess Asati took from the sacred river, although he is a Hebrew, is a gift from the gods?"

Every eye turned to Nephura.

"I can only say that this is what all the omens and events appear to say."

Paser did not pursue him on the evasion but pressed on as every eye turned back to him. "Alright, a clarification then. Are you saying that the gods are using this child to tell us that they want to stop the sacrifice of newborn Hebrew males? And is this said as First Priest of Amun-Ra in Memphis?"

Every eye turned back to Nephura.

"Again, I can only say what the omens seem to say, and we are even now debating their meaning. I am sure that every priest here, as I do, would prefer to offer more sacrifices and seek additional signs from the great and noble gods we serve. In addition, I should go to Thebes and sit in counsel with the First Priest of Amun-Ra, but that would take too long. All I can say right now is yes, that is what the omens appear to say."

The silence was broken as voices began to rise from every corner of the hall, mostly in agreement with Nephura. As the noise increased, Sostris stepped forward. He stood there until the din quieted.

"I give way to the honored First Priest of Satis," Nephura said, hoping for a way out of this dilemma, and stepped back into the ranks of priests.

Seti leaned over to Ramses and said, "The gods have given the First Priest of Satis a chance to raise the stature of his goddess in the eyes of the assembled priests."

And put Nephura and the priesthood of Amun-Ra in his debt.

"I thank the gods," Sostris began, "for honoring Satis and her supplicant, Princess Asati, as their chosen messengers. I thank this noble gathering and especially the noble priesthood of Amun-Ra," he said as he extended his hand in the direction of Nephura, "for supporting them and our humble priesthood in this most difficult task.

Who can count the many omens and portents the gods have sent us today? They have whispered to those who would hear, spoken to this assembly with many auspicious signs, and shouted to the whole of Egypt by a heavenly messenger. Can we now agree that the matter is settled? Haven't the gods been clear that they want the edict rescinded? That it offends Ma'at, the foundation of Egypt herself. When the princess came to the temple this morning for prayers and advice from the goddess, she fell to the floor under the influence of a powerful vision. When my priests carried her into the audience chamber, on the floor where she had fallen, I found an ostrich feather."

A murmur of surprise spread through the hall.

Before anyone could respond, the First Priest of Ptah stepped forward and said, "Wait! There is something important we must consider." The hall almost erupted. He raised his hand, waving it as he almost shouted, "Wait!" The commotion began to subside. He turned, faced Seti, and said calmly, "Forgive me, my Pharaoh. But, before we decide, I must remind the assembly of something." He swept his arm around the room. "Have we forgotten the prophecy uttered at the ascension of the father of our Pharaoh, the great Ramses? May he dwell forever with the gods." He waited for the murmuring in the room to quiet down. Most of those present were at that ceremony. It was a turning point in Pharaoh's decision to begin enforcing the edict. It was there that the Seer Priest of the great Ptah prophesied to the whole assembly that a male child would be born to the Hebrews. He foretold that if this child grew to manhood, he would not be an ordinary man. He would be one who would excel above all men in glory and virtue to such an extent that his name would be remembered throughout the ages. But more importantly, he would bring Egypt low and raise up his own people."

The room became as silent as any tomb in the Valley of the Kings.

Sostris's heart sank.

When the turmoil we were facing appeared to have resolved, calling out this divine prediction would upset everything. It should be clear to Seti and the assembled priests as it is to me. Everything that has happened today still points to accepting the child and rescinding the edict. However, this prophecy cannot be swept aside. It had helped those concerned about the law of Ma'at to accept Ramses' decision to strictly enforce the edict. What do we do now?

For the first time, Sostris's resolve faltered, and he began to wonder if the gods were confused or, worse, not in agreement. Could the gods be contradicting each other so openly? Had he, in his zeal, missed something crucial? For the first time in his life, he felt genuinely unsure of the gods' intent, a feeling that terrified him.

The heavy silence quickly gave way to a spirited debate, which soon lost all decorum as separate arguments broke out among small groups of priests. The tension built up over the long and tiresome day let loose all at once. It was getting out of hand when suddenly, Pharaoh's staff struck the stone floor with two resounding thuds. All eyes in the now quiet room turned to Seti standing before them. He struck the floor twice more, the heavy blows echoing throughout the large hall.

Seti looked directly at Nephura and said, "We all agree with the Second Priest of Amun-Ra that the gods have spoken. We all agree with what the omens seem to indicate. Looking at the First Priest of Ptah, he added, "Yes, and we all remember the prophecy given at my father's ascension: may he reside forever with the gods." Then, turning to Sostris, he said, "I would ask if the gods have given the First Priest of Satis, the patron of my sister whose gift is at the center of this debate, a solution to our dilemma?"

Sostris looked at Seti, his mind racing to find a response. He was being given a unique chance to elevate his stature and that of the goddess, but he found himself in an impossible situation. He had no time to think or prepare a suitable argument. Trying to gain a little time to find a more detailed answer, he said the only thing that came to him, "I believe what is most important is that the gods entrusted this special child to the household of Pharaoh." He could think of nothing else to add; his mind was blank, and the silence grew uncomfortable.

All eyes turned to Pharaoh, but Seti instead turned and looked directly at Nephura and said nothing.

Nephura knew Seti was giving him a chance to regain his position, but he had to solve this riddle in a way that didn't put him at a disadvantage. Already, several arguments were forming in his mind. Sostris had given him a possible solution.

"What does Amun Ra have to say," Seti asked, not what Nephura would say, but his god. It was a subtle shift in focus but an important one.

"My Pharaoh," he began, "I believe we can all agree that the gods are not confused or divided on what they have said today. There is no evidence of that."

Sounds of assent came from around the room, but they were more a hope than an affirmation.

"We do not know if this child is the son of prophecy. However, even if he is, we should praise the gods for placing him in the sacred river. He could have been hidden away, raised in secret, allowing him to become a plague on Egypt's future. Instead, the gods, in their wisdom, gave him to the household of Pharaoh. Because of this, he can be raised as a child of Egypt, schooled by our priests to understand our ways, and taught to worship the true gods, the divine protectors of the Two Lands. Remember, nowhere in our sacred texts does it say the prophecy's outcome is written in stone."

As Seti listened to Nephura's argument unfold, he leaned over and whispered to Ramses, "The gods always find a way to accomplish their will, even if they have to work through the duplicitous tongue of the Second Priest of Amun-Ra."

"The gods, by giving the child to Princess Asati," Nephura continued, "have protected the future of Egypt and given to her and the royal household a divine task and a great honor."

Seti expected Nephura to find a way to turn the focus away from him and the Temple of Amun-Ra, and he had just succeeded. He was shifting the attention to the household of Pharaoh, laying everything at the feet of his family. Despite this, Seti could think of no rebuttal to the argument. He was outflanked.

All eyes were on Seti, waiting for his response. If he accepted the interpretation, he absolved all the priesthoods of their responsibility in the matter. He placed the entire burden of what the gods had done on his household, his reign as Pharaoh, and the future reign of his son, Ramses.

Though Seti was Pharaoh, he was also a soldier and hated being maneuvered into a corner; his warrior spirit rebelled at the thought. As a soldier, when faced with an implacable foe, he girded up his loins and strode straight into the battle, bringing everything he had to bear. But this was not a war, at least not in the normal sense, where sword and bow and skill at arms could sway the day; this was the court of Pharaoh, and he was more than a soldier. He had to consider the nation's welfare and the gods' demands; indeed, those had to be his chief concerns. Therefore, as Pharaoh, he did what had to be done, even though letting Nephura get away with this audacious maneuver galled him.

Seti struck the floor twice with his staff and pointed to his scribe, "Let it be written; let it be done. Since there is no disagreement or contrary signs, we will not delay. We will not offend the gods by being unwilling to listen when they speak, no matter how difficult their words may be."

Looking around, he saw no disagreement, only nods of affirmation and expectant looks. He had not anticipated any since he was freeing them of responsibility. "I am satisfied with the interpretation and accept the divine task and great honor that the gods have bestowed upon the household of Pharaoh. Therefore," he paused, giving space to what he was about to say, feeling the weight of all the Pharaohs who had ruled before him. He accepted this heavy burden because Egypt's stability required it. History might judge him, but he would bear it.

"I decree that the edict is rescinded. I command that the notice be published throughout the Two Lands that the newborn sons of the Hebrews shall no longer be sacrificed. I accept the divine commission of the gods that their gift, the son of Asati, will be raised by the household of Pharaoh to be a prince and child of Egypt. Let it be proclaimed that the gods of Egypt have declared it so and that Pharaoh decrees to his people that both he and all the priests of Egypt agree this is their will."

At first, there was stunned silence, but as a wave of relief spread through the room, shouts of acclamation ascended from the assembled priests, ringing throughout the chamber.

Seti waited for his words to have their full effect. After a few moments, he took his staff, struck the floor twice more, and said, "You are dismissed." He briefly saw Ramses watching him, sensing the burden he would pass to his son. The thought weighed heavily upon him, yet he knew he could not refuse this responsibility— his duty to Egypt overrode everything. Besides, there was his dream to consider.

Ramses watched his father as the priests began to disperse, his youthful impatience subdued by awe. Today had clearly shown him how fragile truth could be—how easily the gods' signs might be warped by human ambition. But it also showed him what true leadership was and how truth could prevail against all odds. He was overwhelmed with pride as he looked up to his father, a great Pharaoh of Egypt.

Nephura looked across the room at his Seer Priest, who bowed slightly toward him with a knowing smile. He had done it. He had turned a looming disaster into victory. Yes, he had lost the edict, but with everything turning against him, he had, with one deft move, shifted all responsibility to the household of Pharaoh. Nothing would come of the failed attempt. He was exhausted, yet beneath his fatigue simmered a resolve. Yes, it was time to return to the comfort of his temple, but tomorrow would bring new opportunities—plans that Pharaoh would never anticipate.

Reflections

Tuya had been waiting just outside the Great Hall, listening to the final arguments of the debate. While she disagreed with the sacrifice of the Hebrew sons and favored rescinding the edict, she was concerned that Nephura had succeeded in laying all the concerns about this child's future at the royal household's feet. However, thinking back on her dream and on how her son had been sparring and laughing with a younger Hebrew, she was not surprised by what the gods had accomplished.

Though many priests began to leave, some still mingled in small groups around the room, discussing the implications of what had happened. On the dais, Seti talked with Paser while Osri, his scribe, wrote beside him, preparing Pharaoh's declaration that rescinded the edict.

As Tuya stepped into the room, she saw Ramses leaning in on his father's conversation, the intensity evident on his face. Her heart swelled as she watched her son share this important moment with his father, soaking in the experience of what it meant to be a Pharaoh and speaking words that would have a lasting effect on the future of Egypt.

Pride in both her son and her husband lifted her spirits. The day had begun ominously, but it seemed the danger had passed, both for her family and for Egypt. Whether the Priesthood of Amun-Ra had been right in arguing for the edict, claiming it was the will of the gods, no longer mattered. The wretched business was over, and the gods had spoken powerfully and clearly. They had restored Ma'at to its rightful place, and an ignoble burden had been lifted off the soul of the Two Lands.

Seti looked up and saw his wife smiling at him. He signaled her to come over. As she gained the dais and stood beside him, he turned back to Paser and said, "Did we cover everything? Nothing was forgotten?"

"We have dealt with all the necessary tasks. I will set the proclamation in motion as you have commanded."

"Your Highness," Paser said as he bowed slightly to Tuya. Turning to Seti, he asked, "I will take my leave then?"

"Yes. We will talk again in the morning."

As Paser and Osri left, Seti looked at Ramses and said, "Tell your mother what you learned today."

Ramses turned to his mother, who gave him an encouraging smile. Due to his recent growth, he was almost as tall as she was, and his eyes were now level with hers.

"I learned that it's not easy being Pharaoh. It is hard to be patient and possess the wisdom to be a good ruler, like my father.

"Patience will come with age, my son," Tuya replied. "Don't be too hard on yourself."

"He did well," Seti said. "His insights were excellent. I was pleased he could see past the obvious and question what was occurring beneath the well-chosen words and arguments. He has grown more than even his instructors suspect."

Tuya could see Ramses' face redden as he reveled in his father's praise. In some ways, he was still a boy.

A servant approached, and Seti waved him forward.

After bowing, the servant said, "Nazim, one of the guards from the Great Estate, is here with a message from Semri. He arrived while the final debate was taking place and said it was very important.

Tuya looked across the room and saw Seti's former soldier and Semri's closest friend standing at the far entrance to the hall. Her husband told the servant, "Tell him to come over."

As the servant left, Tuya asked, "Do you want to be alone for your meeting?"

"No. Stay. We should discuss how to proceed now that the gods have given the household of Pharaoh the task of raising this possible prophecy."

Asati's guard approached the dais and bowed.

"Tell me, Nazim, what's so important? But do so quietly, as there are still priests in the hall."

"There was an attempt on the life of the child, disguised to appear as an act of the gods, but Semri killed the two serpents as they emerged from their hiding place in a new crib's bedding."

Tuya gasped, and Ramses added, "Father," as much a question as a reaction to such an outrage.

Seti's grip tightened on his staff, his stomach churning. The snakes could have struck Asati as easily as the child! His mind honed itself into a weapon, slicing through the tangled web of Nephura's schemes even as rage clawed at his composure. "Tell me everything!"

As Nazim described what had happened, Seti could see Nephura's hand guiding this effort. It clarified why he was dragging out the debate and what he had been waiting for. Then, when his plan failed, it explained why he had tried to bow out so gracefully and quickly.

Conflicting emotions rose in Seti: admiration for Nephura's audacious plan worthy of a seasoned general, crossed with anger that he would presume to manipulate what the gods had set out to accomplish while placing Pharaoh's sister at risk. If not for Semri, anything could have happened.

After Nazim finished his report, Seti said, "Go refresh yourself while I decide what message you should take back to Semri."

Nazim bowed and went to find a servant.

Seti knew there would be nothing to tie the attempt back to the Second Priest of Amun-Ra. The assassins were dead, and anyone not in Nephura's intimate circle who knew too much to be trusted had probably already disappeared.

This priest is even more dangerous than I had imagined. I will never again underestimate the man.

The three of them were quiet for a long time. The few remaining priests began to leave, increasing their privacy.

Tuya finally broke the silence. "It was good that you posted Semri as your sister's guard."

"Yes. It was a good choice."

"There are two matters still unanswered," she said. "First—what will you do now?"

"Make sure my sister and the child are protected, but I don't expect another attempt, at least not for a while." Seti decided to change the subject before it further darkened his mood. Looking at Ramses, he said, "Tell your mother what else you have learned today," turning this into another learning opportunity for his son.

As Seti looked at his son, he could see in his eyes the pressure his question had put on him. The toughest thing a leader had to do was gather their thoughts and make sense of what had happened.

After a short wait, Ramses said, "We have learned where most of the priests stand. Some stand for the gods, even when what they demand is difficult. Some sway with the wind and are easily led wherever a strong voice takes them, while some stand for themselves."

"Spoken like a general surveying the battlefield," Seti said, his face breaking into a broad smile. He looked at his wife and said, "See how productive the day has been. Our son shows us he is learning the lessons he needs to know to become a good Pharaoh." Turning back to Ramses, he said, "Whether in war or the intrigues of court, you must understand the combatants before you can successfully execute your plan."

Ramses straightened. His father's words were a rare gift, but they also carried weight. One day, he would stand where Seti did, and the choices would be his alone. He hoped he would be ready.

Tuya interjected, wanting to finish what she had started, "My second question—will you let Nephura's ambition go unchecked? Even after this? Be careful, Seti. A man like him only grows bolder when he believes himself untouchable."

"Patience. I will act, but it will take time and careful planning. However, be assured that we will take the necessary precautions to protect our charge. Eventually, there will be other attempts on his life. But not right now. Tonight, we have other needs." His soldier's mind shifted, recalculating—family before vengeance. His outrage could wait; duty came first. "We should get together as a family and have a meal. We need to discuss this task the gods have given us. Let's invite my sister and her new charge to join us so that we can see the cause of all this turmoil."

"I agree. But there is one thing we have not yet discussed," Tuya interjected.

The question hung in the air as Seti and Ramses looked at her. Then, she added, "And what of Amunthura?" Tuya's voice was calm, but her words carried a heavy weight. "What will he do when he returns to find his wife raising a Hebrew as an Egyptian prince?"

Home

The afternoon had dragged mercilessly. Every passing moment, every unanswered question gnawed at Amram. He had no way of knowing what had become of his son. The keel was at a critical point—leaving early, no matter his excuse, would have been impossible. But the moment they released him, he was gone.

Rather than take the shipyard's ferry across the river, he went into the port of Perunifer in search of information. Even as the sun dipped lower, the marketplace was still buzzing. People were discussing the multitude of signs, the star, speculations about the gathering of priests at the court of Pharaoh, and the death of a well-liked merchant who had died of a snakebite in his shop. Even though some considered that an omen, no one was sure of what.

Here and there, he heard speculation about the baby boy Princess Asati had found, but few seemed to speculate that he was a Hebrew, and no one had heard anything about the child being turned over to the priests of Sobek. Amram's heart bounced back and forth between hope and despair, depending on which person he had last overheard.

He was trying to decide how late he could stay before returning home when he heard a commotion coming from the central common area, where public announcements were often made. By the time he could work his way close enough to hear, the Royal Scribe had stepped off the platform and was leaving.

The crowd around Amram seemed divided in their reactions to the announcement, but he could not gather any specifics from the snippets of discussion he overheard. Then he saw Beerta across the square talking with someone. He hurried over to his Syrian friend, who saw him coming and waved to him excitedly.

"Amram, did you hear?"

"No. What caused the uproar?"

"Then, my friend, I am happy to be the first to tell you that Pharaoh, after consulting with the priests and listening to the gods, has rescinded the edict! The sons of your people are now safe."

His words struck Amram like cool water in the desert. Relief crashed over him as he grasped that his son was saved. "Why?" he excitedly asked.

"I didn't hear it all. Sometimes, the crowd's reaction drowned out the Scribe's words. However, I did hear that it was because of the Hebrew child that Princess Asati found, which the priests are calling a gift from the gods. How strange is that? It seemed that between him, the star, and the overwhelming number of signs occurring throughout the city's temples, everyone agreed that the gods were calling for an end to the sacrifices and for Ma'at to be respected. Even the priesthood of Amun-Ra supported the decision. Can you believe it?"

"I have to go. Thank you. Thank you," Amram called over his shoulder as he rushed away, his heart pounding excitedly. He had to get home and share the good news with his wife. She must be sick with worry.

He hurried through the crowded market to the last ferry near the southernmost gate of the city. Fortunately, only a few people were waiting to leave the port side of the river, but the ferry was almost fully loaded as it approached the dock. Even this late, people were still coming into the city. The ride across the river and the rest of his journey was a blur as he rushed home as fast as his legs and lungs could carry him.

Almost exhausted, he arrived at his village but felt it was worth it as he approached his house. As he burst through the door, calling for his wife, he found Miriam feeding Aaron some bread and goat's milk.

They both started talking at once, Miriam trying to tell him what had happened, Amram wanting to know where Jochebed was, and also trying to tell his daughter that the edict had been rescinded.

Finally, Miriam said loudly, "Forgive me, father, but you have to listen!"

He calmed down, reached out, patted his daughter's head, and said, "What do I have to listen to, Miriam, and where is your mother?"

"As I have been trying to tell you, mother has been hired to be the wet nurse for Princess Asati, who found my brother this morning after we put him on the Nile. The princess believes he is a gift from her gods, and she has decided to keep him as her son. She even named him. She calls him Moses, which means out of the water or something like that."

As his daughter's story progressed, Amram could hardly believe his ears. The God of his fathers had done more than he could have ever hoped. When Miriam finished, he excitedly said, "I have even greater news."

"Father, how could any news be greater than that?"

"It is greater because Pharaoh has rescinded the edict. Our sons will no longer be sacrificed to appease the anger of the priests of Amun-Ra. The Lord God has used your brother to stop the abomination. He has saved his people."

Miriam could not believe what she had heard. This day was beyond anything she could have imagined, even in her wildest hopes. "Father, you need to tell the village!"

"I will. I rushed home, hoping to bring solace to your mother, but obviously, the Lord had already given her consolation. I'll go out and tell everyone about the edict."

As he turned to the open door, a cool breeze stirred against his skin. The hairs on his arms rose. And at that moment—before reason could argue, before he could deny it—he knew. Despite the proclamation, despite the miracle, his son was no longer his. Moses belonged to Pharaoh's house now. Joy and loss collided in his breast, and for a moment, he wanted to resist. But that door had already been shut. He realized nothing had changed except their prayers had been answered. As hard as it was to bear, his son was on a new path, one governed by God's purpose, and he knew, in the marrow of his bones, that God had shut the door to him as his son's father. There was no going back.

"Father, are you all right?"

Amram ran his hand across his forehead and took a deep breath to steady himself. Then he looked at Miriam and said, "Daughter, we still need to keep your brother a secret. That has not changed."

He could see that Miriam was unsure why that was necessary now, but she did not question his words. Instead, she took Aaron's hand and followed her father out the door.

Squaring the Circle

Nephura had sent the Seer Priest ahead in the covered chair Mioa had arrived in. He and his trusted priest took his palanquin and returned to the temple. That gave them time to discuss how to respond to what had happened. His failure still simmered beneath the surface, but Nephura never let emotions rule him for long. This was no time for anger—only strategy. The day had exposed vulnerabilities he could not afford. Now, he had new concerns.

"Tell me, what is the current state of our affairs?"

"I transferred the two priests who assisted Ameny. They should already be well on their way into the desert. One agent we know is dead, and the other should have used his poison before they could get anything out of him."

"Such a loss. They were quietly efficient and, until today, very effective. They will be hard to replace. What about this young priest? Do you think we can use him? It would be a shame to lose such a promising resource."

"He is both ambitious and calculating. Did you notice? He deliberately chose two expendable priests—none of his friends, no one close. That kind of foresight is rare. Ruthless, but rare. He is smart, knows how to seize the initiative, and is discreet. I think he could be a worthy protégé, and if he does not work out..."

"You are right; it is time we found a suitable person to begin training. I noticed from the beginning that his nervousness made him controllable, but it did not prevent him from doing what needed to be done. Instead, it is his motivation to succeed. With all of these new challenges, we need someone who can help us expand our efforts, and no one else has shown as much promise as this young priest. Exposing his talents is about the only good thing that came out of this mess. You should meet with him as soon we get back. We need to see how he is handling the pressure of knowing so much about our business."

"What about his source, the ferry boatman? He sounds too clever to have stayed where we could easily find him."

"He knows just enough to be useful but not dangerous. That makes him manageable. And if ambition drives him, we will ensure he understands whose favor he should seek. We can use him in the future, and after we locate his family and close friends, managing him will be easy. A ready ear at the ferry used by the Great Estate could be important. We should consider engaging ears on all of the ferries. I am surprised we never considered it before."

"I will see to it."

"One problem remains. Seti suspects us."

Mioa stiffened, but Nephura raised a hand before he could object.

"Calm yourself. Seti has nothing concrete—no evidence, no witnesses. But suspicion is enough. We've lost the advantage of the shadows. He will watch us now, and a man like that only watches when he means to act.

However, our failure has exposed us, and now he will regard us as a real threat, one willing to act against him. We must be very careful, at least until the situation settles down. As much as I dislike the thought, it is in our best interest, given our current exposure, to ensure nothing happens to the child. We need to prevent any of our other agents from taking matters into their own hands if they see an opportunity. Get the word out. He is off-limits...for now."

"As you wish, noble one. I will take care of it immediately."

The litter came to a halt. They arrived at the temple just as the sun approached the horizon.

"Before you go, is there anything else we need to discuss?" Nephura asked.

Mioa shook his head.

"Then I will retire. The day has drained me."

He stepped from the litter as the temple loomed before him, bathed in the fading light of Ra. Tomorrow, he would begin again.

Semri's Charge

Once Semri's search of the house and compound revealed no further threats, he urged the household to return to its normal rhythm. However, Asati would not let the child out of her sight, and it was likely that for some time, she would be overly concerned about her new son's safety. Understandably, she refused to let the child out of her sight. But it turned her bedroom into a constant flurry of movement—servants, guards, and the wet nurse all revolving around her, trying to carry on while she kept Moses close.

As preparations for the evening meal began, the guard on the house's roof spotted Nazim running up the cart path toward the compound. Worset sent one of the men to alert Semri and then opened the gate.

As Nazim entered the compound, exhausted from his run from the palace, he said to Worset, "I have a message from Pharaoh for Semri."

"He is upstairs with the women and the child in the princess's bedroom."

After taking a moment to catch his breath, Nazim crossed the courtyard, entered through the kitchen, passed one guard, and then ascended the servants' stairs, passing another guard outside the princess's bedroom.

The heavy security made it clear—Semri was taking no chances.

The door was closed, but instead of going in, he called out, "I have a message for Semri from Pharaoh."

"I am coming," he heard Semri reply, and a few heartbeats later, he came through the door.

Nazim handed him the papyrus scroll, closed with Pharaoh's seal. "I came as fast as I could. Is there anything you'd like me to do?"

"Get your bow and go upstairs and relieve the guard. I would prefer your experienced eyes scanning the fields. I'll come up, and we can talk after I've read the message."

"Is there water up there? I am parched."

"Yes, but I will bring more when I come."

As Nazim went to get his bow, Semri broke the seal and opened the scroll. He stepped into the bedroom, where the high western windows provided the light that remained from the setting sun. All three women watched him as he read the message.

Faithful Semri. Nazim told me of your heroic actions and how you rewarded the trust I placed in you when I assigned you to look after the safety of my sister. Your Pharaoh thanks you and calls on you to continue your faithfulness. Bring my sister to the palace tonight for the evening meal. There is much to discuss, and we desire to meet the child who has caused all this uproar. The edict has been rescinded, but I still charge you for their safe arrival. Come as soon as you can prudently do so.

Semri looked at the princess.

There will be little rest tonight.

"What does my brother have to say?" Asati asked.

"Much has happened. First, you need to know that the edict has been rescinded."

Asati, with a prayer of thanksgiving forming on her lips, smiled at Nari as the wet nurse said a quiet "Thank God."

Asati looked at Semri and said, "What else did he say?"

"Pharaoh wants you to bring the child to the palace for the evening meal. We should leave as soon as we can."

"We will get ready. I will take Nari and the wet nurse. We will all fit in the palanquin."

"I will make preparations and send a messenger ahead to alert the Ferry Master," Semri said, then bowed and left the room.

Nari was already giving Moses to Jochebed when Asati called for the servants.

Jochebed turned away, the weight of what had happened settling deep in her chest. Her prayers had been answered, but the deeper truth cut just as sharply—though the edict was gone, the son in her arms would never again be hers.

Temple Joy

By the time Sostris and his Seer Priest returned, the temple was already alive with the news—the edict had fallen. Word of Satis' role had spread, and a jubilant crowd pressed against the temple gates, eager to join the priests in the Hymn of Thanksgiving. The sheer mass of people made it simpler for them to go around to the side, to the garden entrance, where they were let in.

Sostris's servant was waiting for him as he stepped from the litter.

"Noble one. The pure priest has already prepared thanksgiving offerings to the goddess, and the Khenerit have arrived. We have been waiting for your return."

Sostris paused, scanning the crowd. Smiles stretched wide, voices lifted in praise—relief and triumph mingled in every face. Their most pressing problem, Princess Asati's barrenness, was no longer an issue, and the edict, which had weighed heavily on all their hearts, had been rescinded. Ma'at had been vindicated. In addition, the blessing of Amun-Ra, as stated by Nephura himself, had significantly elevated Satis's stature. The people waiting to get into the temple were visible evidence of the change.

"Suspend all other duties. I want every priest and wa'eb gathered— families, bearers, servants. No one is absent. Tonight, Satis must hear the full voice of all her people."

As his servant ran off, Satirah and several senior priests hurried over to him.

Sostris raised his hand, barely containing their excited questions. Starting toward the temple, he said, "Yes, it is exciting, and there is much to discuss, but first, we must offer the celebratory offerings. Then, when everything calms down, we must retire the goddess for the night. We can talk over dinner. That way, I won't have to repeat myself, and everyone can ask their questions."

They reluctantly left him and went into the temple.

Sostris saw Saisa heading toward the priest's entrance and motioned him over.

The young wa'eb bowed and said, "How may I serve you, my lord?"

"I haven't had a chance to talk with you since this morning when you told me the story of the star."

"It has been a momentous day, my lord."

"Yes, it has. Saisa, I have been thinking. Stay. I know you feel bound to your village, but the gods have called you here. We will find someone to aid them—but your path may differ. I believe the gods have marked you, Saisa—a destiny tied to this day and Satis herself. You saw the star fall; perhaps you're meant to rise with it. Stay with us, and we'll seek the goddess's will together... Now, let's celebrate her triumph."

Before Saisa could respond, Sostris added, "Don't try to decide right now. Wait. Consider it and pray to the goddess for guidance, but for now, let's go in and celebrate."

Saisa quietly bowed and followed Sostris through the priest's entrance to the temple. Those inside and those still entering stopped and turned in the direction of the First Priest, expectant. He could feel the energy in the air. It was as if you could touch it. He looked around and saw that everything was ready, and the remaining priests, their families, and the temple servants were entering the great hall. They had cleansed the temple to prepare for the Great Thanksgiving, and now it was time to open the main doors and let the people in. It was time for Satis to receive her due.

"Let Satis receive her worshippers."

Four wa'ebs heaved the great locking bar free. The heavy doors groaned open, and a wave of people surged inside. At the priests' direction, they parted, filling the temple like the waters of the Nile in flood. Arrayed in the center stood the white-clad Khenerit, their sistra raised, their feet poised, waiting for the signal to begin.

Changes

The sun had already set, and the last light was disappearing from the western horizon when Asati's palanquin, escorted by Semri and four guards, arrived at the palace of Pharaoh. The palanquin bearers knelt, lowering their burden with reverence. Asati stepped onto the stone, her movements deliberate, the weight of the day pressing against her shoulders. Nari adjusted her robes, smoothing the delicate folds as Asati composed herself. Tonight, she did not enter as a sister alone—she entered as the mother of a child the gods had claimed. After receiving assurances that everything was in order, the princess reached out to Jochebed for the child. The wet nurse gently placed Moses into the princess' waiting arms. The rhythmic motion of the bearers, as they took them through Memphis, had put him to sleep, and he lay quiet and oblivious to the important people he was about to meet. After sending the bearers, Jochebed, and the escort to the servant's kitchen, Asati nodded to Nari and Semri, and they started up the steps.

Although the edict had been rescinded, and they had agreed that another immediate attempt on Moses' life was improbable, Asati was still concerned for his safety. It did not matter that the priests had supported what the gods had demanded; the princess did not trust the maneuverings of the Egyptian priests, especially Nephura.

Nari gave the princess' arm a gentle stroke of support as she moved to her proper place behind her mistress.

Composing herself, Asati approached the guard standing to the right of the entrance. The guard bowed, and as the other guard opened the door, Asati went inside.

The dining room was to the right, off the main entrance hall. There were five finely upholstered low chairs surrounding a low table. Several large lamps lit the room, including one that hung from the ceiling over the table. Danar, her brother's servant, was waiting for them.

"Welcome, Your Highness. The royal family will be with you shortly."

Almost before he finished, Tuya and Ramses came into the room, followed by Seti, who looked at her as if sizing up a battlefield. His queen's smile or her greeting did not show the same measured reserve.

"So, this is the source of all today's excitement," Tuya said softly, coming over to Asati to get a better look at the child.

Asati, buoyed by the gentle inquisitiveness of Tuya's words, shifted Moses into her left arm and spread the white linen covering to give her a better look at the resting child. He was sleeping soundly. Asati brushed a lock of hair from his forehead, and, lifting her face to Tuya, she then looked past her to Seti and said, "Have the gods not given me a handsome gift?"

Since her marriage and his family's ascension to the throne, Seti had lost the special closeness they had shared throughout Asati's youth. It was not because he loved his sister any less, but after the death of their mother and then their father, the divine Ramses, all of Seti's energies had gone into Egypt. Indeed, he had less time than he would have liked to spend with his wife and son. Asati's voice held a subtle, urgent tremor—a sister's unspoken plea slipping beneath the surface of royal decorum. For a moment, Seti was not Pharaoh but the brother who had once shielded her from childhood fears. He was still her protector, but could he still keep her safe as he once had? And if the gods had already decided, was this protection even his to give? He could see in Asati's eyes the question of trust, asking whether the deepest needs of a sister, especially a sister who was also a daughter of Pharaoh, still held sway in his heart. Fortunately for them, Seti knew that nothing—neither the gods, the priests, the portents, nor even the opinion in the streets of Memphis and Perunifer—gave her reason for concern. Despite the attempt on the child's life earlier in the afternoon, the only remaining problem of immediate concern would be Amunthura, her husband.

Tuya reached out and stroked his forehead. "He is a handsome child."

Ramses stepped around his mother and, looking at Moses, asked, "How old do you think he is?"

"We think he is between three and four months old," Asati replied.

"May I hold him?" Tuya asked.

Asati smiled and gently placed Moses in Tuya's waiting arms.

As Tuya took the child, something ancient and instinctive stirred within her. A mother's arms never forget. The weight of him, the warmth—so small, yet so full of possibility. Her breath caught a flicker of something she dared not name. Was it fate? Or was it the gods whispering through the tiny heartbeat resting against her chest? She looked down at his sleeping face, so innocent in her arms.

Are you the child of prophecy?

"It is time we ate," Seti said, pointing to one of the two chairs on the other side of the table. Then, adding, "Semri, you are to join us."

Nari moved forward. Tuya gave her the child and then sat down to the left of her husband while Ramses took the seat to his right. Asati took the seat opposite Semri. Seti decided that sending Nari and the child away would cause his sister too much distress, so he gave her a nod, after which she quietly moved to a group of cushions placed a short distance away, to the princess's right.

"There is nothing to fear, my sister," Seti said, seeing the question in her eyes. "Your gift is secure. All have agreed that the child is a gift from the gods. The rescission of the edict has been published, and even the priesthood of Amun-Ra is in agreement."

Hearing her hopes confirmed directly from her brother's lips calmed Asati's anxiety and freed her spirit. The great weight she had been carrying, made even more severe by the attempt on Moses' life and only slightly lessened by Semri's earlier announcement, seemed to flow down the length of her body and out her feet with a tingling release.

"Thank you, my brother," she said, as her heart remembered the love they had shared since childhood. "The gods have been merciful to me today."

"We'll talk after we eat," Seti said, smiling at his sister and then nodding to Danar. A small clap caused servants to appear immediately, carrying trays overflowing with fruit and vegetables, succulent meats and sweet bread, a pitcher of wine, and five golden cups.

Seti knew that despite his cautiousness, ears were straining throughout every nook and cranny of the palace for any hint of gossip. The servants were still buzzing over the events of the day. Rumors were as thick as flies at the slaughter pens and had been a distraction during the meal preparations. The Chief Baker was only now beginning to calm himself. Numerous buttocks had felt the sting of his cane, yet rumors still flitted from ear to ear around the servants' kitchen as they began to serve the evening meal.

There was a fountain built into the northern wall, whose primary purpose was to provide privacy. The falling water created a pleasing sound that hid their conversation from anyone not seated at the table. Everyone who saw it, though, marveled at the beautiful and intricate flow of water that cascaded from pool to pool set into the high wall. Sometimes, Seti enjoyed simply sitting in the room, watching and listening to the water as it descended.

Tonight, there was no music or dancers at the meal. Instead, it was a quiet family gathering. At first, their pleasant conversation avoided the events of the day and instead focused on the food, the weather, hope for the coming inundation, and how much Ramses had grown. Semri remained silent, unable to relax his vigilance. At least he could enjoy the exceptional food the Chief Baker had prepared. Only once, in response to Seti's comment that he appeared in excellent health, did he give a short response.

After the servants had taken the main dishes away and brought out a platter of honeyed pastries, Seti nodded to Danar, and everyone else left the room, leaving the royal family, Semri, Nari, and the child alone.

Looking at his sister, Seti said, "There are still important issues to discuss, my sister. You may recall the prophecy given during our father's ascension: May he live forever with the gods, concerning a Hebrew male child."

He could see the tension spreading across Asati's face as she recalled the event.

"Some have argued that this child might be the prophesied one. However, before you become upset, the consensus was that the gods have given this child to the household of Pharaoh so that, if he is the one foretold, we can raise him as a child of Egypt and turn the prophecy to Egypt's advantage."

As concern spread across her face, Asati said, "What does that mean, my brother?"

"It means that the weight of everything that has happened today has been shifted to our household. The family of Pharaoh now carries the entire burden. The priests argued that the gods had entrusted us with this important task. By raising this child as a prince of Egypt, schooling him in our ways, to revere our laws and worship our gods, we will bring the prophecy to no effect."

"That is a heavy burden, my brother. How can we know whether he is the one?"

"We cannot know. We can only follow the path the gods have laid out for us. This should not diminish your joy, my sister. I tell you only to remind you of the seriousness of the task that lies ahead of us. We all will have a part to play." Looking at Ramses, he added, "Even you, my son."

"What will I do, father?"

As Seti explained the two dreams, Tuya's and his own, he made plain to his sister and his son how the gods had shown them that Ramses' future was intimately intertwined with this Hebrew child. He made sure his son understood that the gods had foretold that one day, this child would save his life.

"So, you can see that this child is more than a royal burden."

Despite this assurance, Seti could see the mixed feelings in the faces around the table.

Hearing a cough, Seti saw Danar signaling him from across the room. Standing beside him was an exhausted-looking man carrying a messenger's satchel. He had given orders they were not to be interrupted, so Seti knew this must be important and waved him over. Pharaoh's servant sounded decidedly upset as he apologetically approached his lord.

"Divine one, forgive me for interrupting, but a serious situation needs your attention. This messenger has come from the fortress of Buhan."

Looking at Semri, Seti said, "Come with me." To those left at the table, he added, "I will not be long. Eat some dessert, and we'll continue when I return."

With Semri following, Seti went to a private room off the dining area and sat down. Semri went and stood beside him. The messenger followed Danar into the room and stopped before his Pharaoh with his head down.

"My Lord," Danar said, "This messenger has flown with the wings of Horus. He has been on the water for nine days."

The messenger opened his leather satchel, took out the sealed scroll, and handed it to Danar, who passed it to Seti.

The seal carried the insignia of the commander of Buhan. Seti used his fingernail to break the wax and unroll the scroll.

Silence hung heavy in the chamber as Seti's eyes scanned the scroll. His brow furrowed. The muscles in his jaw tensed. A flicker of something unreadable passed over his face—then came the shift: dark, then sad, then burning with controlled fury. Seti rolled up the scroll and handed it back to Danar. Looking at the messenger, he said, "What is your name?"

"I am called Sunsamen, my Pharaoh."

"Well, Sunsamen, you have done your Pharaoh a great service. Danar, see to his needs and send a messenger to Paser telling him to come to the palace at once. Send for the Royal Scribe, and when he arrives, give him the dispatch."

"As you command, my Pharaoh," Danar said, and then he escorted Sunsamen out of the room.

Seti's gaze locked onto Semri's, the weight of command pressing between them. "You know why I placed you in my sister's service?"

Semri straightened. "To protect her, my Pharaoh."

"Yes." Seti exhaled slowly. "Then hear me now—your duty has become more than guarding a princess. The Nubian gold caravan was overrun. A large force of men descended on it like jackals on easy prey. The chariot force defending it was slaughtered. Two men escaped, and although wounded, one of them lived and was able to reach the fortress. And Amunthura...Amunthura is dead."

Semri gasped.

Set continued, "The commander at Buhan sent this messenger asking for help, and he has been journeying with almost no rest for nine days. The survivor said a force of over 500 men had attacked them. These were not bandits but Khetan soldiers. It appears that King Saparura has broken his treaty with my father. I need to call a council of war and will leave for the south as soon as we can gather the army. My sister is alone now, and with me gone, you will be her and the child's only protection."

As Seti watched the situation sink into Semri's understanding, he began playing out various scenarios in his mind. He needed to set aside the issues of the upcoming war for the moment. He would gather an army and Saparura would be dealt with but the sun or gold fever must have addled his brain for him to do something so stupid. However, there were more immediate considerations.

Was this a coincidence, or had the gods planned this and used the rebellion to remove the last impediment to my sister's new child?

Although he had never liked Amunthura, Asati had wanted him, and it had been a good political match for his family, especially before his father became Pharaoh. Now, her husband's ambitions and arrogance were a thing of the past, as was his sister's barren shame. However, it would be dangerous for them when he left. Asati and the baby would be alone, and despite the agreement reached earlier in the day, there were factions in Egypt that might try to arrange another act of the gods. Semri had become even more important to the Royal household.

Semri bowed and said, "You may depend on me and my men. However, with this additional burden, we could use a few reinforcements if you will allow it."

"Will six be enough? We don't want to make it too obvious."

"Yes, my Pharaoh."

"Choose any six men you want before I leave for the south."

Seti got up and, with Semri following, strode back into the dining area. As he crossed the room, his wife and sister stood up. Looking at him, they both said, "What is wrong?"

Seti looked at Tuya, then at Asati. His voice was measured, but in its depths lay the shadow of war, of shifting fates. "We need to talk, my sister. The gods have moved their pieces, and nothing will be the same."

Fulfillment

The journey back from the palace had been arduous. Princess Asati wept most of the way, and though Nari attempted to console her, her sorrow was unrelenting. Moses briefly comforted her, but her sorrow soon overtook her again, and from then on, she clung to Nari. The queen had urged Asati to stay at the palace, but she refused. She longed for the familiarity of her own bed and the solace of home. Tuya bid her farewell, promising to arrive early the following day at the Great Estate.

The bearers moved swiftly, and Semri dispatched a guard ahead to ensure no delay at the ferry. When they arrived at the compound, Asati kissed Moses before dissolving into fresh tears. She fled inside and up to her room, with Nari following close behind.

Semri escorted Jochebed to the nursery. After thoroughly checking the room and shutting the door, he placed a guard in the hall and left.

The house had fallen into stillness. The only sounds were soft sobs coming from the princess's room. As soon as Semri left the nursery, Moses stirred, obviously hungry. Jochebed decided to try out the nursing chair next to her bed. It was surprisingly comfortable, as the sloped back allowed him to lie comfortably on her chest while he nursed.

As she reflected on the day, she marveled at everything that had happened in such a short span of time. Sadness, danger, joy, and deliverance, all in a few hours. Who could have known? Looking down at her son, now asleep in her arms, Jochebed whispered to him, "Your father was right. The God of Abraham, Isaac, and Jacob did bring you into this world to save your brethren. Today, you have succeeded in delivering your brothers from destruction, and because of you, the edict has been rescinded. Through you, God has brought joy again into the households of the Hebrews. May his compassionate and mighty deliverance be told everywhere and written forever on the hearts of his people."

Jochebed lifted the sleeping child and rose. The fading memory of the agony she had felt earlier that morning when the same action had torn at her heart rose to the surface. It was immediately overcome by the joy that now flooded her being as she laid him gently in the hanging cradle beside her bed. So many things had changed. She bent and pressed a kiss to his brow. His face was serene, his breath soft and steady. She stepped back and said, "Good night, my sweet Moses. Sleep well, deliverer of your people and favored of the Most High God."

Her duties were complete. Extinguishing the light, Jochebed slipped into the warm embrace of her new bed. Beyond the high eastern window, the faint fluttering of wings stirred the air. Before two breaths had passed, the Hebrew nursemaid was sound asleep.

Historical Background

Since this story is set in an unfamiliar time and place and is about the Egyptian beginnings of one of the most important people in the ancient world, the Hebrews, this section provides some background necessary for a better understanding of the story.

There is no way to determine when Moses was born or when the subsequent events of his life occurred. Popular entertainment (The Ten Commandments, The Prince of Egypt) has set its story during the life of Ramses II. The Lawgiver Chronicles use a similar time frame, though Moses is younger, and the Exodus takes place later, during the reign of Ramses II's son, Meremptha.

Titus Flavius Josephus

From the writings of the first-century Jewish historian Josephus, we know that the Egyptians knew from the moment Moses was taken from the water that he was a Hebrew. Josephus also tells us that during this time in their history, the Egyptians were concerned about prophecies foretelling the coming of a Hebrew who would pose significant problems for Egypt. Therefore, any male child who was not destroyed by the edict described in the Bible could be the one that was prophesied.

> *Antiquities of the Jews* by Titus Flavius Josephus: Book II: Chapter 9:2 "One of those sacred scribes, who are very sagacious in foretelling future events truly, told the king [pharaoh], that about this time there would a child be born to the Israelites, who, if he were reared, would bring the Egyptian dominion low, and would raise the Israelites; that he would excel all men in virtue, and obtain a glory that would be remembered through all ages."

> *Antiquities of the Jews:* Book II: Chapter 9:7 "...God himself, whose providence protected Moses, inclining the king to spare him. He was, therefore, educated with great care. So, the Hebrews depended on him, and were of good hopes great things would be done by him; but the Egyptians were suspicious of what would follow his education."

The knowledge that Moses was a Hebrew contradicts the storyline employed by the two productions mentioned above, as well as most other authors who have written stories about Moses' life. The Lawgiver Chronicles has attempted to remain faithful to Josephus's evidence. In doing so, it had to solve the problems that being Hebrew created for

Moses and his people, as well as for the Pharaoh and the priests of Egypt, including, from the very beginning, the problem of the edict.

Relevant Events Timeline

You may want to refer back to this timeline as you read the story.

Our story unfolds during one of the most tumultuous periods in Egyptian history. The year is 1292 B.C., and for over a generation, religious and political conflict has battered the institutions and people of Egypt.

The chaos began sixty years earlier, in 1352 B.C., with the institution of the Pharaoh Akhenaten (Amenhotep IV). His wife was the well-known Nefertiti (*the beautiful woman has come*), whose sculpture resides in Berlin's Altes Museum. In the fourth year of his reign, Akhenaten began to restructure the Egyptian religion toward monotheism, declaring to all of Egypt that there was only one god, represented to the people by the sun. The name of this supreme god was Aten.

Initially, Akhenaten elevated Aten to a place of preeminence, placing him first among the Egyptian deities while granting the other gods a lesser status. In Aten, Akhenaten saw a merging of the three most important aspects of deity found in the main Egyptian gods: Ra, Amun, and Horus. These included light and sun, creator and wind, and protector and savior.

In year five of his reign, this disruptive Pharaoh began constructing a new capital city called Akhetaten (The Horizon of Aten), creating a religious and political center free of what he saw as the corrupting influences of the former gods of Egypt.

Then, in the ninth year of his reign, he declared Aten the sole god of Egypt and made himself the sole intermediary between Aten and the Egyptian people. While this built on the previous position of the pharaoh as the primary link between the gods of Egypt and her people, the difference this time was that Akhenaten placed himself between the people and the one whom he claimed was the one and only god.

A significant effect of Akhenaten's actions was that they removed the priests of Egypt from their former influence as secondary intercessors to the gods, which ultimately destroyed their primary source of religious and political power. A short time after declaring Aten as the sole god, Akhenaten issued a universal ban on all idols representing the former gods and began defacing the temples of Amun, who was Aten's chief rival in the minds of the people. At that time, the priests of Amun were the most powerful religious force in Egypt.

While trying to bring such a radical change to the religious/political face of Egypt, Akhenaten had three serious problems:

First, internal opposition arose among the priests of Amun, who, by the time of our story, had united with the priests of Ra to form the priesthood of the combined deity, Amun-Ra.

Second, external opposition developed from Egypt's traditional allies and the enemies who had begun encroaching on her borders. This problem became even more severe with the rise of a new power to the north and west, the Hittites, who started to flex their military and diplomatic muscle.

Lastly, one of the first recorded pandemics struck the ancient world. Modern investigators believe it was an influenza virus that originated in Egypt and subsequently spread throughout the Middle East. It killed the Hittite king, temporarily slowing that threat. Still, the Egyptian people saw this devastating epidemic as the revenge of the historical gods of Egypt on what they now began to call Akhenaten's heresy.

Towards the end of Akhenaten's reign, his wife, Nefertiti, was elevated to co-regent. After the pharaoh's death in the year nineteen of his reign, Nefertiti ruled alone and, for a short time, was the most powerful woman in the ancient world. To stabilize Egypt's religious and political turmoil, she abandoned the god Aten and the religion of her husband and moved the capital of Egypt back to Thebes. She hoped this would placate both the people and the still-powerful priesthood of Amun. Nefertiti ruled only for a short time, disappearing from the official records less than a year after her husband's death. However, the move back to Egypt's historic polity had begun.

After Nefertiti, Tutankhamun (the King Tut of recent renown) ascended to the throne in 1336 B.C., marrying Nefertiti's daughter, Ankhesenamen. He built many temples devoted to the one he declared the true sun god, the combined god Amun-Ra, and he issued a royal decree rejecting the cult of Aten. During the reign of Tutankhamun, Egypt undertook a concerted effort to restore its historic religious heritage and reestablish the traditional gods in their rightful place in Egyptian life. The young pharaoh died in the tenth year of his reign, probably from a gangrenous infection of his leg several days after severely breaking it in a chariot accident.

His wife, Ankhesenamen, sent messages to the Hittite King, seeking one of his sons as a husband to help her rule. The Hittite King accepted, but the prince was murdered on his way to Egypt. In desperation, Ankhesenamen married Ay, a commoner who had risen to power under Akhenaten and was Tutankhamun's Grand Vizier. Ay succeeded in outmaneuvering the General of the Armies, Haremhab, to become the new Pharaoh in 1327 B.C.

Ankhesenamen quickly disappeared from the records, but her husband, Ay, continued to rule for four years. He sustained the efforts to restore the traditional gods of Egypt to their former glory and actively courted the favor of the priests of Amun-Ra, whom Tutankhamun had championed. After Ay's death, Haremhab, the formerly passed-over general of the armies, succeeded in sweeping aside Ay's chosen successor and taking the throne for himself. Haremhab had always believed that he was destined to be Pharaoh, and he made his conviction a reality in 1323 B.C.

Haremhab went further than his predecessors, beginning to remove all references to Akhenaten's former beliefs. He also desecrated the tomb of Ay, whom he believed to be a traitor, smashed his sarcophagus, and even usurped his mortuary temple for his own use. With the support of the priests of Amun-Ra, he began washing the memory of Aten and Akhenaten from the memory of Egypt. He was so successful that Akhenaten became viewed as a heretic and was referred to as the "*Pharaoh Who is Not Named.*"

Haremhab embarked on a period of broad reform in which the centralized power of those who had risen to prominence under the "heretic" was broken. He succeeded in deposing most of the former officials of Akhenaten, confiscating their lands and property. As a result, many of the former first families of Egypt were reduced to the level of ordinary servants. In our story, the chief maidservant of Princess Asati, Nari, is the daughter of one of those deposed officials.

The Chronicles of the Lawgiver and the speculative history used for this story postulate that Haremhab was the Pharaoh who initiated the edict against the newborn sons of the Hebrews. He acted at the behest of the priests of Amun-Ra, though he was very lax in its enforcement. Our story, which works within the available historical information, states that the priesthood of Amun-Ra believed the Hebrews were responsible for infecting the *Pharaoh Who is Not Named* with their monotheistic religious ideas. This fact, coupled with the prophecy that the Hebrews would produce a leader who would cause great hardship for Egypt (recorded in Josephus), lent weight to the argument of the priests of Amun-Ra that the Hebrews must be destroyed and their heresy eradicated from Egypt's memory. To diminish the hardship on the economic and social fabric of Egypt (who depended on the Hebrews for much of the menial labor), they would accomplish this purification by killing all of the newborn males, which would effectively wipe out their enemy in one generation as the existing Hebrew male population grew old and died off.

Haremhab, however, had a serious problem: he was sterile. Even though he took several wives in succession, he was unable to produce an heir. After reigning for twenty-seven years, in which Egypt effectively regained its former social and religious heritage, Haremhab passed the throne to his chosen successor with the support of the Egyptian priests. He selected a military man like himself, his General of the Army, Pramesse, who already had an heir and strong son, Seti, who in turn had two sons of his own. Following Haremhab's death, Pramesse was instituted as Ramses I, the first Pharaoh of the Nineteenth Dynasty, in 1295 B.C.

Upon Ramses' ascension to the throne, Egypt experienced the greatest inundation of the Nile in living memory, further solidifying the beginning of this new dynasty in the minds of the Egyptian people. In our story, seeking to strengthen the support of the priests of Amun-Ra, the new pharaoh initiated the first rigorous enforcement of Haremhab's edict against male Hebrew births. Soldiers now searched the villages for newborn Hebrew males, no longer relying on the midwives to enforce the will of Pharaoh. However, Ramses ruled for less than two years before his son, Seti I, the Pharaoh of our story, succeeded him. Seti, also needed to solidify the support of the priests of Amun-Ra, so he continued the rigid enforcement of the Hebrew edict despite his feelings that it went against the law of Ma'at, the Egyptian concept of law, morality, truth, justice, and the will of the gods.

Into this perilous scene, a unique Hebrew boy is born, a child who is destined to change the future of the human race to set the stage for the world as we know it. While his parents initially were able to keep his birth a secret, his discovery and horrible death were only a matter of time. In an effort to save him, his parents set in motion a bold plan that succeeded beyond their wildest dreams. Our story takes place on the day that their plan was set in motion.

Cartouche of Moses and Maps

Moses

Our story takes place in Memphis, the northern capital of Ancient Egypt. Because the Nile River is one of those rare major waterways that flow from south to north. The Egyptians considered the north to be Lower Egypt.

Memphis was located 12 miles south of the modern city of Cairo, on the West Bank of the Nile. Founded around 3100 B.C. as the first capital of Egypt, it stood slightly off the river to the west. A huge city by ancient standards, Memphis was surrounded by towering white walls punctuated with massive gates. The city was filled with temples and had an extensive canal system that supplied water from the Nile. In the expanse of ground between the city wall and the Nile River to the east stretched the port of Perunifer, a major shipping destination where goods arrived from all over the known world to be sold in its thriving market.

To the east and west of Memphis and along the banks of the Nile to the north and south of the city, there was fertile farmland, regularly enriched by the yearly inundation that flooded the land and replenished the soil with rich sediment. Egypt depended on these annual surges of the sacred river for a good harvest and enough food to maintain its people and kingdom. Low inundations led to small harvests. Several consecutive low inundations would lead to extreme shortages, while large river overflows would result in an abundance of crops. Egyptians viewed the annual rise of the river as a sign from the gods, indicating whether their relationship with their deities was good or ill.

Story Locations and Routes

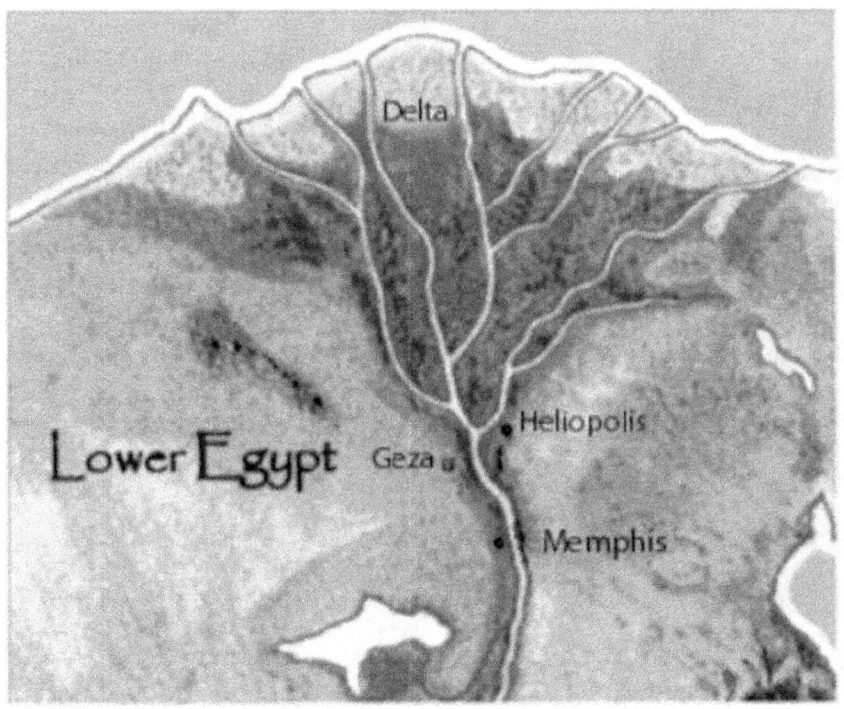

Lower Egypt

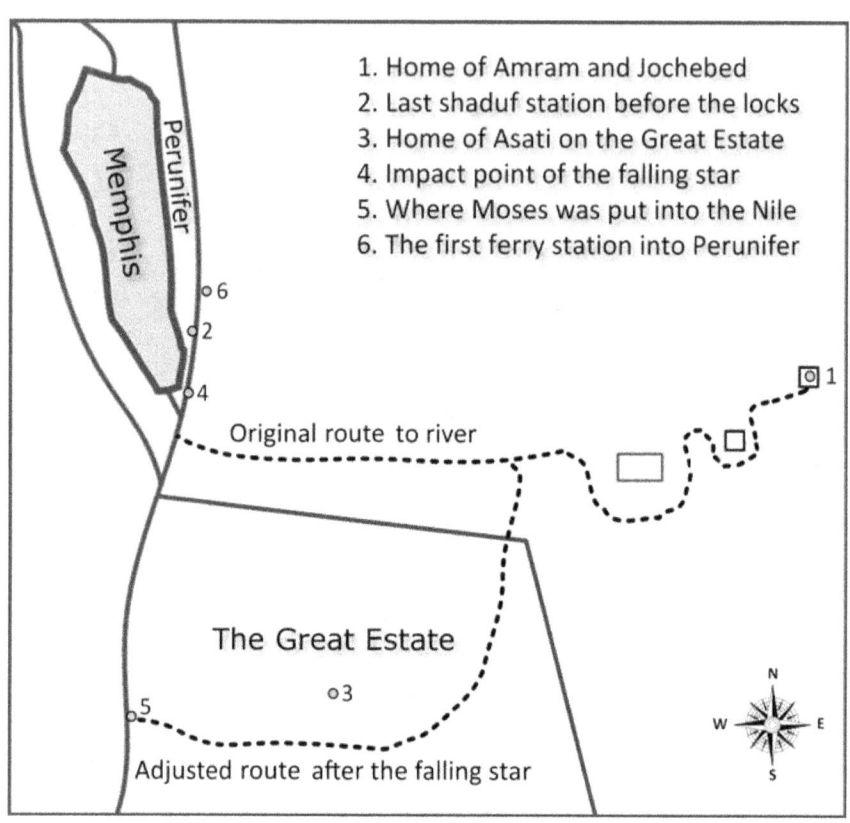

1. Home of Amram and Jochebed
2. Last shaduf station before the locks
3. Home of Asati on the Great Estate
4. Impact point of the falling star
5. Where Moses was put into the Nile
6. The first ferry station into Perunifer

Memphis

Perunifer

o 6

o 2

o 4

Original route to river

The Great Estate

o 3

o 5

Adjusted route after the falling star

N
W   E
S

Jochebed's Route to the Nile

Character and Place Listing

Akhenaten – The "*Pharaoh Who is Not Named*"-attempted to convert Egypt's religion from a polytheistic system to a monotheistic one centered on the god Aten, represented by the sun. He almost drove Egypt into ruin before his death. He was succeeded by Tutankhamun, who helped Egypt begin the long road to recovery.

Ameny – The young priest of Amun-Ra who becomes entangled in the intrigue on the day he gathers information for the temple.

Ammuti – The short, stocky assassin who is speared by Semri and takes poison to prevent being questioned.

Amram – Husband of Jochebed and father of Moses, he worked as a carpenter in the Memphis shipyards. He was able to secure enough pitch to seal the ark basket that carried Moses down the river.

Amunsa – Personal servant of Nephura, Chief Priest of Amun-Ra in Memphis.

Amunthura – A prince and husband of Asati, the sister of the Pharaoh - comes from a long line of supporters of the throne. His family had resisted the religious novelty of Akhenaten, and they remained loyal to the traditional gods of Egypt, especially the priesthood of Amun-Ra.

Apophis – Also known as Apep, this snake god was regarded as the enemy of order and, consequently, the nemesis of Ra and Ma'at. He was the perfect deity for assassins, especially those who preferred using vipers.

Asati – Daughter of Ramses I and sister of Seti. She is married to Amunthura and infertile, despite being dedicated to Satis, goddess of the First Cataract and emblem of fertility.

Aten – The sun god, whom Akhenaten sought to establish as the sole god of Egypt. In our story, many of the priests of Egypt believed that this new god of the *Pharaoh Who is Not Named* was taken from the God of the Hebrews, and therefore, they blamed these foreigners for the pharaoh's heresy.

Buhan – Egyptian fortress located a short distance north of the Second Cataract on the trade route from the Salima Oasis. The most northern of Egypt's large garrison forts, it supplied patrols and protection to the gold caravans coming from Nubia.

Danar – Personal servant of Seti I, Pharaoh of Egypt.

Hapi – A god identified with the inundation and sacred water of the Nile itself, and in its divine characterization, represented by the hippopotamus. He was seen as the source of all fertility, as the Nile itself provided life to Egypt and her people.

Haremhab – The Pharaoh who preceded Ramses I, who was childless and chose a loyal general from the army to succeed him. Haremhab was the head of the military under Akhenaten (the "*Pharaoh Who is Not Named*") and finally succeeded in bringing relative stability to Egypt after the turmoil caused by Akhenaten's heretical actions.

Jochebed – Mother of Moses and wife of Amram, she became a wet nurse to Moses in the household of Asati.

Kamwaset – The Chief Priest of Ptah who resided at the god's primary temple in Memphis.

Memphis – The city of white walls, it was the first capital of Egypt and the current residence of Pharaoh. Its port, Perunifer, was the main port for all of Egypt and contained a thriving international market and trading center.

Merba – Night shift supervisor of the Memphis police under Sekmet, he was a superior investigator.

Mioa – Priest of Amun-Ra who was confidant and co-conspirator in whatever Nephura, the Chief Priest in Memphis, needed to accomplish.

Nakhti – The household steward of the Great Estate who had gone south to Buhan to help Prince Amunthura return home after his service.

Nari – Chief maidservant of Princess Asati, whose family had been an important follower of Akhenaten's monotheistic god, Aten. As a result, her family was disgraced and lost its position in Egyptian society. Because she still secretly followed the rejected beliefs, she was favorably predisposed toward the Hebrews.

Nazim – A guard at the Great Estate, he was one of the best bowmen in Egypt. He had served in the army with Semri, who was his closest friend.

Nephura – Second Priest of Amun-Ra and First Priest of the god's temple in Memphis, he was a mortal enemy of the Hebrews. He despised their monotheism, which he claimed was responsible for the aberration of the "*Pharaoh Who is Not Named*," Akhenaten. He sought the Hebrews' complete annihilation.

Naos – The inner shrine of an Egyptian temple, where, for safekeeping, the god's statue was placed at night.

Nubia – A resource-rich African country that was directly to the south of Egypt.

Obekka – First Priest of Sobek, the crocodile-headed god, and overseer of the sacrificial offerings of the newborn Hebrew males.

Osahar – The Seer Priest of Asati, who accompanies the Chief Priest Sostris at the gathering at the palace.

Paser – Seti's vizier and the one who oversaw the lessons and training of Ramses, preparing him to become the next pharaoh. A soldier who had served under Seti, he was loyal, sharp-witted, and adept at navigating the court's intrigues.

Perunifer – The port which stood between Memphis and the west bank of the Nile. It was an international trading center and was always filled with foreigners and merchants.

Pramesse – Asati and Seti's father, made Pharaoh by Haremhab; he took the name Ramses I on his ascension. He was the first pharaoh to initiate the serious enforcement of Haremhab's edict against newborn Hebrew males.

Ptah – The primordial god who called creation into being. His cultic center was in Memphis, where he was revered as the god of craftsmen and reincarnation, hence his ability to bring things back again, such as Queen Tuya's lost dreams.

Sahal – An island in the middle of the Nile, seven river units downstream from the First Cataract. It is where Pramesse first met Sostris, First Priest of Satis, who became the patron of the future Pharaoh's daughter, Asati.

Saisa – a priest and magician-in-training from the Temple of Satis, who, while collecting clean water from the Nile, saw the falling star strike the Nile in front of him.

Salima – An oasis along the caravan trail used to ship gold from the mines in northern Nubia to the treasury of Egypt and near where the gold caravan was attacked.

Satemra – An orphan raised in the Temple of Satis, who, in the city market, overheard the story of what had happened that morning in the Temple of Amun-Ra.

Satirah – One of the older priests of Satis and a chief confidant of Sostris.

Satis — The Goddess of the First Cataract and sender of the inundation — was the patron of Asati. She rose in power alongside the rise of the Pramesse family.

Satyu – Brother-in-law of Sostris, who went to the Temple of Hapi and heard about the birth of twin hippopotami.

Sekmet – Chief Scribe of Investigations and Secrets, he was the Chief of Police for the city of Memphis. He was short-statured but quick-witted and a solid investigator.

Semri – Chief of the guards at the Great Estate, he was appointed to that position by Seti, whom he had served under in the army before Seti's ascension to Pharaoh. He is a natural leader, an accomplished close combat fighter, and spear thrower.

Sephra – A young woman and servant of Asati, who had been informally adopted and raised by Nari, the princess's chief maidservant.

Seti – Pharaoh of our story, brother to Asati, and the father of the most famous Pharaoh in Egyptian history, Ramses II.

Setia – A young servant of Asati who accompanied Sephra on her shopping trip to Perunifer, where they got items for the nursery.

Shasu – A people group that threatened the northern trade routes to Syria until Seti subdued it in the first year of his reign.

Sobek – The deification of crocodiles; he represented the fertility the Nile brought to the land and could undo evil and cure ills. He was also the patron of the army, representing Egypt's strength and power. It was to him, in an effort to undo the evil Akhenaten had done and reinvigorate Egypt's strength and power, that the Hebrew newborn males were sacrificed.

Sostris – Chief priest of Satis, goddess of the First Cataract of the Nile, and a patron of Asati. Known first to Asati's father, Ramses I, her brother Seti I also came to rely on his sound judgment. He had recently moved to Memphis, where a new temple to Satis was under construction, initially supported by Ramses I and later continued by Seti when he became Pharaoh.

Sunsamen – An official courier sent from the Buhan fortress with news for the Pharaoh.

Sutekha – The tall assassin whom Semri fights below the Shaduf station and is killed by a crocodile.

Thebes – The southern power center and sometimes capital of Egypt, it was the seat of power of the priesthood of Amun-Ra. It was often called the city of a hundred gods since each of its one hundred gates was named after a god.

Tutankhamun (Tut) – Pharaoh after Akhenaten died in a riding accident at a young age, leaving Egypt without an heir and causing a political crisis. It was not until the reign of Ramses I and his son Seti, which marked the beginning of a new royal dynasty, that real stability returned to Egypt.

Tuya – Wife of Seti I and mother of Ramses II, she was an intelligent, accomplished woman. Due to the death of her first son, she was overly protective of Ramses.

Upina – Purification partner of Saisa, student and magician/priest at the Temple of Satis.

Wasur – Rower on the north Memphis ferry, he passed information to Ameny, priest of Amun-Ra and new spy for Mioa.

Worset – A friend of Semri and a powerful swordsman and hand-to-hand fighter, he was part of the guard at the Great Estate.

Glossary of Terms

cubit – 45.72 centimeters (about 18 inches). The average length from the elbow to the tip of the longest finger of an adult male.

hem-netjer – Servant of the god, these were the common priests of the temples of Egypt. They made the offerings and assisted at ceremonies and processions. They could enter the Naos, where the god's image was kept, and they controlled who entered the temple.

Khenerit – Women who assisted in worship at temples, serving as singers and sacred musicians. They sang hymns and played their sistra to drive away evil during the temple rituals and prepare a favorable place for the god to inhabit. They did not reside in the temple but lived with their families and led a normal life. They were required to serve on specific days and for only a few hours and were then released from their duties after the ceremonies.

kher heb priest – The lector priest who read the ritual and religious texts during temple practices.

Ma'at – The Egyptian concept of law, morality, truth, and justice rolled into one, maintaining the proper balance and order of everything. When personified, Ma'at was a goddess who regulated the stars, seasons, and actions of mortals and deities. From the moment of creation, this feminine stabilizing force drew order out of the roiling chaos. Everyone, even pharaohs and the gods themselves, was subject to the demands of Ma'at.

mesniti – Egyptian blacksmith or metalworker. An important member of a large estate, he could do everything from fixing a plow to repairing a sword or spear or crafting rough offerings (stelae) like the ones used by Asati to make her offering to Hapi.

Neheb tree – A common sycamore tree that was found in all Egyptian districts. When fully grown, the width of its canopy can be equal to its height; therefore, they were highly prized for their shade.

Open the Mouth ritual – The awakening, washing, and preparation of an Egyptian god to meet the new day so that they could receive their petitioners.

papyrus – A tall reedy plant that grew along the banks of the Nile and its tributaries. Used for a wide range of purposes in Egypt, from boats and baskets to making paper.

Pure Priest – The priest responsible for the morning's "Open the Mouth" ritual. He had to maintain ritual purity, and because the duty was so demanding, all of the senior priests took turns.

river unit – A long unit of measure equal to 20,000 cubits or about 10.5 kilometers.

Sau-Priest – Worked protective magic, preparing amulets and potions.

Seer Priest – Interpreter priests; their office was prophetic, as they read signs and portents and interpreted dreams.

shaduf – A device for lifting water that utilizes the principle of leverage and a rotating pivot.

Sirius (Alpha Canis Majoris) – The brightest star in the sky, Canis Major, the Greater Dog, it represents Orion's larger hunting dog and is commonly called the "Dog Star." It was only visible for a part of the year from within Egypt. The first glimpse of Sirius in the dawn sky after its absence signaled the expected rising of the Nile and the beginning of the inundation.

sistra – A long-handled musical instrument with a large hoop at the end, strung with beads and small cymbals on cords that stretch across its face. When struck along its rim, it sounded similar to a tambourine, and the Khenerit used its noise to drive away evil during temple ceremonies.

Toilet—Everything it took to get ready to appear in public, especially the intricate makeup worn by both men and women, particularly Egyptian royalty. Everything had to be done perfectly and touched up whenever necessary.

wa'eb priest – A priestly (hem-netjer) assistant who performed maintenance of the temple and assisted in its rituals. All priests began as wa'eb as they started their course of study. Some priests stayed at this level for their whole life.

 **Wedjat Eye** – The most powerful magic symbol in ancient Egypt, it was often formed into amulets and worn for protection.

www.ingramcontent.com/pod-product-compliance
Lightning Source LLC
Chambersburg PA
CBHW071305210626
46818CB00015B/3020